Dream
Big,
Stella!

ASHLEY FARLEY

ALSO BY ASHLEY FARLEY

Hope Springs Series

Dream Big, Stella!

Show Me the Way

Mistletoe and Wedding Bells

Stand Alone

Tangled in Ivy

Lies that Bind

Life on Loan

Only One Life

Home for Wounded Hearts

Nell and Lady

Sweet Tea Tuesdays

Saving Ben

Sweeney Sisters Series

Saturdays at Sweeney's

Tangle of Strings

Boots and Bedlam

Lowcountry Stranger

Her Sister's Shoes

Magnolia Series

Beyond the Garden

Magnolia Nights

Scottie's Adventures

Breaking the Story

Merry Mary

Clear Bottom Lake

Summer House &
Wellness Center

Cottage
Row

Carriage House

The Barn

The Cottage

The Inn

Hope Springs
Farm

Bek Cruddace

ONE

Three jobs in less than a year. I'm living proof that a college degree is no guarantee for success. My BTech degree in Hospitality Management from CUNY is a bogus degree by some people's standards. For years, I attended school part-time and worked full-time in the shoe department at Bloomingdale's to earn it. I'm a born and bred New Yorker, the ideal person to greet tourists upon their arrival and accommodate them while they're here. I know the best shops and five-star restaurants, and I can score prime seats to sporting and entertainment events. Concierge is my dream job. If only I could get promoted from guest service agent. Which isn't likely to happen at my current gig, a boutique hotel on Fifty-Second Street near Madison Avenue. The guest service supervisor is looking for a reason to fire me.

I can feel Mr. Moran's eyes on me from where he's positioned at the far end of the counter. He's watching my every move, waiting for my next screwup. I've been taking too long with my current guest, a supercute guy whose brother plays for the New York Knicks. Mr. Cannon is in town for the Knicks' game against the Detroit Pistons at Madison Square Garden. While I may be flirting with him just a little, he asked for my recommendation on the best nightclubs in Manhattan, and I certainly can't be rude.

When I hand Mr. Cannon his key folder, he steps away from the desk and disappears into the crowd. Guests arriving for the weekend flood our lobby. Throngs of people swarm the bank of elevators, stand in line at the reception counter, and wait for seats to open up at the bar.

An attractive couple in their fifties moves forward, and I greet them with my brightest smile. "Welcome to The Sydney. Checking in?"

The man gives me a curt nod. "Last name, Davis."

My fingers fly across my keyboard as I locate their reservation. "What brings you to New York this weekend?"

Mrs. Davis looks to her husband to answer. When he doesn't, she says, "We're here to see our daughter. And meet her fiancé."

My hand flies to my chest. "A wedding! How exciting for you. Congratulations. Where are you from?"

Mrs. Davis lifts her head high and proud. "Texas."

Her husband casts a disgruntled look at the fat snowflakes falling outside the lobby windows. "Houston. Where spring is in full gear."

"Don't be such a grump. I love the snow." Mrs. Davis hugs her husband's arm. "It's so romantic."

I smile at her. "It is, isn't it? Late season snow showers are common for New York. I consider this the perfect kind of snow, pretty to look at without the headache of event cancellations and travel delays."

Shrugging his wife off, Mr. Davis glances at his gold wristwatch. "Can we hurry this up? I have a conference call in fifteen minutes. I'd like to take it in my room."

"Of course." I print out their paperwork and slide it across the counter for him to sign.

I take this opportunity to study the woman. Teardrop

diamonds dangle from her earlobes, a Chanel crocodile bag hangs from her shoulder, and a silk scarf in vibrant shades of pinks and blues is knotted at her neck. I'm no fashionista, but I know a lot about labels and brands from my best friend, Rachel, who works for the hit reality show *Say Yes to the Dress*.

I touch my fingertips to my collarbone. "I love your scarf. Hermès?"

She bobs her coiffed blonde head. "A Christmas gift to myself."

Her husband clears his throat in irritation as he thrusts the paperwork at me.

"Right, your conference call. We'll have you settled in your room momentarily."

I encode two plastic key cards in the machine, and hand the folder to Eric, the most senior member of our bell staff who is hovering nearby, his cart piled high with an obscene amount of Louis Vuitton luggage. "The Davises are in room 326."

Panic overcomes me. *Or was it room 324? Nope. It was definitely 326.*

I turn back to the Davises. "The fitness room is on the second floor. Breakfast is served in the lounge from seven until ten in the morning. And we offer twenty-four-hour room service if you're in the mood for a midnight snack."

The Davises follow Eric to the elevator, and the next guests in line approach the counter. I've served three couples and the fourth pair is stepping forward when Eric returns with the Davises and their luggage. Mrs. Davis wears a smile of amusement, as though she's keeping a naughty secret. Meanwhile, her husband's head is ducked with phone glued to one ear and hand pressed to the other to block out the cacophony of noise in the lobby.

Eric, his neck disappearing into hunched shoulders, says loud enough for Moran to hear, "You gave me the key to the wrong room."

Mrs. Davis is quick to explain, "We walked in on a man and a woman in a compromising position. I assume she was his wife. She was . . . well, it was all rather embarrassing."

Mr. Moran appears at my side. "My apologies for the inconvenience. I'd like to upgrade you to a suite at no additional cost to you."

Mrs. Davis drops her smile. "Interesting. There were no suites available when I booked my room a month ago."

"As it happens, I've just gotten off the phone with one of our regular guests. She's had an unexpected death in the family and won't be able to make the trip this weekend. The suite is all yours." Without giving the Davises time to resist, he keys two new cards. "The suite is on the concierge floor. The view is magnificent. I'll take you up myself."

As he passes by me, Mr. Moran snarls under his breath, "I'll see you in my office when I return, Miss Boor."

My spirits plummet as I traipse home to Greenwich Village. I love the snow, and I don't mind the cold, but today the gray weather feels dreary. I'm not worried about finding another job. There are over seven hundred hotels in New York. However, without a reference from Moron Moran—and he made it clear one would not be forthcoming—the past ten months were a waste. I'm right back where I started from, applying for entry-level positions. I'm nearly thirty years old, and I have nothing to show for my life.

The smell of garlic and onions greets me in the vestibule of my apartment building. Home sweet home. A decade ago, when my parents moved to Red Hook, I opted to stay in the village. I've lived here all my life. And, even though the building is rundown and my apartment is a five-hundred-square-foot studio, I don't aspire to live anywhere else. With the loss of income, I don't know how I'll pay next month's rent. The apartment is a hand-me-down, my parents' former art studio. To move would mean giving up a rent-controlled space in one of the most sought-after areas in New York. No one in their right mind would do that.

I check my mail, removing three past-due bills from the brass box and stuffing them in my bag, and climb the stairs to the third floor. I'm pausing at the top of the stairs to catch my breath when I notice a gentleman waiting outside my apartment. With ankles crossed, his back is against the wall, overcoat draped across folded arms and black leather messenger bag at his feet. He must be lost. No one in this building wears tailored suits and expensive silk ties.

When he sees me, he pushes his lanky frame off the wall. "You're Stella Boor," he says, a statement not a question.

"I am. Who are you?"

He offers his hand. "I'm Brian Powers, an attorney from Virginia. I'm representing your father's estate."

As I place my gloved hand in his bare one, thoughts swarm my brain, but only one sticks. *Virginia.* My mother is originally from Richmond, Virginia. Powers's piercing blue eyes are on me, watching closely for my response. I'm grateful he can't see my heart pounding against my rib cage. "There must be some mistake. I don't have a father. I have . . . had . . . a sperm donor."

"Is your mother Hannah Boor?"

"One of them, yes. She's my birth mother." I was raised by lesbian mothers, living as an openly gay couple long before it was widely accepted to do so.

I can't put an age on this man. His dark hair is streaked with gray and he has crinkles around his eyes. While Mom's in her mid-fifties, I estimate this man to be close to sixty. Although he's way more dignified than Hannah, it's possible they were friends. "Did you know my mom?"

He either doesn't hear me or chooses to ignore me. "May I

come in?" he asks, nodding at the door. "We should discuss this matter in private."

"Of course." As I'm fumbling with the lock, I remember that my apartment is a disaster. I overslept this morning and didn't have time to straighten before leaving for work.

"Give me a minute," I say and close the door on him, leaving him standing alone in the hall.

I fold the mattress into the sofa, tossing the cushions on top, and gather the clothes strewn about the room. When I let the attorney in, he turns his nose up at the stench. "It's the litter box. Sorry."

My cat jumps down from his perch on top of the refrigerator and slinks over to our guest, leaving orange fur on Powers's suit pants when he brushes up against his legs. Powers appears both irritated and a little afraid.

"I'm not much of a cat person either." Scooping up the cat, I toss him into the bathroom and close the door.

"Why you have a cat if you're not a cat person?" Powers asks with an amused smile.

"The cat found me. He appeared on my fire escape one day. I made the mistake of giving him some milk. I haven't even named him. I call him Cat."

I don't tell Powers about Cindy, the little girl with the sad brown eyes who lives across the hall. She's the reason I haven't taken Cat to an animal shelter. She visits him nearly every single day. I've tried to give Cat to Cindy, but her mother refuses to let her keep him.

"Please, have a seat." When I motion Powers to the sofa, I notice a pair of my thong underwear peeping out from between two cushions. As I'm lowering myself to the sofa beside him, I stuff the underwear out of sight.

"Forgive me, Mr. Powers, but this is all a little overwhelming. How do I even know you're legit?"

From his wallet, he removes a business card that states he's an estate attorney with a law practice by the name of Zimmerman, Harrison, and Powers in a place called Hope Springs, Virginia. "After seeing you, there's no doubt in my mind you're Billy Jameson's daughter." Sliding an iPad out of his messenger bag, he thumbs a few keys and hands it to me. "This was taken in his much younger years."

A man about my age stares out at me from the iPad. The resemblance is eerie, like looking in the mirror. We have the same unruly brown hair and high cheekbones. But our eyes are different. His are a beautiful golden color while mine are big, blue, and round like Hannah's.

So, my father isn't some random dude who sold his semen to a sperm bank to buy drugs or pay for his education. This man, this Billy Jameson, is an actual person. Someone my mother knew in her past life. The fact that she's gay only adds to my confusion.

The realization that Billy Jameson is dead, that I'll never have the chance to know him, strikes me hard, and I fall back against the sofa. "How'd he die?"

"He had a congenital heart defect that didn't show up until his late thirties. He was ill for a very long time. His passing was a blessing." Powers's handsome face is full of sorrow, as though he and Billy were close friends.

"Is this condition hereditary?"

"I've been told that it isn't," Powers says. "But I'd advise you to discuss it with your doctor to be certain."

My mouth is suddenly as dry as the Sahara. Handing him back the iPad, I spring to my feet. "Can I get you something to drink, Mr. Powers?" Then I remember I don't have anything to offer him. "I'm sorry, but I only have water."

"I don't need anything but thank you anyway. And please, call me Brian."

In the galley kitchen, I fill a class with water from the tap and gulp it down. Refilling the glass, I take it back to the sofa.

In my absence, Powers has removed a file folder from his bag and opened it on his lap. He waits for me to get settled before he says, "You're the primary beneficiary of Billy's estate, the magnitude of which is substantial."

I wonder if *substantial* means I can now afford to pay next month's rent. But I immediately feel guilty for even thinking it. A man is dead. My father is dead. "Does Billy not have any other family?"

"His parents are deceased, and he never married. The principal concern is a historic inn that has been in the Jameson family for generations."

I move to the edge of the sofa. "Did you say inn? As in a hotel?"

He hands me two 8x10 photographs. The first is of a three-story stone building with cupolas and dormer windows, green awnings, and sweeping verandas.

"The main building has thirty guest rooms, ten suites, a restaurant, and multiple lounging areas."

I move on to the next image, an aerial view of the property.

Powers continues, "The inn is located on seventy sprawling acres in the mountains of Virginia, just outside the small college town of Hope Springs. The outbuildings include a barn, caretaker's cottage, carriage house, and summer house."

I hand him back the photographs. "Charming. But I'm not sure what any of this has to do with me."

"The Inn at Hope Springs Farm, including seventy acres of grounds and various outbuildings, now belongs to you. It's your responsibility to manage it."

"I'm a city girl. What would I know about managing a seventy-acre farm in the mountains of Virginia?"

"Based on your interest in hospitality, I would think you'd consider this a golden opportunity."

Unfortunately, this *golden opportunity* comes with a price tag

I'm not willing to pay. "Thanks, but no thanks. I'm not leaving New York."

Powers closes the photographs in the file and tucks the file in his messenger bag. "Take some time to think about it before giving me your final answer. Coincidentally, I stopped by The Sydney on my way here. They told me that, as of today, you're no longer employed there." His eyes travel around the room, taking in my collection of cast-off furniture and the rolling garment rack that serves as my closet. "Looks to me like there's not much keeping you here."

He has a point. "If this farm now belongs to me, can I sell it?"

Powers's face tightens. "I was just getting to that. There is one major stipulation of the will."

"Of course. The catch. I knew this was too good to be real." I fall back against the cushions.

He chuckles. "In your case, it's not a catch but a provision. You're prohibited from selling the property for three years."

"What if I refuse your offer?"

"I'm not making you an offer, Stella. This is your inheritance. Billy let things slide during his illness. He left things in a state of disrepair. If you don't give the property the attention it deserves, the inn will close for business. What is worth twenty million dollars today may only be worth five in three years."

My eyes grow wide. "Did you say twenty million dollars?"

Powers shifts his body toward me. "That is bare minimum at today's market price. The property is on the outskirts of town. The opportunities for development are limitless."

I study the attorney, looking for a twitch or a smirk, a sign that he is lying. But I only find sincerity in his face. "Why didn't Billy contact me while he was still alive?"

"He was a very sick man. He didn't want to burden you with his illness."

"Why did you come all the way to New York to tell me this? Wouldn't it have been easier to just to call?"

"Billy left strict instructions for me to deliver the news in person."

My father sounds like a control freak. "I have to give this some thought, Mr. Powers. I can't make such a split-second decision without talking to . . . without thinking it over."

Who would I talk to about this? Certainly not my mothers, the women who kept my father from me all my life. Or my boyfriend, who isn't really my boyfriend. Rachel is the only person in the world I trust. And she's in a serious relationship, soon to get engaged and be lost to me forever. I'm all alone in my so-called wonderful life in New York.

"I understand. But don't take too long. In terms of the condition of the farm, time is of the essence." Powers stands to go. "Who knows, Stella. You might find you like living in the mountains. The fresh air and beautiful scenery. And, if it interests you, you'll have the opportunity to learn more about your ancestry."

TWO

I send Rachel an urgent text, asking her to meet me at our favorite coffee spot as soon as possible. She responds that she'll be there in an hour. I wait at a table by the window, sipping a caffe mocha I can't afford and learning as much as I can from googling on my phone about Hope Springs, Virginia.

Two hours pass, and I'm about to give up on Rachel when she arrives, breathless and irritated.

"This better be good, Stella." Rachel has changed—and not for the better—since she started working for her reality show and dating Bert, a total snob with family money and a high-pressured finance job.

"It's better than good. I inherited twenty million dollars today."

She flicks her dark hair over one shoulder. "Are you kidding me right now? I dropped everything and came rushing over here—"

"Look at me, Rach," I say, pointing at my face. Does it look like I'm making this up?"

She glares at me. We're lifelong friends. She knows when I'm lying and when I'm telling the truth. "Wait. You're serious. What's the catch?"

"I have to move to Virginia."

"Damn, girlfriend!" She calls out to Ron, the barista, to bring her a double shot of espresso and drops down to the chair across from me. "Start talking."

Rachel listens with wide eyes and slack jaw as I tell her about my biological father and the will and the stipulation that I can't sell the inn for three years.

When I'm finished, she says, "So the sperm donor has a name and a face, after all."

"It appears so. The attorney showed me a picture of him. Except for my eyes, I look just like him."

"Are you going to tell Hannah and Marnie?" My parents have always insisted my friends call them by their first names.

"Eventually. I have so many questions for them, but I'm too furious to talk to them right now. They kept my father from me. How will I ever forgive them for that?"

"Don't you wanna know if Hannah did the dirty with your father?"

"Geez, Rachel, do you have to be so crude?" I say, but I laugh, because heck yes, I want to know if Hannah and Billy were romantically involved. "The very idea of Hannah having sex with a man blows my mind. She's just so . . ."

"Gay. Hannah is totally gay. Are you gonna take the offer?"

"It's not an offer. It's my inheritance," I say, repeating Brian's words from earlier. "I have a responsibility to look after the property. Besides, there's nothing keeping me here."

"What about Vince?"

I hang my head. "I mean nothing to Vince. I'm merely his late-night booty call."

"You have me."

Looking away from her, I stare out the window. Snow continues to fall, and with a plunge in temperatures during the past hour, it has started to stick on the awnings of buildings across the street. "When's the last time we spent any time together? You're too busy with your career and Bert. Don't get me wrong. I'm happy for you. But your full life is a reminder of how empty mine is. I got fired from my job today."

"Ugh! Stella. Again?"

"Unfortunately." I tell Rachel about the key mix-up. "I suspected I'd entered the wrong room number, but I gave the keys to the bellman anyway. I'm not stupid. But I keep doing these stupid things. I keep pushing the envelope. Maybe, deep down inside, I was hoping I'd get fired, because I hated that job." I stare down at my folded hands. "When I was a teenager, old enough to go out on my own, I used to sit on a park bench across from the Ritz, watching the well-dressed men and women coming and going. I wanted to be a part of that world, and since I could never afford to stay in luxury hotels like the Ritz, working in one seemed like my next best option. But now that I've earned my degree, I'm not sure that's what I want. I enjoy meeting the customers. The nice ones, anyway. Most of them aren't. Most of them are stressed out, or in a hurry, or have their faces glued to their phones."

"You're always talking about being a concierge," Rachel says. "You'd be perfect in that role. Why not apply for those types of jobs?"

"Hotels rarely hire for concierge positions from the outside. They usually promote from within." My tears are close to the surface. "I don't know how to describe it. I just suddenly feel like something is missing from my life."

"You need a man. Vince isn't the one. You need someone you can count on. A serious relationship. Someone you can build a future with."

"How can I make a man happy when I can't even make myself happy?"

Rachel tosses her hands in the air. "Then go to Virginia. Maybe you'll find whatever you're looking for there."

I remember what Brian said. *You'll have the opportunity to learn more about your ancestry.* "I admit I'm curious about my biological father, the man who gave me half my DNA. I want to know more about him. His life. His illness. His home in Virginia."

Rachel's lips part in a smile. "You've already made your decision."

I slide back in my chair, arms crossed over chest. "No, I haven't."

She points a black-lacquered nail at my face. "You totally have. I know you, Stella Boor. You're wasting time arguing with yourself. What have you got to lose? You can always move back if you hate Virginia. If this property is really worth twenty million dollars, how can you not go?" She picks her phone off the table. "What's the name of this inn?"

"The Inn at Hope Springs Farm. It's in Hope Springs, Virginia."

Rachel looks up from her phone. "Kinda hokey, don't you think?"

"Definitely. But maybe hokey is what I need." When Rachel returns her attention to the phone, I say, "The website needs updating. According to the attorney, the place is a wreck. But the town looks adorable. Total population, just under seven thousand. And there's a small private college there, Jefferson College, liberal arts with around three thousand students."

"Never heard of it," Rachel says, thumbs on screen.

Neither have I, truthfully. I'm grasping at straws. The town doesn't even have a Starbucks.

She tosses her phone back on the table. "It doesn't look like twenty million dollars' worth to me. But I'm not a realtor. Who am I to make that judgment?" She plants her elbows on the table. "I say go for it, Stella. Think of the bright side. You have nothing of value to take with you. You won't even need to rent a moving truck."

While her words cut deep, she's right. "I have my wardrobe." Clothes are the one splurge I allow myself on the rare occurrence when I have extra money. I know where to get bargain knockoffs, and I never pay full retail for anything.

"Box up your clothes and ship them to Virginia." She gets up and pulls me to my feet, engulfing me in a hug. "I have a good feeling about this, Stella. I'll even throw you a great big going away party."

I'll be long gone before she'll get around to planning a party. I inhale the fresh scent of her ocean breeze body cream, committing the fragrance to memory. "We'll FaceTime, right?"

"Every day," she whispers in my neck. We've been best friends since second grade, and now we're going our separate ways. At least temporarily. Maybe permanently.

"Promise you'll come for a visit?"

"I promise. Who knows? Maybe Bert and I will spend our honeymoon at your hokey inn."

I hold her at arm's length. "Are you . . ."

"Not yet, but we're looking at rings."

I raise my hand for a high five. "That's awesome, Rachel. I'm so excited for you."

Arms looped, we exit the coffee shop together, and then head in opposite directions. I don't look back. I'm as light as a feather as I float down the sidewalk. Acting on impulse is nothing new for me, and this is a once-in-a-lifetime opportunity. My inner voice is telling me to go for it. For the first time in as long as I can remember, I'm hopeful about the future. As I walk the short distance to my neighborhood, I check the Amtrak schedule on my phone. The next train from Penn Station to Roanoke, Virginia, departs at 12:35 tomorrow afternoon. I click *add to cart* and purchase a one-way ticket in coach.

I stop at the corner market on my block. I've known the

owner, Mr. Webster, all of my life. When I tell him I'm moving to Virginia, he wishes me well and retrieves a stack of broken-down boxes from his stockroom. I use my rent money to buy a roll of packing tape, a large container of cat litter, and enough cans of cat food to fill a brown paper bag. I'll give my landlord the requisite thirty-days' notice to terminate my lease and use my security deposit to cover my last month's rent. I don't expect much pushback from my landlord. He'll be thrilled to rent my apartment at today's market rate.

Outside the market, I'm waiting for the pedestrian light to change when I spot Vince in the window of our favorite happy hour hangout on the opposite corner. Although our relationship is mostly about late-night sex, Vince has taken me out on a few real dates. He even treated me to a nice Italian dinner once. I'd planned to text him later, to invite him over for a quickie and tell him about my move. But since he's here, I'll buy him a farewell drink instead.

The light signals for me to cross, and laden with boxes and cat supplies, I walk slowly to the other side. As I draw nearer to the bar and look through the window, I see that Vince is not alone. He's with a beautiful blonde, who looks vaguely familiar, but I can't quite place her.

Surprisingly, I'm not upset. I wasn't in love with Vince or anything like that. The sex wasn't even that great. But I'm disappointed. This is just one more measure of my failed life.

I'm covered in sweat by the time I climb three flights of stairs to my apartment. I put fresh litter in the litter box and coax the cat down from the top of the refrigerator. I take the cat, the litter box, and the bag of canned food to the apartment across the hall. Cindy's mother works nights as a waitress in a diner, and I'm banking on the babysitter being here.

Cindy answers the door and her eyes light up a million watts when she sees Cat in my arms.

"Hi, cutie pie. Is your mommy home?"

Chin dropping to her chest, she shakes her head.

I kneel down in front of her. "So, kiddo, I have to leave town suddenly, and I was wondering if you'd like to keep Cat. As your own."

She bobs her head up and down.

"The thing is, I'm not sure if your mommy will agree to let you keep him."

The babysitter appears behind Cindy. I've met her countless times when she brings Cindy for visits, but she doesn't speak much English, and I don't know her name. "We keep Cat," the sitter says. "I buy litter and food myself."

Over the top of Cindy's head, I mouth, "Thank you!"

Unexpected tears fill my eyes when I give Cindy a goodbye kiss on her cheek. I can't explain the soft spot I have in my heart for children. I got fired from my first hotel job for showing a rich kid how to shoot street craps in the posh lobby. Maybe it's because I was so lonely as a child. I always wished for a sibling to keep me company while my parents were out with their artsy friends. Maybe a child is what's missing from my life. But I don't want to raise a kid alone. Who knows? Maybe I'll find love down in Virginia.

THREE

W hen I text Brian to let him know I'm coming to Virginia, I offer to Uber from the train station in Roanoke, but he insists on sending a car to pick me up. My train arrives an hour late, and at nearly eleven o'clock at night, there are few people in the station. I'm relieved to see my driver, bearing a placard with my name, waiting for me by the exit. He's an older gentleman. In his seventies, if I had to guess. Pleasant but quiet. Which is fine by me. I'm not in the mood to talk. During the hour-long drive to Hope Springs, I stare out the window into the black night, pondering the drastic detour my life has taken in the past thirty-six hours.

As my train was departing Penn Station earlier, I sent Hannah and Marnie a group text. *I'm on my way to Virginia to manage the inn my father left me in his will. Thanks to you, I'll never have the chance to know him.*

In response, my parents blew up my phone with texts and calls until I finally block their numbers. I will deal with them when I'm ready.

When we pass the city limit sign for Hope Springs, I press my face against the glass, but it's too dark to see much of anything.

We make our way up a long driveway, and the inn appears in front of us, much larger and more charming in person than in the picture Brian showed me. The combination of stone facades and wide verandas is so cozy and inviting.

Parking under the portico, the driver helps me with my one suitcase. I shipped the rest of my wardrobe in boxes, which are scheduled to arrive on Monday. I wait for the driver to speed away before entering the building. There's no one in sight, not a guest service agent or a single hotel guest. A wide entryway leads to a reception area. An envelope bearing my name in chicken scratch is waiting for me on the marble-topped desk. Inside the envelope is a key attached to an oval-shaped brass key ring, etched with the number 310.

The lobby branches off in opposite directions from the reception area, but I'm too exhausted to explore tonight. I drag my suitcase down the hallway to my right to a bank of elevators. The elevator cart smells of stale cigar smoke, and I brace myself against the wall as it jerks and rattles me to the third floor. Stained wallpaper and filthy carpet greet me when the doors part. My mothers are old movie buffs. The 80s horror film *The Shining* comes to mind and goose pimples crawl across my skin as I hurry down the dimly lit hallway toward my corner room. I imagine eyes watching me as I fumble with the key. Brian neglected to tell me the inn was haunted.

Locking the door behind me, I lean against it until my breathing steadies. What have I gotten myself into?

But I'm pleased to see that my room is actually a suite with bedroom and sitting area. While spacious, the bathroom is nothing special—tub, toilet and counter. The fabrics are worn, and the carpet soiled, but the building itself has nice bones. The Inn at Hope Springs Farm needs a face-lift and an exorcism. And I'm not sure I'm the right person to oversee either.

I have trouble falling asleep, and when I finally drift off, I dream of phantoms chasing me down dark tunnels. Surprisingly, I wake feeling refreshed. Regardless of whether or not I stay in Hope Springs, the view from my hotel room at dawn is worth the trip to Virginia. The sun turns the sky pink, then purple, and finally yellow as it rises above the mountain range. The landscape is washed in the bright green of new spring foliage. A red brick sidewalk stretches down to a large lake at the foot of the mountains. Buildings of various sizes with the same wooden stone architecture as the inn are situated on either side of the sidewalk.

I stand at the window for hours, wondering how I made it through nearly thirty years without ever visiting the mountains. Or the Grand Canyon. Or the white sandy beaches of the Caribbean. When I was a child, Marnie took me to California once to visit her family, but that turned out badly. Other than that trip and annual trips to Cape May with Hannah and Marnie every summer, we never went anywhere else. When I got old enough to travel on my own, I was too busy working or studying. Besides, I always found plenty to explore in the city.

Around nine o'clock, the need for caffeine drives me out of my reverie. Taking my toiletry bag into the bathroom, I turn on the shower faucet, but I'm unable to get any hot water. I consider not showering but change my mind when I catch my reflection in the mirror—greasy hair matted to head and mascara smudged under my eyes. I feel grimy from the train trip, and before I chicken out, I strip off my pajamas and step under the cold stream of water. I stay in long enough to shampoo my hair and wash my body with the tiny bar of soap. My lips are blue and teeth chattering when I emerge from the shower. I dress in cropped jeans and a black crew-neck sweater, and when I can't find a hair dryer, I towel my wet corkscrews into a frizzy mess.

If I were a paying guest, I would totally complain. I venture down to the lobby where I discover an elderly couple venting a litany of grievances to the stunning woman at the front desk.

Their list is long, and the agent comps them their room with an apologetic smile. But when the couple steps away and the woman turns her attention to me, her lips turn downward.

"I'm Stella Boor. I'm—"

"I know who you are," she says in a clipped tone. "I hope *you* don't have a complaint. Your suite is the last remaining fully functioning room we have."

I hold my tongue about the icy shower.

Naomi, according to her name tag, is Whitney Houston gorgeous. She wears her hair in a sassy cut, short with long bangs that dip over sultry eyes. While I have so many questions for her and I could really use an ally, she is throwing out some serious back-off vibes. But I'm a New Yorker who can cop an attitude with the best of them. "I need coffee. I gather Starbucks is outta the question." I mean it as a dig, since I know from my Google search the nearest Starbucks is thirty miles away.

Her arm shoots out, finger aimed at the large lounge area to her right. "Dining room's that way."

Thanking her, I move from reception into the lounge where comfortable seating areas are arranged in front of floor-to-ceiling windows to take advantage of the stunning view of the mountains. Oriental rugs in muted colors adorn worn wooden floors. And while the upholstery is shabby, most of the furnishings appear to be high-quality antiques. Meandering my way through the lounge, I admire the artwork hanging on the walls. I've visited most of New York's major museums many times, and these are some of the most unusual paintings I've ever seen. The soft colors are pleasing to the eye. All are nature scenes—stands of tall trees, a shimmering lake with the mountains in the background, a tranquil stream of water bordered by lush greenery. The signature in the bottom corner of each painting bears the same name. Opal. No last name.

As I pass by the bar, I notice thick layers of dust coating the liquor bottles on the glass shelves on the wall. How long has it been since anyone had a drink in here? The lounge dead-ends into the dining room. The wall of windows continues in here where streams of sunlight highlight outdated lattice wallpaper on the ceiling and faded green carpet on the floors.

Tables and chairs are scattered about the room in no particular order. Only two tables by the window are draped in linen and set with flatware, drinking glasses, and coffee mugs. The elderly couple I encountered earlier in the reception hall is seated at one. I take my place at the other and stare out the window, across the veranda to the grounds. While I'm eager to explore, I'm nervous of what I might discover.

Naomi appears within minutes, dropping a chipped plate bearing a sad-looking muffin on the table in front of me.

"Don't you have someone that can help you serve?" I ask.

"Nope," she says as she fills my mug with thick, dark coffee. "I'm a one-woman show around here. Server, reservations manager, housekeeping. The rest of the staff quit, except for Bernard, the groundskeeper. And he can barely keep the grass mowed."

The elderly couple signals for Naomi, but before she can escape my table, I ask, "Would it be too much to ask for a tour of the property?"

Naomi hunches a shoulder in a why-not gesture. "Come find me after breakfast."

Gulping the muffin down with stale coffee, I beat Naomi back to the reception desk.

In a disgruntled voice, she says, "All right then. But I warn you, I can't be away from the front desk for long."

I think back to when I arrived last night. The door was unlocked and the front desk unsecured.

I follow her out the back of the building, across the wide veranda, to a semicircular stone patio with a fountain in the center that has ceased to spew water. She turns to face the inn. "There are thirty rooms and ten suites in the main building. In addition to the bar, lounge, and dining room, which you saw, we have a library, a solarium, and a wine cellar in the basement." Doing an about-face, she points to the three closest outbuildings. "There's the barn, the carriage house, the caretaker's cottage, and the lake."

"Does the lake have a name?"

"Not a very original one," Naomi says. "Clear Bottom Lake. The water is so clear you can see all the way to the bottom."

"And what's that down by the lake?" I ask of the plain-looking low-slung building.

"The summer house, a glorified porch used for bingo nights and dances back in the day."

I know little about building maintenance, but it doesn't take an expert to see all four are in need of major repairs. Shutters hang askew. Paint is either faded or peeling off the sides. Shingles are missing from roofs. A gutter has fallen off the carriage house. "Are these buildings in use?"

Naomi's lips are thin and her jaw tight as she explains. "Bernard houses all the lawn equipment in the barn. The carriage house is divided into two suites that haven't been rented in years. And the ceiling is caving in on the summer house."

"And the caretaker's cottage?" I ask, thinking the cottage might make a nice home for me. Anything is better than the creepy inn.

"Billy lived there. You're welcome to it, if you can get through the door. He was a bit of a hoarder."

"Oh," I say, imagining stacks of newspapers and magazines and black plastic bags of trash barring the door. "How bad is business?"

She stares past me, her gaze fixed on an object behind me. "We average two or three bookings a week. We have 50 percent occupancy for the upcoming college's graduation, but I have no idea where we're going to put the guests. As I mentioned earlier, most of the rooms are uninhabitable."

"How did things get into such bad shape?"

"Billy's heart wasn't into running the inn. He made sure everything was maintained in good working order, but when he got sick, he lacked the strength to even do that. I guess he was waiting to die, to hand this mess over to you." Her brown eyes are full of sadness. She obviously cared about him. Was their relationship strictly professional? Were they friends? Or something more?

"Where was Billy's heart, if not here?"

She huffs out her irritation. "Ask someone else. There are plenty of people around here who would love to tell you what made Billy Jameson tick."

I stare with mouth wide open as she reenters the building. Why does she dislike me so? Does she consider me a threat? She's technically my employee. I should fire her for being so rude. But, in her own words, she's a one-woman show. At the moment, she's all I've got.

FOUR

The caretaker's cottage, located a hundred yards from the main building, is one story with a blue front door and a wide porch that wraps around two sides. Inside, I'm relieved to discover that my father was not a hoarder. He was a lover of rock and roll, and his cottage houses a museum-worthy treasury of memorabilia. Signed and framed album covers and posters of all the greats adorn the walls. There's Mick Jagger, John Lennon, Bono. The list goes on. Three guitars are mounted over the sofa—two electric and one acoustic. On either side are shadowboxes containing ticket stubs and guitar picks from world famous tours. A bomber jacket once worn by Led Zeppelin, also framed, takes up space near the entrance to the kitchen. One side of floor-to-ceiling bookshelves is home to an extensive vinyl collection while the other side houses glossy programs from concerts and biographies of superstars' lives.

I'm studying a framed photograph of Billy with Elton John when I sense someone behind me. I turn to see Brian Powers peering over my shoulder. I jump. "You scared me. I didn't hear you come in."

He nods at the photograph in my hands. "He was something, wasn't he?"

I'm surprised when my throat swells with emotion. I didn't even know Billy Jameson, yet I feel this strange connection being in his home. "He was . . . not what I expected. What kind of musician was he?"

"Billy was a legend around these parts. Ever heard of the Wild Hollers?"

My jaw hits the floor. "Shut up!" I jab my finger at the photograph. "You mean this man, my father, was *that* Billy Jameson?"

Brian smiles. "The one and only."

"I know his music well." I study the photograph in my hands. "No wonder he looked familiar when you showed me his picture the other day. Out of context, I didn't put two and two together."

"Billy wasn't famous worldwide. His following was mostly local. I'm surprised you've heard of him."

"My mom introduced me to his music when I was just a kid. That makes sense now given the circumstances."

"What do you think of the cottage?" Brian asks before I can press him for more information about my mother and Billy.

I return the Elton John photograph to the end table. "I haven't gotten past the living room."

I follow him into the adjoining bedroom, which is surprisingly uncluttered with a queen-size bed, chest of drawers, and lounge chair.

"We removed Billy's clothes and brought in a new mattress," Powers says.

I want to ask him who the other party in *we* is, but I assume he's referring to Naomi.

He opens a door on the far side of the bed. "This is the only updated bathroom on the property. We put in a shower stall to make it easier for Billy."

I peek around the doorjamb at the marble bathroom, relieved to see modern fixtures capable of producing hot water.

We pass back through the living room to the kitchen, which is outdated but quaint with linoleum on the floor, a sink under a small picture window, and a narrow pine farm table along the opposite wall.

Brian opens a half-paned door and we step out onto a side porch. A pair of rockers and small round table with the kind of chairs you'd find in an ice cream parlor occupy the small space.

We stand side-by-side, looking out toward the mountains. "I trust you'll be comfortable in the cottage."

I look over at him. "Are you sure it's okay for me to live here? Naomi mentioned it, but I wasn't sure."

"Of course. It's the caretaker's cottage. And you're now the caretaker. I'm sorry there's not more room for your things. We'll eventually need to figure out something to do with Billy's collections. But for now, his valuables are safer here."

"I agree. I wouldn't want anything to happen to his collections. I don't need much room, anyway. I only have my clothes." I don't tell him I left the rest of my possessions in a heap on the curb for the trash men. "Can you give me a more detailed job description for the caretaker's position?"

"Certainly. Why don't we sit a minute?" He motions me to the small table, and we sit opposite each other. "You need to stop thinking of this as a job, Stella. You are the proprietor of the inn." He spreads his arms wide. "All this belongs to you."

I press my hands against the sides of my head. "I'm having a hard time wrapping my mind around that. You told me the property was in a state of disrepair. You didn't tell me it was in worse shape than the Roman ruins."

Brian laughs. "I didn't want to scare you off before you had a chance to visit the property. You have to admit it has potential."

I cut my eyes at him. "I remain unconvinced. I'll be honest with you, Brian. I'm in over my head here. I know nothing about

27

construction. And this building needs a major overhaul. As in, we should lock the doors and not allow any guests in until everything is restored to working order. In my humble opinion, you're doing the inn a disservice by allowing anyone to see it in its current condition."

A relaxed smile crosses his face. "I agree completely. Cancel the bookings and lock the doors."

I blink hard at him. "Are you serious? I can't believe you'd give me that kind of authority when you know virtually nothing about me."

"I know plenty about you, Stella. And Billy had faith in you. He believed you're the right person to give Hope Springs Farm the tender loving care it deserves."

"But Billy—"

Brian holds up a hand, silencing me. "You are his daughter. His and Hannah's. You come from a long line of strong-minded characters on both sides."

"Obviously, Billy and my mother were involved. Sexually, I mean. But were they in a relationship?"

His face registers surprise. "Did you not talk to Hannah about all this?"

"I'm not currently speaking to her." I don't elaborate. It's none of his business.

"Your mother and Billy were once close." He hesitates, and I get the feeling he's trying to decide how much to say. "I won't give you all the answers, Stella. You'll have to figure some things out for yourself. This is your journey, your discoveries to make. This is what Billy wanted for you. Billy wasn't just my client. He was my friend. We talked about his plans for you at considerable length."

While I resent having my life manipulated without my knowledge, I'm totally intrigued that my father cared so much about my future.

"Were you and my mother friends?"

"Friends?" He pauses, as though considering how to answer. "No. Hannah and I were definitely not friends."

I have so many questions, but his expression has become guarded, and I don't yet know him well enough to pry. "All right then. So, tell me . . . where do I start? After I lock the doors and cancel future bookings. I have a little over two hundred dollars in my checking account. I don't know how much these things cost. That might buy several boxes of nails and a hammer at the hardware store."

He laughs out loud. "You might be able to add a screwdriver and a gallon of paint to those purchases." He removes a debit card from his wallet and slides it across the table. "I took the liberty of opening an account for you at the local bank. You can create a PIN number when you activate the card. You'll receive an automatic deposit once a month for five thousand dollars."

I gulp. I didn't make that much in three months as a guest services agent. "Do I need to pay rent on the cottage?"

"Nope. You will live here for free. This is your personal income. You may do with it as you please. If you find you need more, let me know and I'll make the arrangements."

After years of barely getting by, I might actually be able to save a little.

"As for the business expenses, the inn is in a trust with me currently designated as trustee. I will pay all the bills, including the renovations. For planning purposes, it would help if you could come up with a budget. But don't cut any corners. Dream big, Stella. Hire decorators and architects. Renovate the existing outbuildings and build more. Do whatever you want. We're behind you all the way."

There's that we *again.* "Can you give me some guidance as to what type of finished product you're looking for?"

Brian crosses and uncrosses his legs. He's too tall for the chair, and he looks miserably uncomfortable. "My opinion doesn't matter. Billy wanted this to be your vision. The shelves in the library are packed with old photo albums that will help you get a feel for what the inn was like in its heyday."

"I have little to bring to the table, Brian, but I promise I'll do my best."

"I have no doubt but what you will. If you're anything like your father, you possess the gumption necessary to succeed."

Gumption. Not a word I hear often, but I like the sound of it.

Brian stands to go. "I can give you the name of three contractors, but you're wasting your time in contacting two of them. Only one is worthy of a project of this magnitude. Jack Snyder is passionate about historic renovations and demands only the best from his subs. He will get the job done in a professional and timely manner. And by timely, I mean by the beginning of September, when the students return to Jefferson college."

I feel a throbbing headache developing behind my eyeballs. "September? A lot needs to happen in four months."

"Which is why you should get started right away." He digs through his wallet and hands me a business card with the contractor's name and number, email address, and website information. "I've already spoken with Jack about the project. He's waiting to hear from you."

"If I may ask, what exactly is Naomi's title? Is she the general manager?"

"For now." Brian lets out a deep breath, and his body deflates. "I realize she can be difficult. Naomi's been through a lot. Give her the benefit of the doubt until you can prove otherwise."

"She clearly has something against my being here. Do you know what it is?"

"You'll have to ask her."

"Right. My journey. My discovery."

He walks down the short flight of steps, and when he reaches the ground, he turns around, looking up at me. "I'm here for you, Stella. If you need anything, do not hesitate to call."

FIVE

After Powers leaves, I move from the table to the rocking chair, and sit for a long time, staring at the mountain range while I mull over our conversation. What if I fail at this once-in-a-lifetime opportunity? This is a monster project for a notorious screwup like me.

The longer I remain on the porch, the more aspects of the project I imagine going wrong. When my nerves get the best of me, I jump down off the porch and take off on my own self-guided tour of the farm. I roam around the grounds. Narrow roads, intended for service vehicles, wind around the property's perimeter while sidewalks and golf cart paths connect the different buildings. I peek in the windows of the carriage house and walk through the barn. If anything, the groundskeeper is the hoarder. Junk is piled up behind the John Deere riding mower. There are rusty wheelbarrows and broken yard tools and bags of fertilizer. There are also things one would never expect to find in a toolshed—microwave, broken floor lamp, a child's wooden rocking horse. I create a new to-do list on my cell phone's Reminder app. The first item is to have the groundskeeper clean out the barn.

After leaving the barn, I make my way down the hill toward the water. As I draw near the lake, I notice a woman standing at an artist easel under a large tree blooming with white flowers. She wears a paint-splattered smock over faded blue jeans, with a floppy sunhat topping the long gray braid that flows down her back. The subject of her focus is a round wooden hut adjacent to the summer house.

Her head jerks up at the sound of a stick cracking beneath my foot. "You startled me," she says, hand on chest, clutching the fabric of her smock. "I'm used to having the place to myself."

"I didn't mean to scare you." Moving toward her, I get a closer look at her canvas. "You're the artist who painted the lovely landscapes in the inn."

She lifts her chin high. "I am indeed. I'm Opal. And you are?"

"I'm Stella Boor. Billy's daughter."

"Are you, now?" Opal wears a smirk on her lips, as though she already knows who I am. She steps nearer to me to examine my face. "I see the resemblance. It's quite strong, actually. Are you musically gifted?"

I laugh. "No ma'am. I can't hold a tune. Although that doesn't prevent me from singing. While I'm a fan of the arts, I have no creative talents of my own."

"One doesn't have to be an artist or a musician to express one's creativity. Perhaps you like to garden or arrange flowers."

I shake my head. "I'm from New York. I know nothing about either."

"Photography?"

I wave my cell phone at her. "This is the only camera I own."

"Cooking?"

I shake my head. "Limited to the basics."

She pats my arm. "Don't worry. You're still young. You have plenty of time to discover your hidden talents."

There's the word *discover* again. Does she belong to the *we* conspiracy?

Opal wipes sweat from her brow with the back of her hand. "It's warm out today. Would you care to sit a spell?" she asks, gesturing at a nearby moss-covered bench."

"Sure! I have nothing but time on my hands."

We sit down side-by-side on the bench, and I angle my body toward her. She's in her late seventies or early eighties, but she carries her age well. Aside from a few wrinkles around her eyes, her skin is taut across her face. She's trim and seemingly agile, the type of woman who chooses healthy food and attends yoga classes regularly.

She removes a bottled water from the pocket of her smock and takes a long swig. "So . . . tell me, my dear, how're you finding Hope Springs Farm so far?"

"The property is beautiful." I let out a little laugh. "The buildings, on the other hand, are in desperate need of fixing upping."

Screwing the lid back on her bottle, she says, "And from what I hear, you're just the person to manage the renovations."

Aha! She is a member of the *we* conspiracy. "So, you're aware of my situation? About why I'm here?"

She nods but doesn't elaborate.

"Brian Powers—I assume you know Brian—keeps telling me I'm the right person for the job, even though I'm grossly unqualified."

"Yes, I know Brian. And you don't need qualifications to do this job, Stella. You need strength of character."

"Ha. Do you know where I can get some of that?"

She barks out a laugh. "Your sense of humor will serve you well. I can tell you're a likable young woman. Use your personality to your advantage."

"I'll keep that in mind. I need to first figure out how to get people to overlook my age and pitiful résumé."

"No one cares about your résumé, Stella. As for your age, if you speak with the voice of authority, others will respect you."

I pick at an imaginary speck of lint on my sweater. "You make it sound so simple."

"Few things in life are ever simple, my dear. But hard work is gratifying. If you have faith in yourself, you can accomplish anything. You young folks have a useful tool we didn't have when I was your age. Use the internet to your advantage. Educate yourself. Do your research."

I wave my phone at her. "As it happens, I'm a professional Googler."

"I knew it," she says, slapping her thigh. "This is Hope Springs, Stella. You can be whoever you wanna be here." She jumps up and pulls me to my feet. "Come with me. I want to show you something."

We practically run down across the grass to the wooden hut in her painting.

"I was wondering about this place. What is it?"

"You'll see." Opal removes a key from over the top of the doorframe and inserts it into the padlock. Shoving the creaky door open, she steps out of the way for me to enter.

A small pool with water that smells not of chlorine but rotten eggs takes up most of the interior. Cobblestone coping surrounds the pool while two sets of wooden steps on opposite sides allow for easy access. A sign on the wall reads Swim at Your Own Risk, but one would be hard-pressed to swim three strokes from one side to the other. I move in for a closer look. The water is blue green in color and so crystal clear I can see down about eight feet to the rocky bottom.

"What is it?"

"A natural hot spring, water that has been heated by the earth's interior before rising to the surface. According to legend, Native Americans were the first to discover the spring, but Europeans who arrived in 1746 were the first documented settlers. They built a lodge where the inn now stands."

"That is seriously cool, Opal." I drag my fingers through the water. "It's so warm."

"It averages about ninety degrees. The water is thought to have special healing powers."

"Hence the name, Hope Springs," I say.

Opal nods. "Exactly. The farm came first and then the town. The townsfolk view the spring as a symbol of hope for the future. If the inn were to close, it would be devastating not only for the town's business but for morale."

"No pressure there." I dry my hand on my jeans. "Do you ever soak in the spring?"

"All the time." She presses her fingertips to her lips, hiding a smile. "On occasion, I even get in butt naked, but don't you dare tell anyone. You should try it. The water is reinvigorating."

"Are guests allowed to soak?"

"Adults over the age of eighteen."

My mind spins with ideas for capitalizing on the hot spring. "This would be the perfect spot for a spa."

"That's a brilliant idea. Your father would be proud." Opal smacks me on the back. She's strong and the slap stings, although I don't admit it to her.

"Did you know my father well?"

"From the time he was a little boy," she says, her fondness for Billy obvious in her soft smile. "We were good friends. I miss him dearly."

"According to Naomi, Billy wasn't into running the inn. Is that because he was so into his music?"

"Suffice it to say, Billy's life didn't turn out as he'd planned."

"Do you know my mother, Hannah Boor?"

"In a manner of speaking." I wait for her to say more, but her expression has become guarded. The discussion is closed.

Taking me by the elbow, Opal guides me out of the spring

house. When we emerge, something in the distance catches Opal's eye.

"What is it, Opal?"

"Just the groundskeeper, Bernard." She locks up and returns the key. "He's drunk again, passed out under the oak tree at the top of the hill. He ain't done a licka work in decades."

"Why didn't Billy fire him?"

"Billy had a soft spot for the old buzzard. Bernard started working here as a boy, when Billy's grandparents ran the place. There's more to maintaining the grounds than mowing and blowing. You'll need to hire a whole grounds crew."

"Good to know," I say, adding this task to my mental to-do list.

We walk back to Opal's easel in silence. "I should let you get back to work. Is there a grocery store nearby? I'd like to pick up a few things for the cottage."

"There's one in town. Take Main to the first stoplight. Go right on Maple. The local market is four or five blocks on your right. You can drive Billy's car. Ask Naomi for the keys."

"I don't have a driver's license."

I think she's making fun of me when she laughs, but then she says, "Of course, you don't. Why would you need a license when you live in New York City? We'll have to remedy that, though. If you can give me a few minutes to clean up, I'll drive you to the store."

"I can't ask you to stop painting. I'll walk. The weather is nice, and it'll give me a chance to get better acquainted with the town. Thanks for the pep talk." I lean down and kiss her cheek. My show of affection surprises me. I'm not the lovey-dovey type. Definitely not with strangers. But I feel a connection with this old woman I can't explain.

SIX

Opal is at the forefront of my mind as I walk back to the main building for my purse. Growing up, I would've given anything for a grandmother like her. A hip and energetic older woman to take me on trips to the zoo and spoil my dinner by buying me ice cream cones. To invite me for sleepovers and cook me stacks of blueberry pancakes for breakfast the following morning. To share Christmases and birthdays and all the other holidays.

When I was eight, Marnie took me out to California to visit her family. In addition to my grandparents, I was to meet my aunts and uncles and cousins. But Marnie picked a fight with her mother our first night in San Diego, and we had to cut our trip short. We left the next morning, before I even got to go to the zoo.

All my life, I've pestered Hannah to tell me about her family, but she refused to talk about them except to say she doesn't have any siblings. And she only shared this information to commiserate with me when I complained about being an only child. I was the kid who had no siblings or grandparents, two mothers but no father. In today's world, same-sex parents are widely accepted, but back then, my classmates thought I was a freak.

When I enter the building, I hear music. Have new guests arrived? I follow the sound to an octagonal-shaped glass room at the end of the hallway. Beams of sunlight stream down from the ceiling, glistening off the streams of water spewing from a trio of bronze cherubs in the center of the room. A little girl in full ballet garb leaps and pirouettes across the black-and-white checkered marble floor to the music from Swan Lake. Naomi—the child's mother, I assume—stands off to the side, wearing an expression I can't read.

When the music ends, I clap loudly and call out, "Bravo!"

Realizing she has an audience, the child performs a delicate curtsy. Perfectly poised, with head high and spine ramrod straight, she glides on her toes toward me. Her glossy dark hair is fastened in a high bun, and she's dressed all in white—leotard, chiffon skirt, and tights—with the exception of the blush-colored ankle wrap ballet shoes. Her complexion is lighter than her mother's—butter pecan versus Naomi's milk chocolate—with eyes the color of cognac. The child is so positively scrumptious, I want to eat her alive.

When she stops in front of me, I say, "I'm Stella. What's your name?"

"Jazz. It's short for Jasmine."

"A pretty name for a pretty girl. How old are you, Jazz?"

"I turned six in March."

"In that case, happy belated birthday. I'm a big fan of ballet. I've seen the New York City Ballet perform many times. I think you're very good for someone your age."

Jazz flashes me a snaggletoothed grin. "Really?"

"Really," I say with a vigorous nod.

From behind her daughter, Naomi shakes her head and mouths, "Don't encourage her."

My eyes narrow in confusion. What the heck? Her daughter obviously has talent.

Placing her hand on Jazz's back, Naomi gives the child a nudge toward the door. "Run get your things, Jazz. Your father is waiting to take us to dinner."

Naomi watches her daughter leave the room. "A year ago this past Christmas, her father and I took Jazz to see the Richmond Ballet's presentation of *The Nutcracker*. When she begged for ballet lessons, I thought it would be a good way for her to make new friends. I never dreamed she'd become so obsessed. Or that she'd have such natural talent."

"Isn't that a parent's dream come true? For their child to be passionate about something they do well?"

"I'd rather Jazz be dissecting frogs. Her time is better spent studying biology to become a doctor. To choose a career in entertainment is to choose a pathway to heartache."

Her face is stone. Nothing I say will change her mind. And since I'm not a parent, who am I to argue?

"On a different note, I've decided to close the inn for renovations."

Her brown eyes pop. "*You've* decided?"

Opal's voice echoes in my mind. *Speak with the voice of authority.* "With Brian Powers's blessing. As of today, the doors are locked. All future bookings will be canceled."

Her eyes fall to the floor. "I can't do this?"

"Do what, Naomi? I thought you'd be excited. Your position here won't change. We'll work together to prepare for the renovations, and once construction is underway, we'll start planning for the grand reopening."

Her nostrils flare, and a vein in her neck pulses. "You wouldn't understand."

"Then explain it to me."

No words come out of Naomi's mouth, but she pins me with a

stare so full of hatred my knees go weak. She views me as a threat, and I don't blame her. I came along out of the blue. But I won't apologize for something that has been imposed upon me. Until two days ago, I'd never heard of Hope Springs Farm and Billy Jameson was the lead singer in a rock band, not my father. I'm terrified here. Brian is expecting a lot of me. I need an ally, not an enemy.

She spins on her heels and leaves me gaping at her back. I'm standing in the same spot minutes later when she returns with a set of keys. She tosses them at me. "This headache is all yours. Have fun!"

I'm on her heels as she hurries back toward reception. "At least think about it for a few days, Naomi. We can work through our issues."

Jazz is waiting for her by the check-in counter. Naomi takes her by the hand, nearly jerking her little arm out of its socket, and drags her toward the entrance. She bursts through the double doors with enough force to knock them off their hinges.

Tears sting my eyes as I lock the doors behind her. What was it Powers said about her? *Naomi's been through a lot. Give her the benefit of the doubt until you can prove otherwise.* Whatever she's been through has nothing to do with me. I only met the woman yesterday. I tried to give her the benefit of the doubt, and she walked out on me. I would prefer to have her on my team. I know virtually nothing about the way this inn works. But I draw the line at begging.

I return to the solarium where I spend an hour contemplating the many possible uses for the space. This is one of the few rooms that doesn't need renovating. The retro vibe works here. I've watched all the classic greats with Hannah and Marnie, and I expect to see Ginger Rogers and Fred Astaire waltzing across the floor. Left empty, the solarium would be the ideal place to host cocktail receptions. Furnished with wicker furniture and floral print fabrics, it becomes an inside garden for special occasion breakfasts and afternoon teas.

I create a new file on the Notes app on my phone and record my ideas before moving on the wood-paneled library next door. Aside from the stench of cigarette smoke permanently permeated in the carpet and drapes, I find this room old-world handsome with its stone fireplace and leather upholstery. Two walls of bookshelves showcase first edition copies of classic novels as well as more contemporary romances and mysteries written and signed by authors who were previous guests at the inn. A whole section is dedicated to oversized hardcover books with glossy photographs—coffee table books—documenting the life and times at Hope Springs Farm. I set several of the more intriguing ones aside to study later tonight at the cottage.

The cabinets beneath the shelves are full of photo albums chronicling events held at the inn, dating from the twenties until a few years ago. Seated with my legs crossed on the floor, I study the albums, reliving the inn's history through the ages. At its prime, the inn was a hotspot for famous politicians and movie stars. The albums from the late eighties and nineties sport pages of photographs of Billy Jameson performing in the lounge. I add those albums to my stack of glossy books for the cottage.

From what I can tell, conditions at the farm began to deteriorate around the turn of the century. And Powers expects me to restore it to its glory. A tall order for a girl from New York who can't hold down a job.

Around seven o'clock, my stomach reminds me I haven't eaten since the stale muffin I had for breakfast. I got so distracted that I never went to the market. Since it's too late to go now, I order a veggie pizza from Domino's and summon the nerve to go to my room for my suitcase. Being alone in this hotel freaks me out. I imagine an ax-wielding Jack Nicholson waiting for me when the elevator doors part on the third floor, and the spooky twins in blue dresses watching me hurry down the long hallway to my room.

I waste no time in throwing my belongings in my suitcase and hightailing it back down to the lobby. I wait for the pizza deliveryman out front, under the portico. After he leaves, I manage to transport my pizza, suitcase, and the stack of books from the lobby to the cottage in a single trip.

With doors locked and lights on, I feel safer in the cramped quarters of my new home. Rolling my suitcase into Billy's room, I unpack the few clothes I brought with me in the antique chest and small closet. Changing into my pajamas, I return to the living room. Clicking on the gas logs in the small fireplace, I curl up at one end of the sofa with the pizza box and stack of books on the coffee table beside me.

I activate my debit card, and after confirming the balance of five thousand dollars, I spend a few minutes researching laptops before purchasing a basic, thirteen-inch MacBook Air. My dinosaur Dell PC went to its final resting place at the electronics recycling center months ago. Almost instantly, I get an email notifying me of my new computer's arrival tomorrow. And not a moment too soon, considering the amount of research I need to conduct.

I spend hours studying the photographs in the glossy books and making lists and notes on my phone. When I finally turn out the light and go to bed, I have the strangest feeling I'm not alone. There's not a soul on this seventy-acre farm except me, but instead of being afraid, I'm oddly comforted by Billy's prized memorabilia. I'm at home in this small cottage. Billy wanted me here. Even though he didn't know me, he trusted me with this monumental task, and I will do everything in my power not to let him down.

SEVEN

First thing Friday morning, I tick off the top item on my to-do list by calling the contractor Jack Snyder, who sounds excited to hear from me. When I ask about his availability to meet on Monday, he says, "Is there any chance you're free this afternoon? I'd like to take the weekend to work up some numbers."

Once I commit to meeting with him, there's no turning back. "This afternoon works great. How does three o'clock sound?"

"I'll see you at three."

Seated at the reception desk, I spend some time acquainting myself with the reservation system, which is similar to the ones I've worked on in the past. We have only thirty-six bookings on our calendar from now through the end of August. Twenty of those are for Jefferson College's graduation in May. I place the dreaded calls and cancel the reservations. For the guests I'm unable to reach, I leave detailed messages explaining the situation. I offer our sincere apologies for any inconvenience and invite them back for a complimentary weekend after we reopen in the fall. Of those I speak with, a few are angry, but most agree the inn is way overdue a face-lift. I make meticulous notes in each of the reservations for future reference. No more sloppy work from me.

By eleven o'clock, having consumed a whole pot of coffee and two stale muffins, I'm ready for a healthy lunch. I set out for the grocery store but get sidetracked by the flower bed in the center of the circular drive where only a few sad daffodils and tulips remain amongst clumps of weeds. In the past, I know from the glossy books that this bed was always planted with bright flowers —in yellows and oranges during the fall and reds, whites, and blues for the Fourth of July.

I'm snapping images with my phone for the before and after album I'm planning when a lemon-yellow Mini Cooper convertible careens up the driveway with an old Wild Hollers song blasting from the radio. Opal blows the horn and waves at me over the top of the windshield. Cupping her hands around her mouth, she yells, "Have you been to the grocery yet?"

"I'm on my way there now!"

She waves me over to the car. "Get in, and I'll give you a ride."

Something about this woman warms my heart. And I'd be crazy to turn down a lift to the store.

I slide into the passenger side, and she speeds off before I can buckle my seat belt. At the end of the driveway, she zips onto Main Street. She turns down the volume but still has to shout to be heard over the sound of nearby car engines. "If the wind is too much, you can roll up your window."

I nod, but the fresh air feels good, and I leave my window down.

"How's your day been so far?"

I offer her a thumbs-up. "How about yours?"

"Just dandy."

Dandy. I repeat the word in my head. Another word I don't hear often, but it fits her spunky personality.

Yesterday, she instructed me to take a right at the light onto

Maple to get to the store, but today, she continues straight. "Why don't I give you the nickel tour of Hope Springs before we go grocery shopping?"

I smile. "I'd like that."

As we drive down Main Street, Opal directs my attention to various points of interest. There's the town's only coffee shop. An art gallery that frequently exhibits her work. An old-fashioned theatre with a retro billboard announcing show times for the spring's hot new movie, *I Still Believe. And a multitude of* men's and women's clothing boutiques displaying high-end merchandise in their windows, suggesting an upscale clientele.

"Can college kids afford to shop in those places?"

"Some of them can," Opal says. "Their parents certainly do. We also get a lot of tourists who come just for the day to shop."

"There's certainly no shortage of eating establishments for the tourists to have lunch."

"Some of the restaurants cater primarily to the college students. Like that one." Opal points to a corner restaurant with an outdoor seating area. "I wouldn't be caught dead in the Town Tavern, but I order takeout from there a lot. They make a mean hamburger."

"I'll keep that in mind."

"Nothing can compare to the restaurant at the inn when Chef Hugo was alive," Opal says. "The inn itself was once a hubbub of activity for our townsfolk."

"My goal is to make it that again one day."

"I have no doubt that you will."

The noise level dies down as we leave the busiest part of Main Street. I tie my knotted hair back with a scrunchie. "As of yesterday evening, the inn is officially closed for business. All reservations from now until September have been canceled, and I'm meeting with a contractor this afternoon."

She smiles her approval. "Good for you! You don't waste any time."

"I already made one screwup. I somehow managed to run Naomi off."

"She'll come back," Opal says in a dismissive tone. "And if she doesn't, it's not the end of the world. I've been trying to get rid of that one for years."

"Opal!" I can't help but laugh at her lack of restraint. "I thought it was just me. I take it you had a problem with Naomi as well."

"Naomi has a problem with me. She cops an attitude with everyone. Not the guests, of course. She's very gracious to them. She's good at her job. She knows this inn better than anyone." Opal grips the steering wheel. "I'm being unfair to her. The truth is, I owe Naomi a huge debt of gratitude for the kindness she showed Billy during his illness."

She says this in such a territorial way I can't help but wonder if Billy was more than a friend to Opal. Maybe he was family. According to Powers, Billy's parents—my grandparents—are deceased. I want to press her for more information, but the faraway look in Opal's eye warns me against it.

We make a loop through the Jefferson College campus. Ivy-covered stone buildings form a rectangle around a central common area. Students in shorts with backpacks slung over their shoulders move about on the sidewalks and stretch out on blankets on the grass.

As we're exiting the campus, Opal asks, "Do you have time for me to show you one more thing before we head to the store?"

"Sure! I'm free until my meeting with Jack Snyder at three."

"Oh good! I'm glad you're meeting with Jack. You'll like him."

We exit the college campus and drive back through town. As we're passing the inn, heading toward the mountains, I ask Opal about the house that appears to be a mini version of the inn.

"That's the manor house. Your great grandfather built it as his primary residence. Both your father and grandfather grew up here."

"Who lives there now?"

"I'm not sure."

Opal punches the accelerator, and within minutes, we're on open road, passing rolling fields and horse farms as we race toward the mountains. Zipping around in a sporty convertible is the most alive I've felt in as long as I can remember.

Opal navigates the curving roads with ease. We drive for miles, and my ears are beginning to pop, when she veers off the road onto an overlook. She kills the engine and stands up in her seat, helping me to my feet. Three picnic tables are lined up directly in front of us. Beyond the picnic area is the town of Hope Springs.

"There's your farm down there." She sweeps her arm in front of her. "And that's just the thirty acres that have been cleared. There's an additional forty wooded acres of hiking paths and fishing streams."

I'm rendered speechless at the sheer magnitude of what's been handed to me. *My farm.* Wanting to better understand Billy's motivations, I ask, "Why would Billy gift such valuable property to someone he never met?"

"I can't answer that, child," she says, in a tone so genuine I believe her.

Neither of us speak on the return drive. When we make a left onto Maple, Opal says, "These neighboring streets are mostly residential. If you go a mile down this road, you'll find chain stores like Walgreens, Target, and Lowes. There's even a Kroger. We can go there now if you'd prefer, but the local market carries everything on a smaller scale."

"The local market it is."

When we pull into the parking lot, I laugh at the words scripted on the plate glass window. "I didn't realize the name of the market was actually *The Local Market.*"

"We're simple folk around these parts." Opal parks the car, and we enter the store. "They have a made-to-order sandwich bar. If you like, we could grab some sandwiches and have a picnic." Her face reddens. "Perhaps I've taken enough of your time already."

"I would love to have a picnic with you, Opal."

She places our order at the sandwich bar while I shopped the aisles for supplies. The cupboards and refrigerator in Billy's kitchen are empty, and I quickly fill a cart with the basics—coffee, yogurt, salad ingredients, protein bars. I pay for my groceries—Opal insists on buying the sandwiches—and we load my six bags of groceries in the Mini Cooper's cargo space.

We're almost back at the farm, when, at the base of the driveway, Opal stops suddenly and gets out of the car. "What're you doing?" I ask when she comes around to my side.

"It's your turn to drive." She opens my door and tugs on my arm.

"No way." I say, jerking my arm back. "I've never driven a car in my life."

"Gotta learn sometime. Come on."

I let her drag me out of the car, and I reluctantly go around to the driver's seat.

"Consider yourself lucky," she says. "Back in my day, we learned to drive with manual transmissions."

I put the car in drive, but when I take my foot off the brake, the car starts to roll backward. "Give it some gas!" Opal demands.

I press my foot on the accelerator and the little car jerks forward. It's easier than I thought, and I get the hang of it right away. When we near the portico, Opal instructs me to take a right onto a narrow road off to the right and I follow it around the main building. I've never approached from this direction, and I'm surprised to see a gray Jeep Wrangler parked beneath my bedroom window.

"Park behind Billy's Jeep," Opal says, pointing at the Wrangler. "Which belongs to you now. After you get your learner's permit, you'll have to wait a period of time before taking the test for your license. In the meantime, the roads around the farm are perfect for practicing your driving."

After lunch on the porch, Opal heads off with her easel and supply tote bag. She reminds me of Mary Poppins the way she dances a little skip as though preparing to fly off into the clouds. I smile to myself. Just watching her makes me happy.

I take in my new surroundings, the mountains and trees and blue skies, so vastly different from New York. I wonder if it's possible for a person's sense of place to be genetically transmitted like the color of their eyes. Hannah and Marnie love New York, and because I am their daughter, they taught me to love New York. But that is nurture. I woke this morning with a sense of belonging and purpose I've never known before.

One thing's for certain, Virginia has New York beaten hands down when it comes to pleasant weather. The sun beams bright in a cloudless sky, and a breeze delivers the sweet fragrance of flowers. I don't know one flower from another, but with an hour to kill before my meeting with the builder, I set out on foot to find the source of the heavenly scent. I stroll the perimeter, listening to birds chirping the arrival of spring and watching the buds on trees practically open before my eyes. I'm departing the lakefront, trudging up the hill through a ground cover of leftover autumn leaves, when I trip over a log and nosedive to the ground. The knees of my jeans are dirty, but I'm otherwise unhurt. I get back on my feet, and I'm brushing off my pants, when the log moves. I jump back ten feet when a man emerges from beneath the leaves.

"Are you outta your mind? You scared me to death. You

tripped me just now. You're lucky I wasn't hurt. Who are you? And what're you doing hiding in the leaves?"

"I wasn't hiding. I was taking a nap. I'm Bernard, the groundskeeper. And who the hell are you, missy?"

Missy? Did he just call me Missy? I catch a whiff of whiskey, and my anger escalates. "I'm Stella Boor, Billy Jameson's daughter, the new owner of Hope Springs Farm. Which makes me your new employer."

"I ain't working for no dame, especially one who's barely old enough to have her period."

My brow hit my hairline. *Is this dude for real?* I don't care if he is my elder, I refuse to be talked to in such a derogatory manner. "Then you won't be working here anymore. Pack your things and get off my property."

"Make me, little lady."

I'm seriously angry now, but also a little intimidated. "I'll let the police handle that." I whip my phone out of my pocket and stab the numbers nine-one-one on my screen. When the operator comes on the line, I say, "This is Stella Boor at the Hope Springs Farm. I have a disgruntled, drunken employee threatening violence. Can you send the police right away? We are on the property behind the red barn."

A long moment of silence fills the line. "I've dispatched a unit. They should be there momentarily. Do you need me to stay on the line with you until they arrive?"

"Please!" I say.

My eyes follow Bernard's hand to the gun holster attached to his belt. "So, what? You're gonna shoot me now?"

"Shoot you?" the operator says in an urgent tone in the phone. "Does your employee have a gun?"

I grip my phone. "He does."

Removing the handgun from its holster, with arms locked in front of him, Bernard trains it on me. "Pow, pow!" He jerks the gun up as though firing it, and I nearly pee in my pants while I wait for the bullet to hit me.

"Bernard! You old fool! Put that gun down right now." Opal's voice comes from somewhere off to my right, but I don't take my eyes off him to look for her.

"This ain't none of your concern, Opal. Mind your own business."

Behind me, I hear the sound of car doors slamming followed by the crunch of leaves. Two officers appear in my peripheral vision. One remains by my side while the other marches up to Bernard with an outstretched hand. "Give me the gun, Bernard," he says in an indulgent tone of voice a parent might use with his child.

Bernard reluctantly hands over the gun. "Ain't nothing but snake shot, Pete. I wasn't gonna shoot her."

Are you serious? These two know each other?

I glare at the old man. "How was I supposed to know that? I don't even know what snake shot is. You used your weapon to intimidate me, which I view as a direct threat."

Brian appears on the scene. *Where did he come from?* He comes to stand beside me in what I consider a show of allegiance. "Are you okay?"

"I think so."

"What happened?"

I open my mouth and the words tumble out. I feel like a tattle-tale, but will do whatever's necessary to get rid of this old drunk. "I was walking up from the lake, and I tripped over him. He was passed out drunk in the leaves. He wanted to know who I was, and when I told him, he said, and I quote, 'I ain't gonna work for no dame, especially one who's barely old enough to have her period.'"

Brian tenses, but I continue, "When I asked him to get his things and leave, he refused, and I called nine-one-one. That's when he pulled out the gun."

"Come on, Brian," Bernard says with pleading in his voice. "You know me better than that. I ain't never hurt a flea."

Brian moves over to the groundskeeper. "While that may be true, Bernard, you and I both know it's way past time for you to retire. Billy's been warning you about your drinking for years. You've let things slide around here. We can't keep you on any longer. We'll work out a generous retirement package. You can spend your days doing something you enjoy, like fishing."

"Billy never would've fired me," Bernard says in a childlike disgruntled voice.

Brian squeezes the man's shoulder. "We're not firing you, Bernard. You quit, remember?"

Understanding crosses the old man's weathered features. Brian is offering him a way to save face. "Right. I quit."

"Now, let's go get your things." With his hand still on Bernard's shoulder, Brian walks him toward the barn.

Once they're gone, Opal rushes over to me. "Are you okay, sweetheart?"

I can't find my voice, so I nod. But then I shake my head as my eyes fill with tears. Once my body starts to tremble, it won't stop. For the first time since leaving New York, I want to call my mommies.

Opal places an arm around me and pulls me in for a hug. I'm tempted to give into my fears, to collapse against her and ball my eyes out, but I don't want Brian to see me cry. I push away from her and move about in circles, shaking my limbs out and taking deep breaths until I've calmed down. "Okay. I'm better now. Sorry for the meltdown."

"Honey," Opal says, cupping my cheek. "No need to apologize. What happened to you here was terrifying. Anyone would react the same way."

"I'm not anyone. There's no telling what kind of crazies I'll encounter when I'm managing the inn. I can't afford to show weakness."

"You're being entirely too hard on yourself, sweet girl."

Opal's words hang in the air between us. *Sweet girl.* That's exactly what I am. A girl. An inexperienced one, totally out of her league.

When Brian motions me up to the barn, I wave a finger at him, signaling I'll be there in a minute. "Thanks for coming to my rescue, Opal." I give her a quick hug.

"Anytime. I'm going back to my painting. I'll be down by the lake if you need me."

The police cruiser is driving off with Bernard in the back seat when I approach the barn. "Are they arresting him?" I ask Brian.

"No. They're taking him home. He's too drunk to drive." Brian turns his back on the retreating squad car and faces me. "I don't have any reason to believe Bernard would try to hurt you. He's a harmless, old curmudgeon. But I've taken the police up on their offer to periodically patrol the premises throughout the weekend. We had a night security guard until a few months ago. He moved to Florida to be closer to his aging mother. Naomi was working on finding a replacement. We'll ask her where she is in the process."

"About Naomi . . . she left, and I'm not really sure why. I gave her the benefit of the doubt like you suggested. Yesterday afternoon, when I told her I'd decided, with your blessing, to close the inn for renovations, she said she couldn't do this. When I asked her what *this* is, she refused to say. I told her to take a few days to think about it. But I haven't heard anything from her today."

"She's a bit of a hothead. She's run off before, but she usually comes back. I'm not worried about Naomi, only in that I don't want all the responsibility of the inn to fall on you."

"I'm figuring things out. I'll let you know if I get in over my head. Thanks for backing me up just now with Bernard."

"You're welcome. Firing him was the right thing to do." Brian starts off toward the main building, and I step in line beside him.

"I was on my way over, anyway. I hope you don't mind if I sit in on your meeting with Jack Snyder."

"Not at all. I'd like to hear your thoughts on the project."

So, Brian doesn't trust me to handle the renovations, after all. And I don't blame him. I don't trust me either.

EIGHT

Jack Snyder is waiting outside the locked front doors when Brian and I cut through the main building from the courtyard. I open the door for him, and we make our introductions in the entryway. He's mid-thirtyish with tiny lines around his hazel eyes and a spattering of gray mixed with his dark beard stubble. I don't usually go for older men, but I'm drawn to his rugged good looks. I'm glad to see he's wearing a wedding band. Mixing business with pleasure already cost me one job.

Jack studies me closely. "Wow. The resemblance is uncanny."

My face heats. "Do you really think so?"

"You are 100 percent Billy Jameson's daughter."

"I take it you knew my father," I say.

"When I was growing up, every kid in Hope Springs idolized Billy Jameson. My friends and I, aspiring to be the next Wild Hollers, took guitar and voice lessons. None of us were ever any good," Jack says with a snicker. "I got to know Billy better in recent years. I priced out a few projects for him, but he never followed through on any of them. He just didn't have it in him."

We talk about New York for a few minutes, and Jack tells me about the time he visited with his family as a boy.

Brian, ready to get down to business, finally interrupts us. "I realize you've only been here a couple of days, Stella, and at the risk of putting you on the spot, I would appreciate your initial thoughts on the project."

He's totally testing me. Time to sink or swim. Remember, speak with the voice of authority.

"Certainly. I've been studying some of the albums I discovered in the library, and I have some ideas. As you know, the hotel was built in 1925. From what I can gather, minor renovations were made in the late forties with a more extensive remodeling in the early sixties. Since then, it appears as though changes have been made here and there without a cohesive plan."

Brian's facial muscles relax. "Excellent observations. Go on."

"I'd prefer to wait until I've selected a decorator before I share my ideas for decor. I'm thinking upscale with a tendency toward swanky without compromising the overall traditional feel."

They nod in unison, and I can tell by their rapt expressions, I have their approval thus far.

"Can we do a quick walk-through of the main floor? I'd like to tell you my thoughts about construction."

Brian nods and Snyder says, "Of course."

I lead them down the hall to the solarium. "Overall, this room appears to be in good shape. We need comfortable seating with a few tables scattered about, furniture we can easily adjust to accommodate various functions. I'm thinking Santa brunches for the locals and welcome parties for large groups of guests."

Snyder is taking notes on a legal pad, his pen flying across the paper while I talk.

We move down the hall. "The library is peaceful and inviting with the fireplace and dark paneling while the adjacent room is so blah. Do we really need a conference room, Brian?" I ask, referring to the beige rectangle with the large conference table next door.

"To the best of my knowledge, the room is hardly ever used," Brian says.

"What if we knock out this wall?" I knock on the wall that separates the library from the beige rectangle. "I understand there are certain restrictions on renovating historic properties. But if we could combine these two rooms, we would have enough space for a small bar and a pool table with a big screen TV over the fireplace for watching major sporting events."

"There are so many." Brian ticks them off his fingers. "The Super Bowl. Masters Golf Tournament. The NCAA football and basketball championships. What do you think, Jack? Can it be done?"

"I'm not sure about knocking out the whole wall, but we can definitely get away with creating a framed opening to combine the two."

I snap my fingers. "I like that idea even better. A set of folding doors would come in useful if we ever want to close one of the rooms off or use them for separate events."

"I'm all for it," Brian says, and Snyder makes a note of it.

As we cross through reception, I say, "I don't envision this room needing much in the way of construction. As far as decor, I'd like to come up with something really wow to greet our guests."

We continue into the lounge. "Opal's artwork adds a local flavor. We might consider adding some smaller pieces by other area artists."

"Brilliant suggestion," Brian says, and Snyder adds, "We have quite a few talented artists who would be proud to have their work featured."

"We could even host art shows followed by a cocktail reception and dinner," I say.

"Yet another brilliant suggestion," Brian says.

"We'll come back to the bar," I say as we bypass it and continue on to the dining room. "To attract patrons who aren't staying at the hotel, the restaurant needs a name, its own identity instead of the dining room at Hope Springs Inn. A magnet or theme would help. I have no idea what that might be. Fly fishing or a historic event that happened at the hotel." I move to the center of the room. "I envision a farm-to-table modern grill room, elegant yet casual, with a variety of seating—banquettes and free-standing tables, a long community table stretching down the middle of the room." I cross to the far wall and open the swinging doors leading to the kitchen. "We'll never attract a prominent chef with this kitchen. We need to gut it and start over with high-end commercial appliances."

"That's a no-brainer," Brian says.

I throw open the french doors, and we walk out to the veranda. There are a few rickety rockers but no tables or lounge chairs. "What better place for our guests to enjoy coffee in the mornings than looking out at the mountain range. Was the veranda ever used for dining? I couldn't tell from the photographs."

Brian massages his chin. "Not that I remember."

"We need to make outdoor dining a priority since everyone wants to be outside these days. Is there a way to widen the veranda?"

Stepping down off the porch, Snyder cranes his neck as he looks up at the building. "I don't see why not. For balance purposes, you would want to extend it the entire length of the building."

Brian says, "This side will be for dining and the opposite end for relaxing in hammocks and rockers."

Snyder turns toward the stone patio. "You might consider enlarging this area as well. Get rid of the fountain to accommodate tables and firepits. You wouldn't necessarily have to serve your guests out here. Just offer them a place to hang out."

"These are all wonderful ideas." We cut back through the dining room, and when we reach the lounge, I say, "I have an idea for the bar, but I'm not sure what you'll think of it. You won't hurt my feelings if you hate it."

Brian leans against the granite-topped bar, arms folded and eyes on me. "You have my undivided attention."

"I saw dozens of pictures in the albums of Billy performing here. What if we line the walls with Billy's fabulous collections as a special tribute to him? We could call it Billy's Bar, or something catchier."

When no one says anything, I look closely at Brian. Are those tears in his eyes?

He swipes at his eyes with the backs of his hands. Definitely tears. "I love it." Brian looks over at Snyder. "What'd you think, Jack?"

Jack, too, appears choked up. "Billy would be honored."

Brian pushes off the bar. "I'll leave the two of you to continue the discussion." He leans down and kisses my cheek. "You have done your homework, young lady. I'm impressed with you and your wealth of ideas. Keep up the good work."

"Thank you," I say, beaming. I take his compliment to mean I've passed his first test.

Brian turns to Snyder, extending his hand to shake. "I'll look for those numbers on Monday."

"You'll have them." Snyder claps his shoulder. "If we can agree on the numbers, we'll get started right away. Pulling this off by September will be no small feat."

Jack and I spend two hours inspecting nearly every inch of the main building, starting on the ground floor and working our way up. We take extensive notes, Jack on his legal pad and me on my phone. We agree to give the guest rooms and suites a face-lift, with new carpeting and fresh paint, and to gut the bathrooms, tearing out the old and putting in marble tile and new fixtures. Jack is thorough and I enjoy watching him work. Specifically, the way his Wrangler jeans hug his butt. I have to remind myself repeatedly that he's married.

On the top floor, we discover water-stained ceilings and wallpaper in many of the rooms. "You have a leak or leaks in the roof," Jack says. "I'll get my roofer over right away to give us an estimate."

When our assessment is complete, we take the elevator back to the lobby. Jack turns to me at the front door. "This project means a lot to me, Stella. I don't need this job. I have homeowners waiting in line for my services. But I spent a lot of time at the farm as a child. I have fond memories of birthday dinners and coming to see Santa. Billy's family used to host a great big picnic right before school started every August. They'd invite the entire town for free hot dogs and hamburgers, watermelon and fireworks. That was back in the good old days before . . ." His voice trails off and he stares out the front door.

"Before what?"

He hesitates, as though struggling with how much to say. "I don't want to get into all that now." His gaze shifts back to me. "In the interest of full disclosure, I've convinced Brian not to get bids from other contractors. For two reasons. One, there is no other capable builder in Hope Springs. He would have to hire a firm out of Roanoke or Richmond, and the travel expenses would be a large factor in the bid. But also, because I've promised him I'll do the work as economically as possible. He trusts me to keep that promise. I have every intention of meeting our early September deadline. In order to do that, I need your cooperation. While I like what I heard from you today, I don't really know you. Your age and inexperience are concerns."

I lift myself to my full height, feigning a confidence I don't feel. "That's fair. And I appreciate your honesty. You have my word that I will give this project my undivided attention. However, because I am inexperienced, I will need guidance. Can I count on that from you?"

"Absolutely," Jack says with a sigh of relief. "Once Brian approves the numbers on Monday, I will immediately set things in motion."

"Which brings us to my first question. What do we do with all the furniture during construction?"

"You'll need to hire a mover and rent warehouse space. Talk to Brian about that. He may have one lying around."

I raise an eyebrow. "You mean, a warehouse?"

Jack smiles. "Yes, an empty warehouse. Powers is a resourceful man."

"I wonder if he has an interior designer lying around."

"I might be able to help you with that. My sister is an architect in Richmond. She works with commercial designers all the time. I'm sure she'd be happy to offer recommendations."

"That would be great." I add decorator to my long list of topics to research when my computer arrives. "So, your sister is an architect? I have a project in mind that will require an architect. Is she any good? That's a stupid question for me to ask her brother. Of course, you think she's good. Since we're going to be working together, you should know that I'm an expert at putting my foot in my mouth."

He chuckles. "You're too hard on yourself. I've known you now for several hours, and that's your first blunder. You handled yourself well with Brian. He's a tough audience."

"You seem to know a lot about Brian. Are the two of you close?"

"This is a small town, Stella. Everyone is close."

"Brian doesn't seem to want to talk about himself. At least not with me."

"He'll open up," Jack says. "Give him some time."

Jack props himself against the front door, as though not yet ready to leave. "Tell me more about this project you have in mind. Why do you need an architect?"

"I'd rather show you. Do you have time to walk down to the lake?" When he glances at his watch, I add, "It's getting late. I understand if you need to get home to your wife."

He thumbs his wedding band. "I can make time."

With legal pad tucked under his arm, he follows me out the back door, across the stone patio, and down the stairs to the sidewalk. I see the lawn and flower beds through a different set of eyes now that Bernard is no longer with us. In all the confusion, no one, including Brian apparently, thought to consider what we will do without a groundskeeper. According to Opal, we need a whole crew. "You don't happen to know a groundskeeper looking for work, do you?"

"Not off the top of my head. What happened to Bernard?"

I quickly explain the events from earlier in the day.

"Whoa! That must have freaked you out, having him pull a gun on you like that. Bernard has been here since I was a child. I can't believe he'd do something like that." Jack's arm shoots up, finger pointing at the sky. "I take that back. Last time I saw Bernard, he was drunk outta his mind. I say good riddance."

"I agree. Surely, it won't be too hard to find a replacement."

Jack slows as we pass by the carriage house. "I haven't been inside that building in years. Do you know what condition it's in?"

"I don't." I dangle my set of keys. "Care to have a look?"

"Sure."

The carriage house door is stuck, and Jack has to use the force of his body weight to open it. I enter the building ahead of him. Two sets of stairs flank the small foyer, and as I cross the threshold into the main living area, I duck my head too late, running smack into an enormous spiderweb. Sticky cobweb coats my hair and my mouth.

"Here. Let me help you." Removing a red bandana from his

back pocket, Jack wipes the goo off my face. His cologne smells like patchouli and sandalwood. His touch is gentle, and as his hazel eyes meet mine, a spark passes between us and we jump apart.

To hide my embarrassment, I rake the cobweb out of my hair, tying it back with an elastic band, while Jack circles the room with his legal pad. He's back to business, our moment forgotten, which is just as well. The man is forbidden fruit.

We spend fifteen minutes checking out the identical suites—each with two bedrooms connected by a sitting area—on the second floor. We exit the building, and I'm locking the door behind us, when Jack says, "I'll give Brian a separate estimate for remodeling this building. Then he can decide whether to proceed now or wait until later."

"That's a good call."

Neither of us speaks as we continue down to the lake, our easy banter from earlier noticeably missing.

I lead him to the summer house. "This is just an idea. Not worth mentioning to Brian yet."

Jack drags an imaginary zipper across his lips. "Mum's the word."

"We should capitalize on the hot spring since it's such a unique feature. I'd like to convert the summer house into a spa, a multistory building with lots of windows overlooking the lake. A casual restaurant would occupy the ground level. The spa would take up a whole floor and the other would be dedicated to fitness with all the latest exercise equipment, yoga rooms, and an indoor lap pool."

"To add authenticity, we could incorporate the hot springs hut. If you widened the pier, you could offer kayaks and paddleboards."

Tingles of excitement dance across my chest. "So, you approve of my idea for a spa?"

"Wholeheartedly. Your spa would create enormous opportunity for growth." Shielding his eyes against the falling sun, Jack looks off in the distance. "I've always wondered why the Jamesons allowed Cottage Row to deteriorate. Those were once the best accommodations on the property."

"What's Cottage Row?"

"Come with me, and I'll show you," Jack says and starts off down a gravel path bordering the lake.

When we come to a stand of trees, Jack steps out of the way for me to enter the woods.

I shake my head. "No way. I'm not going first."

"Chicken," he says and ducks below the low-hanging tree branches. We fight through sticks and brambles for a short distance. When we enter a clearing, six cottages in a row—each standing one and a half stories tall and having a front porch and dormer windows—stretch out in front of us.

"Why would anyone wanna stay back here?"

"Believe it or not, those woods were once a manicured rose garden. Tennis courts were over there." I follow his finger to where the top of a green chain-link fence peeks out from the trees. He draws a line through the air. "There was a pool and playground over there." All evidence of both are now gone. "From what I understand, families spent whole summers here."

We walk over to the nearest cottage and peek through the window. On the inside, the ceiling and walls have begun to collapse.

"So why *do* you think the Jamesons allowed Cottage Row to deteriorate?"

"Billy had so much tragedy in his life," Jack says, leaning back against the porch railing. "I can only—" The railing gives way beneath his weight and he scrambles to prevent himself from falling.

"Are you okay?" I hold onto his arm while he steadies himself.

"I'm fine, but the cottages are in worse shape than I thought."

Stepping to the safety of solid ground, we move to the edge

of the water. A boardwalk runs along the lakefront, but we don't dare test it, to see if it's sturdy.

"What were you saying about Billy having tragedy in his life?"

Jack lets out a sigh. "Sometime in the late eighties, Billy's older brother, Ethan, was killed in a plane crash. He was living in DC at the time. He'd chartered a small plane to fly him home for his wedding. Ethan was the golden child in the family, a hotshot lawyer who one day hoped to run for congress. The family was grief-stricken, especially Billy's parents. Even though they were still young at the time, barely in their sixties, they both died a few years after Ethan—his mother from a massive stroke and his father from a heart attack."

My heart aches, as though I knew these people. They were my grandparents. Ethan was my uncle. His bride would've been my aunt. Their children, when they had them, my cousins. "That is the saddest thing I've ever heard."

His lips turn down. "Isn't it? Ethan was Billy's idol. And to lose his parents so soon afterward. He was a mess for a long time. Just as he was showing signs of coming out of his depression, he became ill."

"So that's what Naomi meant when she said, 'Billy's heart wasn't into running the inn.'"

Jack nods. "There were too many ghosts here. He couldn't escape them."

NINE

Rain sets in during the night on Friday. The dim glow of headlights from the police cruiser patrolling the grounds offers some comfort, but I feel unsettled, not only by my run-in with Bernard but by what I learned about the Jamesons and their family's tragedy. Even though I stay up late, creating Pinterest boards and researching interior decorators on my new computer, I get up early on Saturday morning.

I find an old quilt in the linen closet, and wrapped up against the damp air, I rock for hours on the porch with the rain pounding the tin roof. I can't stop thinking about my father and how difficult it must have been for him to lose his brother and parents in a matter of years. I yearn to know more about the Jamesons. My family. I don't feel comfortable asking Brian. Opal might tell me, but she won't be painting in the rain.

Around ten o'clock, I dress in jeans and a hoodie. My raincoat will arrive with the rest of my wardrobe in the shipment of boxes on Monday. I make a dash across the lawn and up the stone steps to the main building where I discover an umbrella and a mildewy yellow slicker in a closet in the manager's office. My office now. Seated at the mammoth wooden desk, I run my hand across the smooth leather top. Billy once worked here and his father before him. I know from the glossy books that my grandmother's name was Janis and my grandfather was Ethan, like his eldest son. Ethan Senior was the last successful manager of Hope Springs Farm. Before the plane crash, Ethan Junior's career path had taken him into law with the possibility of a future in politics. Where did that leave Billy? Was he teed up to become his father's successor? And what about his music? Would he have gone on to become a rock and roll star if his music career hadn't been cut short by the untimely death of his father?

Coming from behind the desk, I study the framed black-and-white photographs lining the walls of the Jameson family posing with famous people who have visited the inn over the decades. Maybe it's wishful thinking, but I see something of myself in my grandmother. Janis was an elegant woman, poised and immaculately dressed.

More eager than ever for information about my long-lost family, I set off on foot to the public library. I stop in at Caffeine on the Corner for a hot beverage to take with me. The interior of the coffee shop is cheerful with ochre-colored walls and gas logs burning in the fireplace. Customers of every age occupy the booths and free-standing tables as well as stools at the counter that stretches across the front window. As I stand in line to place my order, I eavesdrop on a group of Jefferson College students rehashing last night's big party.

When my turn comes, I ask the attractive barista for her opinion of the caffe mocha.

"It's my personal favorite." She raises her right hand. "And I promise I'm not just saying that."

She's about my age with thick honey-colored hair and flawless skin. Her blue eyes twinkle, and even though I don't know her, I'm drawn to her easygoing manner and smile that hints at mischief. Is it possible I'm about to make my first friend in Hope Springs?

I smile at her. "I trust you. One caffe mocha, please."

As she rings up my order, she says, "You're new in town." It's not a question but a statement.

"Do I wear the dazed expression of a city girl in a small-town world?"

She laughs. "Yes! I recognize the expression from my own reflection in the mirror when I first moved to Hope Springs eighteen months ago."

I stick my credit card in the reader, and while it's processing, I say, "I'm Stella Boor, native New Yorker."

"And I'm Cecily Weber, native everywhere else but here." When I squint my eyes at her, she adds, "It's a long story."

The person behind me in line clears his throat, signaling for me to move on. Leaning across the counter toward Cecily, I say in a lowered voice, "What's the public library like here? I imagine gloomy catacombs of dusty classics and World Book encyclopedias. Will I escape alive?"

She whispers back, "You'll survive. I visit the library all the time. I'm an avid reader, but I've never warmed up to e-books. I like the feel of the book in my hands."

"I know what you mean," I say, even though I can't remember the last book I read for entertainment.

The guy behind me clears his throat again, louder this time, and I move to the end of the counter to await my order. Drink in hand, I make the short walk, down a block and over another, to the Hope Springs public library. The two-story stone building nestles between City Hall on the right and the local branch of the Blue Ridge Bank on the left. An older woman at the front desk welcomes me with a warm smile, and when I tell her what I'm looking for, she escorts me to the microfiche room on the second floor.

I spend the afternoon researching old newspaper articles from the town's *Daily Post* for information about the Jameson family as well as the inn. Ethan was killed on Friday, October 5, 1990. He

68

was to have wed Meredith Brown the following day. One newspaper account pictures Meredith, wearing a veil over her face, with Billy and his parents at Ethan's funeral. My grandparents both received quarter-page features at the time of their deaths, Ethan Senior in 1992 and Janis in 1994. Loved by the entire community, Ethan Senior served on boards of many civic organizations and was known for his generosity in supporting nonprofit organizations. A dedicated gardener, Janis served terms as both the president of the Hope Springs Garden Club and the Garden Club of Virginia. I print a copy of *The Virginia Gardener* magazine article that features photographs of a young Janis in her perennial and herb gardens. I've seen no evidence of those gardens during my walks around the farm. My grandmother would roll over in her grave if she knew her hard work had gone to waste.

I pore over every article I can find about the inn, but I don't discover anything I haven't already learned from the glossy books. Nor do I find any mention whatsoever of my mother. Of all the dozens of photographs I've seen in the books and on the walls at the inn, Hannah is not pictured in a single one of them. So, how did I end up in my mother's womb? Was she involved in a relationship with Billy? If so, how does Marnie fit in?

The library is preparing to close when I emerge from the microfiche room around five. On my way through the lobby, I ask the same pleasant librarian for a recommendation on a current best seller. From behind the desk, she presents me a copy of *Where the Crawdads Sing*.

"Been on the bestseller list for months. Certain aspects remind me of *To Kill a Mockingbird*."

Harper Lee's classic was one of my favorites in high school. "I'll take it. Thank you."

When I reach the novel, she jerks it away from me. "You must fill this out first." She slides an application for a library card across the desk. "I'll need to see a valid Virginia driver's license."

"I don't have a Virginia driver's license. I don't have any kind of driver's license, actually. I just moved here from New York." I remove my wallet from my bag. "I have a valid ID card issued by the state of New York."

"I'm sorry, but I need verification of your local address." She hugs the book to her chest possessively. "We must protect our property from theft."

"But I plan to get a license soon. I've only been in town for . . ." When I pause to count the number of days since my arrival, I'm surprised the number is only three, including today. So much has happened during that time. "Three days. Can't you give me a break?" Propping my elbows on the counter, I say, "Would it help if Brian Powers vouches for me? I am Billy Jameson's daughter, the new manager of the Inn at Hope Springs."

"Billy Jameson," she says, her pale eyes glassing over with unshed tears. "Well, I'll be darn. I knew his family well."

She taps the library card application. "Fill it out, using the inn as your local address. I'll issue you a card as long as you promise to bring me your driver's license as soon as you get one."

Once I've completed my end of the process, she scans my card and the book. "The book is due in two weeks. Don't make me come looking for you."

I finger an x across my heart. "I promise. I won't."

She walks me to the door. "I'm Rose Mitchell, by the way. Welcome to town, Billy Jameson's daughter."

"Thank you," I say with a smile.

Tucking the hardback book under my arm beneath my raincoat to prevent it from getting wet, I leave the library and dash across the street to the Local Market. I purchase a loaf of seedy bread, several thick slices of cheddar cheese from the deli, and a container of homemade tomato bisque.

Back at the cottage, I heat up the soup and make a grilled cheese sandwich. While I eat my dinner, with the gas logs keeping me company, I listen to my father's music. His stereo system is antiquated, and even though his vinyl collection is extensive, most of his own music is recorded on cassette tapes. I pay close attention to the lyrics. His music prior to 1990 is upbeat with songs about love and hope and good times had with friends. There's a twelve-month gap in his recordings following the plane crash. From 1991 onward, his songs are dark.

After putting my dishes away, I rummage through the contents of Billy's bookshelves. When I find a relatively new model DSLR Canon camera, I spend two hours watching YouTube videos to learn how to use it.

I download the handbook from the Virginia Department of Motor Vehicles with every intention of studying, but my eyes are too computer weary. A few minutes after nine, I change into my pajamas and crawl into bed with the novel I checked out at the library. I'm hooked on page one, and four hours later, I'm still reading.

TEN

Hannah and Marnie stopped going to church years ago, but I consider myself a regular attendee. By regular, I mean once or twice a month and all the major holidays. But I didn't think to pack a dress, and I don't have anything appropriate to wear to the pretty little Episcopal church with the stone facade and tall steeple I spotted in town yesterday. I dress in gray slacks and a white silk blouse and head over to Jefferson College for the eleven o'clock service in their chapel. As I stroll through town, I think about the six-year-old protagonist in *Where the Crawdads Sing*. One by one, her mother and siblings abandoned her, leaving her alone at their shack in the swamp with only her angry alcoholic father to take care of her. How sad her little life must have been. My anger toward my mother softens. While she and Marnie lied to me about my father, they were always loving parents and good providers.

I'm surprised to find the pews in the chapel filled with students—some who look as though they just rolled out of bed. But I understand the attraction when the young female minister delivers her sermon. All eyes focus on Reverend Malone as she counsels her young congregation about making the most of our

God-given talents. I feel like she's talking solely to me when she says, "At some point in your future, opportunity will come knocking on your door. Don't be afraid when it does. Have confidence in your abilities, commit to doing your best, and put your faith in the Lord."

I leave the service believing in my heart that I've done the right thing in coming to Virginia.

Yesterday's rain is gone, the sky is clear, and the air warm. I stop in at Caffeine on the Corner on my way home. The coffee shop is empty except for a middle-aged man wearing a gray suit, sipping a warm beverage from a fat white mug while reading the Sunday edition of the *Richmond Times Dispatch*.

"Welcome back!" Cecily says cheerfully from behind the counter. "How was the library?"

"Productive. I checked out *Where the Crawdads Sing*. I started it last night. Couldn't put it down. Have you read it?"

Cecily nods her head, her copper ponytail dancing around her shoulders. "Twice, actually. Finish the book, then we'll talk."

"Deal."

"What's it gonna be?" Cecily asks. "Another caffe mocha?"

I smile. "I'm surprised you remember with all the orders you must fill."

"Comes from years of waitressing experience."

I study the menu on the wall behind her, considering several options. "I'll have an iced coffee, please."

She removes a disposable cup from the stack and fills it with ice. "So . . . what brings you to Hope Springs?"

"I inherited the Hope Springs Inn from a father I didn't know I had."

"Seriously." She laughs and then sees from my expression that I'm not joking. "Holy moly!"

"Long story. Remind me to tell you sometime." I remove my wallet from my bag to pay for my drink. "What about you? How did you end up here?"

She slides my drink across the counter. "Mine is also a long story." I pay for the drink and she hands me my receipt. "I'm a trained chef. Why don't I make you dinner in exchange for a tour of the inn? I drive by there every day, and I'm dying to see inside. We can exchange stories while we eat."

"You mean tonight?" I've never had dinner with a virtual stranger before. She must be as desperate for friends as me.

She shrugs. "Sure! If you're free."

"Are you joking? I'm free for the foreseeable future. Does six o'clock work?"

"Six o'clock is perfect."

Back at the farm, I venture over to the main building with Billy's camera slung over my shoulder. My goal is to take *before* photographs for my album, but when I can't figure out how to adjust the light sensor on the camera, and the images turn out yellow, I resort to using my phone to take the pictures.

Outside is a different story. The camera loves the blue sky and natural sunlight. I snap dozens of images, not only of the exterior of the rotting buildings but of the budding flowers and trees. I see the world through different eyes. Through my grandmother's eyes, a woman passionate about gardening, and through Owens's protagonist Kya's eyes, a child living on her own in a swamp with only seagulls and herons for companions. As I walk around the grounds, I look for signs of Janis's gardens, but it's been twenty-seven years since her death, and a few spindly rose bushes are the only signs of her handiwork.

I make my way up to the barn and slide open the heavy doors. I'm terrified I'll find Bernard passed out drunk under the lawn mower, but his rusty pile of odds and ends is the only remaining evidence of him.

I attack the pile, setting aside most of the junk to be hauled off to the dump while salvaging a few useful items. At the back of the barn, I discover a variety of flower containers in all shapes and sizes. I find a charming pair of cast iron urns that are still in good shape despite their obvious age. I drag them one by one across the lawn to the cottage.

An hour later, promptly at six o'clock, I'm in the library of the main building, thumbing through flower books for container ideas, when Cecily arrives with a large basket. Peeking out from beneath a red-and-white checkered cloth is a bottle of red wine and a loaf of french bread.

"You went to too much trouble," I say, taking the basket from her and setting it on the reception desk.

She waves off my compliment. "It was no trouble at all. Now." She claps her hands. "How about that tour?"

We start in the solarium and work our way down the hall through the lounge. When we enter the dining room, she does a little spin, taking it all in. "You *inherited* all this from a man you didn't even know was your father? Stuff like that only happens in the movies. Start talking, Stella. I'm dying to hear your story."

I tell her about being an only child to same-sex parents and my brief and lackluster career in the hotel industry. She listens to my every word without speaking, and when I finish, she peppers me with questions.

"So, we know Hannah and Billy were romantically involved. But were they in a relationship or was it a one-night stand? Maybe he raped her."

I frown. "That's a possibility I haven't considered. But from what I've learned about Billy, he doesn't sound like the type."

"Why don't you just ask Hannah?"

"We're not on speaking terms at the moment. I blocked her number from my phone. Anyway, Brian Powers, the estate attorney, thinks I'm better off figuring things out for myself. In a weird way, I think maybe he's right. I'm putting together a jigsaw puzzle one piece at a time. Now it's your turn. Tell me your story."

"Let's finish the tour first." Cecily grabs my arm and drags me through the swinging doors to the kitchen. She stops short in the center of the room. "Whoa. I've seen some old appliances before, but I'm afraid to even turn these on."

She moves about the room, opening cabinet doors and investigating the walk-in pantry. "The space has potential. Good bones with lots of natural light and plenty of room. Update the cabinetry and appliances and you'll have a kitchen any chef would love to work in."

I watch her with interest. "You clearly know what you're talking about. You mentioned earlier that you're a trained chef. Start talking, Cecily," I say, throwing her words back at her.

Cecily moves to the bank of three windows and stares out across the back lawn. "I have a master's degree in culinary arts. I was working as a sous chef in a five-star restaurant in DC when I made the mistake of hooking up with the head chef one night after work. We'd both been drinking. It didn't mean anything for either of us, but the bastard fired me the next day."

"Ouch." I cross the room to her. "On what grounds?"

"He claims I was sexually harassing him."

"No way!"

"The whole thing was so unfair. He wouldn't even let me use him as a recommendation. I should've contested it, but I was so angry, all I wanted to do was get as far away from him as possible. I threw my stuff in my car, and left DC with no particular destination in mind. When I stopped in Hope Springs for gas, I found the town so charming, I ended up staying here."

I nudge her with my elbow. "We have something in common. Lack of impulse control."

She offers me a sad smile. "This little town feels like home to me, but unfortunately, there aren't enough opportunities for me to stay. I'm certainly not furthering my career by managing a coffee shop. But I can't bring myself to leave."

"Have you applied for jobs with any of the restaurants in Hope Springs?"

"Of course. Even though I'm qualified to be their head chef, the owners don't take me seriously. They say I'm too young."

Something else we have in common, I think to myself, but I don't say it.

"I've eaten in every establishment. Elmo's is the best, but none of them are great. Given the chance, I could really make a difference."

The unspoken hangs in the air between us. She needs a job, and come September, I'll be in need of a chef. The old impulsive Stella would have hired Cecily on the spot. But, with so much responsibility on my shoulders, I can't afford to make a mistake.

If preparing a meal for me is her way of applying for the job, I like her style.

I press my hands together. "Now that I know you're a chef, I'm even more eager to sample the goodies in your basket. Let me show you the grounds, and we'll go to my cottage for dinner."

Exiting the back door, we drop her basket off at the cottage and head down to the lake. "After all that rain yesterday, the grass is growing at a rate of three inches an hour. You don't happen to know anyone in landscaping, do you?"

She thinks before answering. "Not off the top of my head. Surely you already have a lawn service."

"We *had* a lawn service, although I wouldn't necessarily call him a service." I tell her the story of Bernard.

"That must have been terrifying. Aren't you scared living here alone?"

"Not really," I say, but even to my own ears, I sound unconvincing. "Okay. Maybe I'm a tiny bit afraid. The police are patrolling the farm over the weekend, and next week, I plan to hire a private security firm. I've lived all my life in small apartments with hundreds of other tenants in large buildings. But in a weird way, the farm feels like home."

"Did you leave a boyfriend behind in New York?"

"I wouldn't call Vince a boyfriend. I'm much better off without him anyway." When an image of Jack Snyder flashes in my mind, I push it aside. "How about you? Have you met anyone in Hope Springs?"

"I'm not very trusting of men after what happened in DC. But there is this one guy. He's a lacrosse coach at Jefferson College, but he doesn't know I'm alive. Wait! I take that back. He knows I make a mean caramel macchiato."

We burst out laughing at the same time.

When I show Cecily the hot spring, she insists on dipping her feet in. Slipping off our shoes, we sit on the cobblestone coping and dangle our feet over the side.

"The hot springs I've seen are much bigger. Why close it off in this hut? Wouldn't your guests enjoy the view of the lake and mountains while bathing in the healing waters? Imagine it, Stella, illuminated at night by strategically placed landscape lighting."

"Great idea, Cecily. I'm impressed." Jack had mentioned incorporating the springs into the spa facility. Making it open air would be all the more appealing to guests.

Cecily beams. "I'm full of good ideas."

And she proves it throughout the evening by making one innovative suggestion for improving the inn after another. If Cecily is vying for the position as my head chef, she doesn't admit it. Dinner consists of a light but flavorful crab quiche, a mixed green salad topped with assorted berries, and homemade sour-dough bread. Her food is some of the best I've ever tasted, and I devour every bite. Cecily prides herself on tweaking traditional recipes by adding a modern flair and using only the freshest farm-to-fork ingredients. She talks wine like an expert, and pairs the dinner with an excellent dry Riesling. By the time we've finished eating, I have no concerns about offering Cecily the job. I consider her age a bonus, not a disadvantage. She's young with fresh ideas. While we may get some pushback, we'll prove to everyone that we're up for the challenge. Strength in numbers and all that.

"So . . .," I say as we finish the last of the wine. "How do you feel about joining my team as head chef?" I like the sound of that. *My team. My project. My inn.* I break out in chill bumps. How cool is this?

Cecily clinks her glass to mine. "I thought you'd never ask."

ELEVEN

First thing on Monday morning, I put in a call to Brian from the manager's office. Sitting at the massive desk, where so many important decisions have been made in the past, gives me confidence. Even so, I'm still nervous about breaking the news to Brian that I hired a chef.

But he doesn't skip a beat. "Good for you! Bring him onboard as soon as possible. He can be instrumental in developing menus and designing the space."

"*He* is actually a she, Brian. You'll be meeting her soon, so you might as well know, she's the same age as me. But she has a master's degree in culinary arts. I sampled her cuisine last night. It's among the best I've had. And that's saying a lot, having dined in some of New York's top restaurants."

This is not a total lie. While I could never afford fine dining on my paltry salary, I ate in my share of five-star restaurants on birthdays and special occasions when my parents were treating.

When Brian doesn't respond, I prattle on. "Cecily has brilliant ideas about a lot of things, not just cooking. She will be a definite asset to our team. We share the same vision of enhancing the traditional with a slightly modern, upscale flair."

"You don't have to give me the hard sell, Stella. As long as you approve of her."

Despite his endorsement, I detect a hint of skepticism in his voice, and when I thank him for his vote of confidence, I vow all over again to prove myself to him.

I hear the sound of rattling paper on his end of the line. "Coincidentally," he says, "I was looking over Jack's numbers when you called. Everything appears to be in order. I'll give him the go-ahead, and we'll get this project underway."

I feel sick to my stomach, but in a good way. "That's exciting. Hiring a mover is on the top of my to-do list this morning. Do you by any chance know of a large warehouse where we can store furniture?"

"I know just the place. A friend of mine has a warehouse conditioned for heating and cooling. It's been empty for some time. I'll give him a call to see if we can lease it for the summer."

"That'd be great. Jack thought you might have a solution."

Brian laughs. "You can count on my support, Stella. If I don't have a solution off the top of my head, I'll find one for you."

We talk a few more minutes before hanging up. No sooner have I set down my phone, when it vibrates with a call from Cecily. When I answer, the noisy sounds of the coffee shop fill the line, but before I can say hello, Cecily blurts, "Before I turn in my notice, I need to make certain you're serious about the job. We had some wine last night. I totally understand if you were just drunk-talking. I'm offering you an out."

"Chill, Cecily. The job is yours."

"Are you sure? You can walk away, no hard feelings. We'll still be friends."

"I'm positive. I'm thrilled to have you onboard."

Cecily exhales loudly. "This is my dream job, Stella. I was afraid . . ."

"Say no more, Cecily. We're going to make a great team. I

understand you have to work your two weeks' notice, but can you set aside some time soon to brainstorm ideas?"

"I have like a gazillion Pinterest boards. I'll combine some of my best ideas and share them with you. And I'm off on Friday if you want to have dinner again."

"Only if you're cooking."

"Then it's a date."

After ending my call with Cecily, I spend the rest of the morning scheduling Skype interviews with four interior design firms—all of them in Richmond, one of them recommended by Jack's architect sister—and making calls to eleven landscape maintenance services and three moving companies. The lawn services are too busy with their existing clients to take on such a large account, although several of them sound disappointed at having to turn down the opportunity. Only one of the local movers suits our needs, and I schedule an appointment with him for late this afternoon.

I go to the cottage for a quick bite of lunch—a spoonful of chicken salad and a tomato sliced into wedges. When I finish, I go in search of Opal. I find her sitting on a bench near her tree, eating an apple and staring off into space. Her canvas is set up nearby, but it doesn't appear she's painted much on the spring house since the last time I saw it.

I slide onto the bench beside her. "You're a million miles away. What's on your mind?"

She looks over at me, and I think she's happy to see me despite the sadness in her smile. "Oh, you know. Just thinking about years gone by."

"Have you lived in Hope Springs all your life?"

"Off and on." She takes the last bite of her apple and tosses the core across the lawn. "We used to rent one of the cottages every summer."

"By *we*, do you mean your husband and children?"

She ignores my question. "Life happens fast, Stella."

"I'd like to hear about your life, if you want to talk about it."

"No, you don't." She waves her hand in front of her face, as though shooing away a fly. "You have better things to do than listen to an old woman ruminate about the past."

I give up. Opal is either extremely private or she's hiding something. "Actually, I was going to ask a favor. I was up late last night studying the handbook. I was wondering if you'd drive me to DMV to take the test."

"Sure!" She jumps to her feet with the energy of a woman half her age.

I laugh. "I didn't necessarily mean right now. I don't want to interrupt your painting."

"I haven't lifted the brush all morning. I have artist's block." She laughs at her own joke.

"In that case," I say, "can we go before I chicken out?"

"Let me just pack up my things."

We carry her easel and paints up to her Mini, which she parked beside the barn.

"Is DMV far away?" I ask when we're headed down the driveway, wind whipping our hair.

"About three miles outside of town," she says, and turns up the volume on the radio. A song from an early Wild Hollers album is on her playlist, and we sing along with Billy as we drive through town.

My few friends who actually went to the trouble to get driver's licenses have shared horror stories about their experiences at DMV, but I have no complaints about mine. I don't have to wait in line long, and the clerk who assists me in taking the test is pleasant. When I emerge from the testing area fifteen minutes later, learner's permit in hand, Opal is studying a printed copy of the driver's handbook.

She pokes the handbook. "There's a checklist here that describes specific driving tasks you'll need to perform when taking the road skills test. I'm officially volunteering for the job as your driving coach."

"You're hired. Thanks."

We exit the building, and as we zoom back toward town, I point to a garden center ahead of us on the other side of the highway. "Can we stop in there? I found a pair of containers in the barn. I'd love to buy some flowers for them."

"Certainly," Opal says, and whips the Mini across two lanes of oncoming traffic.

"I should warn you, though, I know absolutely nothing about flowers," I say as we enter the fenced-in outdoor area of the garden center.

"Then it's a good thing you brought me a long."

I follow Opal as she circles the tables and carts exhibiting plastic pots and flats of colorful flowers. The choices are overwhelming. "They're all so pretty. How does one decide?"

"You start by narrowing your options based on growth habits and sun exposure." We stand in front of a table of small plants with clusters of flowers in bright summer colors. "Tell me about your containers."

"Well . . ." I pause as I consider how best to describe them. "They're narrow at the base and wider at the top. I guess you'd call them urns. They're about this big." Hands clasped, I hold my arms out in front of me.

"And where are you planning to put them?"

"In front of the cottage, on the sidewalk at the bottom of the steps."

"Good! You'll get plenty of morning sun there." She removes her John Lennon sunglasses and examines the flowers. "I've always had more success with annuals versus perennials in my containers. They're more bountiful and less expensive. You won't feel bad throwing them away at the end of the season. These pretty plants are Calibrachoa, also known as million bells. They would be a good choice for a beginner. As you can see, they come in every color imaginable."

"One of the flower books I found in the inn's library says I should have thriller, filler, and spiller in my containers."

She stares at me from under furrowed brows. "And I thought you knew nothing about flowers."

I laugh. "That's not experience. Only what I read in a book."

"You can take that approach. But there are no set rules when it comes to nature. Plant what you like. If you pick a Proven Winners plant, water it daily and fertilize it every other week, it'll perform well for you all summer long."

We spend a few minutes discussing the pros and cons of the options available. Overwhelmed and frustrated, I decide to keep it simple and plant hot pink million bells in my containers.

"I approve of your choice," Opal says. "A happy splash of color to greet your guests."

We grab a large bag of potting soil and are standing in line to check out, when Opal says, "Perhaps you'll discover a passion for gardening like your grandmother."

"Who knows if I even have a green thumb. I might kill these little guys." I finger a pink flower petal. "I admit, though, after living amongst concrete buildings and sidewalks all my life, I'm enjoying being outdoors."

"Outdoor living is good for the soul."

"I'm beginning to realize that."

When we're finished checking out, we load the flowers and soil into the back of Opal's car.

"You clearly know a lot about gardening," I say on the way home. "Were you and my grandmother friends?"

That same lost-in-the-past expression from earlier returns to Opal's face. "We didn't run in the same social circles, but Janis and I were good friends. Because we shared a lot in common, we enjoyed each other's company."

"What was she like?"

I'd imagined my grandmother to be a real lady, well-groomed and dignified, and I'm shocked when Opal says, "Cussed like a sailor and drank whiskey like it was water. She never put on airs, and that's what drew people to her. One always knew where they stood with Janis Jameson."

"I wish I'd known her," I say in a soft voice.

"You would've liked her. And she would've liked you."

Warmth spreads across my chest. "Thank you for saying that."

At the farm, Opal parks in front of the cottage and we unload the soil and flowers onto the short sidewalk. She shows me how to fill the bottom of the urns with crushed soft drink cans to allow for better irrigation. Once the containers are planted, I step back and admire my work. "Just as you said, a cheerful welcome to my visitors."

For the next two hours, Opal guides me on a horticultural tour of the grounds, naming shrubs and trees and the few perennials showing the tips of their heads in neglected flower beds. I snap dozens of photos with Billy's camera and take detailed notes on my phone. I'm eager to learn. Finally, I've discovered a hobby I enjoy.

"Thank you, Opal," I say, when I walk her to her car. "I really think I'm going to love gardening."

She pats my arm. "Don't get ahead of yourself, my dear. The pruning and planting will wait. Your first order of business is to find someone to mow and blow."

"Trust me, I'm working on it." I give her a peck on the cheek and close her car door.

I check the time on my phone, and seeing that I'm late for my meeting, I hurry over to the main building. The representative from the moving company is waiting patiently at the front door. David Ryan is professional and accommodating. We agree on pricing, but I can only answer a few of his many questions about timing, and I'm grateful when Jack stops by.

Jack explains to David, "Ideally, I'd like to start demo the first of next week. I realize I'm asking a lot, but can you get everything out of here by then?"

"Shouldn't be a problem, since it's a local job. I'll hire extra movers if necessary. My team will be here first thing on Wednesday morning to start packing."

Jack and I stand at the front door, watching the mover drive off in his pickup truck. I wrap my arms around my midsection, hugging myself. "Is this really happening, Jack?"

He flashes a pearly white smile that sends a bolt of electricity to parts of my body totally off-limits to married men. "This is really happening, Stella."

TWELVE

Packing up the inn is a monumental job. All day on Tuesday, I sort through books and dishes and table linens, setting aside items to be donated to charity and junk to be tossed in the trash. From the library, I take several armfuls of books, novels as well as gardening guides and photo albums, to the cottage, stacking them on the floor in the already cluttered living room. There's the issue of what to do with the dusty bottles in the wine cellar, but Cecily and I agree to leave them for the wine steward. I add *Hire a wine steward* to my rapidly growing list.

There's so much to think about. For the guest rooms, we'll need new mattresses and televisions, towels and bed linens. For the public rooms, we'll have to purchase updated lamps, decorative items, and small odds and ends of furniture to contrast with the traditional antiques. While the reception area will get a whole new look, nothing in the manager's office will change aside from a fresh coat of paint and new carpeting. Generations of Jamesons have presided over the inn from this office. Who am I to tamper with family history?

When the movers arrive on Wednesday, I hover over them

while they work, watching closely to make certain they handle every object with care. When I'm not overseeing the packing, I'm narrowing down my choices of interior design firms. I give equal consideration to all of them, but the Richmond firm Jack's sister suggested—it's comprised of two women in their mid-thirties—wins my vote. Not only do they have an impressive résumé of commercial projects of comparable scope, they've successfully implemented the boutique hotel theme at similar properties before. We make a date for the dynamic duo to come to Hope Springs the following Monday for a walk-through.

I receive no word from Naomi and no sign of Bernard. I hire a retired policeman to patrol the grounds at night throughout the summer, but when we reopen in September, we'll need a staff of security personnel.

With each passing day, as the furnishings are removed, the inn becomes a dismal place, dark and gloomy and depressing. By the time Friday rolls around, I'm eager for some fresh air and sunshine. I leave David to oversee the last of the packing and make my way out to the barn.

Every night at bedtime, I read a few chapters of *Crawdads* before falling into a sleep coma. As I wade through the thick ankle-high grass, I think of young Kya, as I often do these days. She seems so real to me, and I have to remind myself she's a fictional character. She's completely stolen my heart, and I root for her through her many trials and tribulations. Although she's not even half my age, her determination inspires me. One way or another, I will cut this grass today.

The movers, as instructed, have hauled off Bernard's junk pile, which gives me a clear path to the John Deere mower. *How hard can it be?* I ask myself as I mount the mower. Twenty minutes later, I've tried everything, but I can't get the machine to start.

When I hear footsteps behind me, I jerk around, expecting to see Bernard training his gun on me. I'm relieved to find Jack instead.

"Going somewhere?" he asks with a sly smile.

I slide off the mower and give the tire a kick. "Blasted thing won't start. The battery must be dead. Or maybe it's out of gas, although I have no idea where to find the gas gauge."

He closes the distances between us. "Here, let me try."

"By all means." I move out of his way, so he can climb onto the mower.

Settling himself into the seat, he says, "Looks to be a relatively new model."

I eye the John Deere suspiciously. "Are you sure? Because, if that's the case, it's the only thing around here that's been updated in the past century."

"I'd be willing to bet it was purchased within the past three to five years. You have plenty of gas. Your gauge is here." He points at a small window between his legs beneath the seat.

I lean in close enough to see the needle pointing to the three-quarter mark. "Oh. There it is."

"Did you choke the motor when you tried to start it?"

Furrowing my brow, I stare up at him. "Huh?"

Jack laughs. Placing his left hand on the red gear lever, he says, "When your engine is cold, you have to push the throttle all the way forward to choke it."

"I wasn't sure what that was for."

"The throttle controls your speed. Now, you have to press down on the brake pedal while you turn the ignition key." He does both, and the engine fires right up.

I roll my eyes. *Naturally.*

In a voice loud enough to be heard over the noise from the tractor, he says, "Once the engine is running, pull the throttle down to the lowest position." He touches his right fingers to a black stick with a yellow handle. "This lever controls your blades. Push it up to engage and down to disengage. Piece of cake." He kills the engine and jumps down. "You'll want to protect your hearing. I'm sure there's a headset around here somewhere."

He locates a set of red headphones hanging on a peg near the mower and puts them on my head. "Cute."

I feel like a child looking up at her father with adoring eyes. I've done an exemplary job of suppressing my attraction to him this week, but now, with the two of us alone in the barn. *There are three of us, Stella. Remember, the man has a wife.*

"You'll need sunglasses to protect your eyes."

I pull my sunglasses out of my pocket and put them on.

"You're all set now. With the grass being as tall as it is, you'll want to bag the clippings. Good thing Bernard's already got the bagger attached."

He gives me a brief tutorial on how to empty the bagger when it's full. "Now climb up, and I'll direct you as you back out."

I turn toward the mower, but my feet get tangled and I slip on the running board. Jack catches me, his hands on my hips. Our bodies are so close together, I want to melt into him, to feel him against me. He spins me around and kisses me. His lips are soft against mine, and every nerve ending in my body is on high alert. My body aches for him, but my mind takes control, issuing commands to my arms to shove him away. "Stop! Jack. What're you doing?"

"Oh god!" He takes a giant step backward. "I don't know what got into me. I'm so sorry, Stella." His neck and face are flushed as he rakes his hands through his thick dark hair. "I'll back the tractor out for you."

He leaps into the seat, starts up the engine, and maneuvers the mower out of the barn. He hops down, and I take control of the wheel. When I start to drive off, he cups his hands around his mouth, but I can't hear what he's trying to tell me.

I turn the motor down and lift the headset off one ear. "What did you say?"

Although he's regained his composure, he refuses to look me in the eye. "The dumpsters have been delivered. My crew will be here bright and early on Monday morning. Enjoy your quiet weekend. It might be your last for a while."

I give him a thumbs-up and drive the mower down the driveway to the main building. Cutting one neat row of freshly trimmed grass at a time, I work my way down to the lake. Jack Snyder forgotten, I fall head over heels in love with the John Deere mower. Is this how Kya felt racing through the swamps in her skiff? I don't even mind wrestling with the bag when I empty the grass clippings. It's dirty work. My clothes are soaked through with perspiration and grass clippings are stuck to my sticky skin. But by the time I finish, I feel like I've truly achieved something.

I shower and dress in white capri jeans and a chambray shirt tied at the waist. Cecily arrives a few minutes after six, gripping a bottle of tequila in one hand and carrying a soft cooler with the fixings for a gourmet Mexican dinner in the other.

"Are you hungry?" she asks.

"Yes! Starving. I just cut every blade of grass on this farm. But I'm not ready to eat dinner yet."

"Then we'll start with homemade guacamole and chips." She brushes past me on her way to the kitchen. "I don't know about you, but it's Friday afternoon and I'm ready to kick back and relax."

"Bring it on!" I lean against the kitchen counter, watching her slice and dice and mash ingredients for the guacamole with utensils she brought from home.

"I have a date tomorrow night," she says with a sheepish grin.

My eyes grow wide. "Yay, you! With the lacrosse coach?"

"Yep." Her face takes on a soft glow. She's totally into this guy.

"See! He did notice you."

"His name is Lyle Nelson. Can you believe it? Like who names their kid Lyle?"

I repeat the name. "I kinda like it. Where's he taking you?"

"To dinner at his boss's house."

"Surely you jest. He's taking you to his boss's house on your first date? No pressure there."

Cecily barks out a laugh. "It's not as bad as I make it sound. Lyle's team has a home game tomorrow, and the head coach is hosting a cookout for players and coaches afterward."

"That actually sounds like fun. Are you cooking for them?"

"Ha! No." She removes a small pottery bowl from her cooler and fills it with guacamole.

"Did you bring your kitchen sink too?"

"Not the sink, but I did bring these," she says, pulling two margarita glasses from her cooler.

"Good thinking. We only have juice glasses. I don't think my father was much of a cook."

Cecily mixes tequila with freshly squeezed lime juice, home-made simple syrup, and orange liqueur into a glass pitcher I locate in the top of a cabinet. She dips the glasses in a concoction of lime, salt, and sugar and fills each glass with margarita. Taking our drinks into the living room, we open all the windows and doors and place *The Best of Van Morrison* vinyl on the turn table. We sit side-by-side on the sofa with the bowl of guacamole and basket of chips between us. A cool breeze wafts through the window bringing with it the scent of freshly cut grass.

"I love that smell," Cecily says, stuffing a loaded chip in her mouth. "It's a sure sign summer is near. There's a lot of grass on this farm. I assume you used a riding mower."

I grin at her. "I did. I had so much fun, I can't wait for the grass to grow so I can cut it again. Is that weird?"

"So weird." She throws a chip at me. "Weirdo."

Even though we've only just met, I feel like I've known Cecily forever. "Speaking of weird, something weird happened to me today. I'm not sure what to think of it." I tell her about Jack's kiss.

When I'm finished, she asks, "Are you sure he's married?"

I shrug. "Why else would he be wearing a wedding band?"

"To ward off aggressive women like you," she says with mischief in her smile.

"Puh-lease." I fall back against the sofa cushions. "Maybe some single women wear fake wedding rings to avoid being hit on by creeps, but what man would do that? Anyway, Jack seemed surprised at himself for kissing me. It was a heat-of-the-moment thing."

"Whether the kiss was spontaneous, or he regularly cheats on his wife, forget it ever happened. You need Jack. This project will not happen without him. From now on, it's strictly business between you."

"Trust me, I get it."

THIRTEEN

On Saturday, I finally get around to unpacking my wardrobe boxes that arrived earlier in the week. The bedroom feels a little more like home with my clothes in the closet. On a whim, I walk to the home goods boutique in town and purchase a comforter set with an abstract floral design in shades of blues, greens, and yellow.

Loneliness sets in when I see couples holding hands as they stroll about on Main Street. The chances of me meeting a guy in a town the size of Hope Springs is slim. For the first time since coming to Virginia, I feel homesick for New York. I can't stop thinking of Hannah and Marnie. I should let them know I'm alive, but their betrayal is still fresh. Without unblocking their numbers, I send a simple group text. *Things are going well in Virginia. I'm sorting through some issues. Will call when I'm ready to talk.*

I click on Rachel's number. She understands my history with losers like Vince. She'll know what to say to help me forget about Jack.

When she answers on the third ring, I hear noise in the background. "Stella! I'm so sorry I didn't call you. It's been such a whirlwind."

I grip my phone tighter, and even though I already know the answer, I ask, "What're you talking about? What whirlwind?"

"My engagement to Bert. Didn't you see my Instagram post? Listen, I'm at brunch with my friends. I'll call you later."

She hangs up on me before I can offer congratulations. I tap on my Instagram app and access her account. Sure enough, there's a pic of Rachel and Bert, gazing into each other's eyes. She's holding up her left hand for the Instagram world to see the ginormous diamond on her ring finger. In all fairness, Rachel and Bert only got engaged last night. But still, we've been best friends most of our lives. I deserve to hear it from her instead of learning about it on social media.

I replay the brief conversation in my head. Rachel said, "I'm at brunch with *my* friends." I've been gone from New York for less than two weeks, and I'm already a distant memory.

That night I eat leftover Mexican food and watch *Casablanca*, which only makes me miss Hannah and Marnie more.

On Sunday, I go to the late service at the pretty stone church in town. The minister is ancient and his sermon a sleeper. I leave feeling more depressed than ever. The weather matches my mood —dreary with off and on showers and cooler temperatures. That afternoon, wrapped in my new comforter on the sofa, I escape to the land of fiction where crawdads sing.

On Monday morning at seven o'clock, I'm waiting at the door to greet Jack's crew with a cardboard travel box of coffee purchased from Caffeine on the Corner. Jack is professionally polite toward me but the easy interaction we previously shared doesn't return.

Once the crew start to work, the banging of their sledgehammers in the guest bathrooms drives me to my office where I stay until the decorators arrive at ten.

Cary and Kathleen are more than partners at Ramsey

Designs. They're sisters. And they are badasses in smart business suits with expensively highlighted blonde hair piled in messy buns. While they're confident in a manner that commands authority, they are in no way condescending. Not only do I strive to be like them in my new role, I trust my project is in excellent hands.

Jack and Cecily sit in for the first part of the meeting. Jack appears antsy and excuses himself after only a few minutes. "I need to be hands on for this first day of demo." He gives each of the designers a business card. "If I can be of any assistance, do not hesitate to contact me."

We take a break after an hour of discussing ideas for the kitchen and dining room. While Cary and Kathleen make phone calls to handle an issue with another client, Cecily pulls me aside. "Jack is seriously hot. But I agree with you. He's totally married. If I were you, I'd keep things between you—"

I hold my hand up to silence her. "Strictly professional."

When Cecily returns to the coffee shop, I give my guests a tour of the building, starting on the top and working our way down. Cary and Kathleen get super excited when I share my thoughts for Billy's Bar. I can almost see gears spinning in their heads as they listen and look around. And then I get super excited as they begin to launch one idea after another, flipping them around like balls in a pinball machine.

"I'm thinking navy as the predominant color," Kathleen says. "With lots of gleaming surfaces—mirrors and marble and high-gloss paint."

Cary scrutinizes the room. "We'll tray the ceiling and choose a bold geometric carpet."

Moving to the rear of the lounge, Kathleen says, "We should think about putting in a parquet floor back here to use for dancing and as a stage when small groups perform. Which reminds me, Stella, we'll give you the name of the firm in Richmond we use for network and Wi-Fi installations. They do audio and video as well."

"Can you show us Billy's memorabilia?"

"Now?" I ask, and they nod in unison.

It's almost two o'clock, and I'm starving. "Can I take you to lunch first?"

"Who has time for lunch? We brought power bars." Cary removes three RX Bars from her oversized designer handbag, offering one to Kathleen and me.

I accept the bars, grateful for anything to satisfy my hunger.

We spend another hour at the cottage. After discussing innovative ways to showcase Billy's collections, we talk about budgets and fees. As I'm walking them back to the main building, I ask, "Do you have any concerns whatsoever about meeting our projected completion date?"

Kathleen, whom I deem to be the older of the sisters, says, "None at all. We know which vendors offer reliable lead times. We'll only order goods that are in stock. We have an efficient staff who will stay on top of all deliveries. While we won't be completely finished, the inn will be in good enough shape to reopen in early September. By the way, do we have an exact date for that yet?"

"Subject to change, of course, but as of now, I'm hoping to have a soft opening the week after Labor Day."

"That seems so far away, but it'll be here before you know it." Kathleen squeezes me in a half hug. "Fasten your seat belt, Stella, you're in for an exciting ride."

My days fall into a routine. When I'm not meeting or talking on the phone with vendors in my office, I find ways to occupy my time outdoors. I give Billy's Wrangler a thorough wash and practice my driving skills on the roads around the farm. I stand for long stretches of time on the grassy hill in front of the inn, imagining Billy and Ethan playing football in the sprawling front yard across the street at the manor house.

When I ask Opal who in the Jameson family sold the manor house, she says, "Billy did. He couldn't bear the memories."

I sit for hours on Opal's park bench, watching her create masterpieces with graceful strokes of her brush. We take long walks around the grounds and picnic at the overlook. Ours is a companionable relationship. We can go for hours without saying a word or have a heated discussion about world affairs. But she makes it clear her past and her family are off-limit subjects. She's never around on weekends, and I assume she's at her home tending to chores. I wonder if she lives in one of the tidy houses lining the streets of downtown. Or if she lives in a cabin in the woods somewhere nearby? When I ask Opal what her last name is, she ignores me, as she always does when she thinks I'm getting too personal. But the name Opal is rare, and when I google the white pages for Opal in the Hope Springs area, my result yields one—Opal Powers. So, Opal and Brian are related. I ask her if she's Brian's mother, and she gives me the first solid answer since we met. Yes.

Yard work is my new favorite pastime. I prune and weed and plant. I learn to use the blower and the leaf sucker and the weed eater. I make countless trips to the garden center for perennials, annuals, and flowering shrubs. Although the improvements are immediate and drastic, the grounds are extensive and my progress doesn't put a dent in the work that needs to be completed in order to return the property to Janis Jameson's standards. There's no way I can do it alone, and I've come no closer to finding a groundskeeper despite my best efforts.

My luck changes on the Friday of Memorial Day weekend. In the middle of the afternoon, I'm shoveling dead leaves into the compost pile when I receive a call from an excited Cecily. "I'm at the coffee shop. Get down here right now! I found you a landscaper."

Certain it's another dead-end lead, I say, "I'm filthy, Cecily. I've been working outside all day. Text me her number, and I'll call her later."

"No way! I'm holding her hostage until you get here. Not kidding, Stella. She's perfect. You'll thank me for this."

A rush of adrenaline surges through me. It would be awesome to finally find someone qualified to take over the grounds. "All right then. I'll be there in a few."

Abandoning my rake, I jog around to the front of the main building, and I don't stop until I arrive, sweating and breathless, at Caffeine on the Corner. Cecily and the landscaper are seated at a table with their heads close together. When I enter, they stand to greet me, and Cecily provides the introductions. Katherine Arnold is about my age, maybe a few years older than me, with medium brown hair, hazel eyes, and a trail of sun freckles across her nose. She's dressed the part in work boots, khaki cargo shorts, and a sleeveless cotton top. A worn straw fedora rests on the table beside her coffee mug.

"Katherine just moved here from Savannah," Cecily explains. "Her husband is the new admissions director at the college. She has a degree in landscape architecture."

Katherine adds, "My landscaping business was just starting to take off when my husband accepted this job. I'm starting over from scratch."

"Did Cecily explain the scope of the property? I'm looking for someone to restore and maintain it."

"I understand," Katherine says with a nod. "I was considering taking the summer off before starting back to work, but this job sounds ideal. Cecily says the farm is within walking distance. Do you have time to show it to me now?"

"Of course!" I turn my attention to Cecily. "Can you come with us? I assume you told Katherine that today's your last day here, and that, as of Monday, you're the new head chef at the Inn at Hope Springs Farm."

Cecily lifts a finger to correct me. "The still unnamed restaurant at the Inn at Hope Springs Farm. And, yes, I told Katherine all about it." She glances around the empty cafe. Aside from the three of us, there's only one other customer seated at the window counter and another barista behind the bar. "Y'all go ahead. I'm not supposed to know this, but my coworkers have planned a surprise going-away party for me when our shift changes at three."

"Well, you certainly can't miss that," I say. "We'll catch up with you later. Maybe for drinks around happy hour."

Katherine tugs her hat down over her head, and we exit the cafe together, walking back toward the farm. "Tell me about yourself, Katherine. Were you sad to leave Savannah?"

"Yes and no. I wanted to support my husband. This is his dream job. And I've lived in Savannah my whole life. I'm excited to try something different for a change."

"This is definitely different," I say with a laugh. "I'm from New York. There's a learning curve for small-town living. Do you have children?"

She offers a despondent smile that lets me know she really wants a family. "Not yet. With the move and all, we decided to stop trying until we get settled."

When we reach the farm, we switch into work mode as we tour the grounds. "Your beds are in desperate need of mulch," Katherine says right off the bat.

"Don't I know it."

"The grass needs attention. We'll fertilize now, and then wait until the fall to seed and aerate." We loop down to the lake, and as we're starting back up the hill, she says, "You have plenty of property to do so many wonderful things. You could put in a maze garden, incorporating hidden sculptures and benches and containers of bright flowers."

"Wonderful suggestion."

"It's a shame to use this charming space for storage," she says, about the barn. "You could rent it out for parties or dances or even weddings. You would need to spruce it up by painting the outside a neutral color and finishing off the interior. I would get rid of the stalls and have one big open space."

"I had the same thought myself, but what do we do with the mower and all the yard tools?"

"Have your builder install a prefabricated commercial storage unit, out of sight somewhere on the edge of the property." Katherine stops circling the barn and faces me. "I don't mean to overwhelm you, Stella. Feel free to tell me to shut up. My husband thinks I have too many ideas."

"There's no such thing as too many ideas. Every idea is worth considering, even if we don't use them all."

"True. But you need to start by getting what you already have under control."

"Agreed." My phone has been vibrating on my hip for the past hour. Removing it from my pocket, I scroll through the string of texts. "Cecily wants to know if you've accepted the job."

There's mischief in Katherine's smile when she says, "Tell Cecily I'm waiting for an official offer."

"I thought that was a foregone conclusion," I say, and take a stab at a salary based on my research. "But that's negotiable. I want you on my team whatever it takes."

Katherine counters for five thousand more a year, and I agree, reminding her about medical and dental insurance.

She points at my phone. "Text Cecily that I accept."

I thumb off the text, and Cecily responds right away. *Celebratory drinks at Buddy's in ten.*

FOURTEEN

Buddy's is what one might expect of a small-town bar and grill. Red-leathered booths and dim lighting. In the back, a pool table surrounded by a group of guys who, judging from their rowdy behavior, have been here since lunch. Against the far wall, a banquet table, draped in a dingy white cloth, is lined with chafing dishes containing today's happy hour specials. A heavy wooden bar with shelves displaying hundreds of liquor bottles occupies the opposite wall.

At five o'clock, aside from the pool players, we're the only other people here. The three of us claim stools at the end of the bar near the window, and Cecily demands a round of tequila shots from the bartender. Pete is his name—shaved head, goatee, and an impressive set of biceps bulging from beneath his tight tee. Placing three shot glasses in front of us, he fills them with tequila and slides a bowl of lemon slices with a saltshaker across the bar.

"One path ends and another begins." Cecily holds her shot glass out to us. "To my dream job," she says and kicks back the tequila with no salt or lemon.

Katherine follows her lead, wiping her mouth on her bare

arm. "This day has been full of surprises. I woke up this morning, wishing I was back in Savannah, and now I have two new friends and a job that may turn out to be my dream job as well."

I raise my glass. "On my first day in town, a wise man encouraged me to dream big. And that, girlfriends, is our new motto. We've been given a golden opportunity. In order to succeed, we will need to reach for the stars. To our dream team," I say and gulp down the tequila.

"To our dream team," Cecily and Katherine say in unison.

I toss my new credit card down on the bar. "Drinks on me."

We order another round of shots and three white wines. We bombard Katherine with questions about her life, and by the time our glasses are empty, we know her history.

Patrons begin trickling in, and before long, Buddy's is rocking. Someone cranks up the volume on the country music jukebox, the pool players send us another round of tequila shots, and we continue to order refills of wine. By the time we get around to standing in line for food, happy hour has ended, and there's not a morsel left.

When Katherine steps outside to call her husband, Cecily and I find ourselves alone at the bar. "How are things with Jack?" she asks.

"Professional." I find this hilarious for some reason and nearly roll off my stool laughing. "No, seriously." I say righting myself and sopping up my tears with a napkin. "When I see Jack, which isn't very often, our conversation is strictly business. Come to think of it, despite the loud construction noises, things have been quiet around the inn. I haven't seen Brian Powers either. He's the attorney I told you about. I thought he'd be dropping by every day to check on progress. Suffice it to say, I'm looking forward to having female company around the farm."

Cecily narrows her eyes. "I've been meaning to talk to you about where I'm going to work. I need to be near a functioning kitchen. I can work from my apartment, but I'd rather be close to you so we can brainstorm ideas."

I sit back on the barstool and cross my legs. "Well, let me think. There's the cottage, but we might get in each other's way. There's also a kitchen in the carriage house. I have no idea if the appliances even work. Why don't you come over tomorrow, and we'll check it out."

Her chin drops to her chest. "Sorry. I can't. I'm going with Lyle to Charlottesville to watch the UVA lacrosse team in the semifinal round of the playoffs."

"That sounds like fun," I say, managing to hide my disappointment. "The kitchen will wait until Monday."

Cecily stares into her wineglass. "Monday is Memorial Day. Lyle is taking me rafting on the river." She looks up again. "But I'll be there bright and early on Tuesday."

"No worries. I totally forgot about Monday being a holiday."

My festive mood tanks at the prospect of another lonely weekend ahead. I survey the other customers in the crowded restaurant. Everyone appears to be coupled up. All the booths are occupied with foursomes. Four gay guys are seated at the table in the window. Even the men and women at the bar down from us are paired up. The guys at the pool table in the back are the only ones flying solo, and they are definitely not my type. I remind myself that I didn't come to Hope Springs to find a man. I came here to find myself.

To rub salt in my wound, Katherine returns with a man whom she introduces as her husband. Dean is handsome, despite his receding hairline, and genuinely excited about his wife's new job. Sitting down beside me, he orders a Devil's Backbone craft beer. "Tell me more about your renovation project at the inn. My new associates in the admissions department are talking about it. As you might imagine, having a five-star property so close to the college is a magnet for our prospective parents. Any chance it'll reopen in time for fall football weekends?"

This brings a smile to my face. "That's our goal," I say and give him a quick overview of our plans.

I notice Cecily's gaze shift to the door, and her face lights up. She hops off her stool and hurries over to the guy dressed in Jefferson College lacrosse swag. She gives him a hug and brings Lyle over to us. Dean is thrilled to meet a fellow college staffer, and the two guys launch into a discussion about sports. While it's probably my imagination, Katherine and Cecily suddenly have much to talk about that doesn't include me. I am the obvious fifth wheel, and when Cecily suggests we move to a table, I seize the opportunity to make my escape.

When Cecily begs me not to go, I say, "I need to rest up. I have a long to-do list for the weekend."

I'm more intoxicated than I realized, and I have trouble walking in a straight line on my way back to the inn. My eyes are glued to the sidewalk, and I don't see Jack locking the front door until I trip over the curb and stumble into him.

He catches me. "Easy, Stella. Have you been drinking?"

"I may have had a teensy bit," I say with slurred words. "We were celebrating. I finally found a new landscaper." I let out a hiccup. "Sorry. I don't usually drink so much. I should go to bed."

"But it's not even seven o'clock. Have you eaten dinner?"

My alcohol-riddled brain jumps to the conclusion that he's suggesting a date. "You should go home to your wife."

He follows my gaze to his left ring finger. "I didn't mean like on a date or anything," he says, shoving his left hand in his pocket. "I was merely recommending you get some food in your stomach. We finished demolition today, and we'll start rebuilding on Monday. We're a few days behind where I'd like to be. With time of the essence, I hope you don't mind if we work on a holiday."

"That's fine." To my horror, another hiccup escapes my mouth.

"This project is a priority for me, Stella," he says in an irritated tone.

"As it should be, Jack." Bringing myself to my full height, I speak slowly so as not to garble my words. "Are you insinuating it's not a priority for me because I had drinks on a Friday afternoon with my coworkers?"

Shaking his head, he turns to leave. "Sleep it off, Stella."

Mortified, I take his advice. I go straight to my cottage, place one of Billy's early albums on the turntable, and crash fully clothed on the sofa.

The sound of sirens jerks me from a deep slumber a few minutes after midnight. When I pry my eyes open, the living room is filled with blue flashing lights.

"What in the world?" Rolling off the sofa to my feet, I hurry outside to see several patrol cars parked haphazardly around the entrance to the barn. I take off jogging up the narrow road, the pounding in my head intensifying with every stride.

I count six policemen gathered around the entrance to the barn, and when I peer over their shoulders, I expect to see a dead body. But it's only Martin, my new night security man, squared off against Bernard. If they start throwing punches, Bernard won't stand a chance.

I recognize one of the officers from the day Bernard held a gun on me. Tapping him on the shoulder, I say, "What's going on?"

"Bernard claims he stopped by"—the officer uses air quotes —"to get some of the things he left in the barn."

I force my way through the policemen. I'm still half drunk, and the alcohol in my system gives me fake courage. "You have no business here, Bernard. I want you to leave."

Bernard puffs out his chest. "Well, now. If it ain't the little missy. I ain't leaving till I get my stuff."

Missy again? "If you're referring to the pile of junk you left behind, I had it hauled off. If you want it back, you'll have to check the city dump." Turning to leave, as I brush past the policemen, I say, "Get this man off my property."

My bravery retreats on the walk back to the cottage. I lock all the doors and turn on the outside lights. I'm only slightly relieved when Martin stops by to tell me the police have arrested Bernard for trespassing and public drunkenness. "You don't need to worry, Miss Boor. He'll be spending the night in jail."

"But will he come back tomorrow night after he's released?"

"I can't guarantee he won't," Martin says. "I recommend beefing up security for the time being."

Goose bumps crawl across my flesh, and I wrap my arms around myself. "Can you take care of that for me, Martin?"

"Yes, ma'am. I know some retired security guys looking for work."

"Hire however many you think we need. I admit I'm a little creeped out. Can you stay nearby tonight?"

"Yes, ma'am. I'll park up at the barn."

After Martin leaves, too wired to sleep, I stay up until well past three finishing *Where the Crawdads Sing*. I feel an ache in my heart that it's over, as though mourning the loss of a friend. Who knew it was possible to be so profoundly affected by fictional characters?

First thing on Saturday morning, I return the book to the library and pay my late fine. Mrs. Mitchell scolds me for not returning the book on time, but when I tell her what an inspiration Kya is to me, she helps me pick out another book. *When We Were Yours*—the story of two orphan sisters separated as children.

FIFTEEN

On Monday, despite being a holiday, the farm is a beehive of activity. Jack's largest crew to date is banging away at the inn while Katherine and the two grounds crewmen she hired are raking out beds in preparation for the arrival of a truckload of mulch. I'm in the carriage house kitchen, wiping down the inside of the oven, when I get the creepy feeling I'm being watched. As I'm backing out of the oven, I bang my head on the stainless-steel frame.

"Ouch!" Rubbing my head, I notice Naomi standing in the doorway with Jazz at her side. "You shouldn't sneak up on people like that." Gripping the counter for support, I slowly get to my feet. I smile down at Jazz. She's wearing white shorts with a pink top, her hair sticking out from her head in a mess of tight coils. "No tutu today?"

She sticks her lip out in a pout. "Ballet is over for the summer."

I frown. "That's a bummer."

Naomi removes an iPad from her purse. She clicks on an app and hands the iPad to her daughter. "Jazz, baby, take this in the other room while I talk to Stella."

Naomi waits for Jazz to leave the kitchen before she says, "I need my job back, Stella, and a place to live."

My eyes travel to the suitcases at her feet. Why should I give her anything after the way she walked out on me three weeks ago? Because, I remind myself, she nursed Billy through his illness. But that doesn't mean I have to make it easy for her.

"I understand about the job," I say, "but why do you need somewhere to live?"

"Not that it's any of your business, but I left my husband."

Something is off here. "You're right. It is none of my business. But I don't understand why a father would turn his daughter out on the streets with nowhere to live. Does your husband even know you left him?"

Naomi's dark eyes are cold. "He'll find out soon enough. But he won't be surprised. He's the one who suggested we split."

Sounds like an act of revenge to me, but I keep my thoughts to myself. "We can work out the job, Naomi, but there are no rooms available at the inn. The main building is torn up."

"What about here?" Naomi's gaze lifts upward, and I know she's talking about the two suites upstairs.

I peer into the lounge through the doorway and notice that Jazz has abandoned the iPad. She's dancing on bare feet around the banquet table I brought over from the main building to use as a conference table for meetings. Any woman who could produce such an adorable kid can't be all bad. "It's a mess up there. But you're welcome to it."

She looks at me with such raw hatred, I almost change my mind. I wait for a thank you, but I get nothing. Not even a grunt. She lifts the two suitcases. "Come on, Jazz. We need to get settled upstairs."

Jazz has stopped dancing and is now doing somersaults on one side of the table. "Do I have to?" she asks in a whiny voice. "Can't I stay here with Stella?"

"Yes, you have to. Stella has work to do."

"Actually, I'm almost finished here. If you can wait thirty minutes, as long as it's okay with your mom, I'll take you for ice cream in town. It is a holiday, after all."

Naomi's features soften, and the transformation in her face is remarkable. She's truly a striking woman. "Are you sure?"

"Positive! I love kids. Besides, you'll need time to clean the suite and unpack." She starts off toward the stairs, and I call after her. "And by the way, Naomi, I've hired a head chef. This kitchen is now her office. I assume you don't mind sharing."

Instead of responding, she keeps on walking. I glance down at Jazz who's looking up at me with adoration. My heart melts. I can put up with her grumpy mom if it means spending time with Jazz. "Okay, kiddo. Finish practicing your tumbling while I clean out the refrigerator. Then we'll go to town."

She nestles up beside me. "I'd rather help you."

"Are you serious? You want to help me clean out the refrigerator?"

"Sure! I clean all the time at home."

Sounds like child labor to me, but I don't argue. "Let's do it! The sooner our chores are done, the sooner we get ice cream."

I tickle Jazz into a fit of giggles and engulf her in a hug. She smells like butter and syrup, and I can't resist kissing her neck.

With Jazz's help, we finish with the refrigerator in no time and walk hand in hand, around the main building and down the front drive to Main Street. Every table in the Dairy Deli is taken, but by the time we choose our flavor and wait for the waitress to fill our order, a two-top near the window opens up.

Jazz takes a big lick of cake batter ice cream. "This is so yummy. Mommy never buys me ice cream."

"What about your daddy? What's his favorite flavor?" When I was babysitting in high school, I learned that most kids have no filters. Ask them the right questions, and they will tell you what you want to know.

"Daddy doesn't like ice cream. Only beer."

I won't touch that one. "Do you know what your daddy does for work?" I lick away on my salted caramel, and pretend to be only mildly interested in her answer.

She lifts a shoulder in a shrug. "Something with computers?"

"It helps to have someone around who's good with computers." I take a bite of my sugar cone. "What are you most excited to do now that school's out?"

Jazz stares up, as though looking for the answer on the decorative metal ceiling. "I can't think of anything. Summer's boring."

"You can't be serious. I've never met a kid who doesn't like summer," I say, but the truth is, I never liked summers either. I was often left at home alone while my parents worked. "Aren't you going to camp or something?"

She shakes her head. "I have to go to work with mommy every day. I'd rather be at school. Except . . ." Her face clouds over.

I lean across the table toward her. "Except what, Jazz?"

"My friends laugh at me, because I can't read."

I immediately think of Mrs. Mitchell at the library. "What grade are you in?"

She holds up her pointer finger.

"So, you just finished kindergarten?" I ask, and she nods. "Don't sweat it, Jazz. Some kids take more time in learning to read. How about if you and I make a field trip to the library this week? We can pick out some books and practice reading together."

She bounces up and down in her chair. "Really, Stella? Can we really go to the library?"

"Sure, we can. I love the library." I stuff the rest of my cone in my mouth and lick my fingers. "This summer's gonna be different for you. Wanna know why?"

Her golden eyes grow wide. "Why?"

"Because I'm here! And I like to have fun."

"Yay. Me too! What're we gonna do next? I'm not ready to go back to mommy yet."

"Do you know how to ride a bike?"

She nods. "Opal taught me."

I laugh out loud. "Of course, she did. Do you own your own bike?"

Jazz furrows her brow. "It's at home. Mommy said I couldn't bring it."

I eye what remains of her ice cream. "Why don't you finish that. Then we'll run an errand on the way back to the inn."

Jazz gobbles down the rest of her cone. She has an ice cream ring around her lips and a smudge of another food substance on her cheek that I'm pretty sure is left over from breakfast.

We throw away our trash, and I steer her to the tiny bathroom in the corner. "Let's wash our hands before we leave."

While Jazz is soaping her hands, I ask, "Do you mind if I clean off your face?"

She smiles at her reflection in the mirror, her little pink tongue licking at the ice cream mustache.

I wet a brown paper towel and wipe her whole face until it shines. Producing an elastic band from my wrist, I ask, "Can we tie back your hair?"

She gives an indifferent shrug.

I gather her hair into a high ponytail that sticks out like a cheerleader's pompom on top of her head. On her, it looks adorable.

We exit the Dairy Deli, but instead of going left toward the inn, we take a right.

"Where are we going?" Jazz asks skipping along beside me.

"You'll see."

At the next corner, we take another right and walk two blocks to Cycle Trail, the bicycle shop I've passed on my trips to the library. A row of cruisers and mountain bikes stretches down the center of the room with racers hanging from the walls. A man of about fifty, with the slim and lean build of a cyclist, comes from behind the counter to greet us. "Ladies, what brings you in today?"

"I'm Stella Boor, the new general manager at Hope Springs Inn. We're in the middle of renovations now, but when we reopen in September, I'd like to provide bikes for my guests to ride around the farm and into town. I was wondering if you'd be interested in working with me to choose the right bikes and give me an estimate on the cost."

He grins. "You bet I would. Years ago, in the late nineties when I was just starting out, I sold the inn a fleet of bikes."

"Right. I saw an old photograph of them, which is what gave me the idea."

"By the way, I'm Allen Farmer, the owner of Cycle Trail." He offers his hand to shake. "For what you have in mind, I recommend cruisers. They're comfortable with reliable mechanical performance and affordable prices. And we have a number to choose from. Shall I truck over a few bikes for you to try out? I can drop them off later this afternoon and leave them with you for a few days."

"That'd be awesome! You're awfully trusting," I say in a teasing tone. "I'm from New York. No bike shop owner in his right mind would make such an offer in New York."

"Welcome to the South, Stella. This is the way we do things down here." Allen smiles over at Jazz. "Should I throw in a few kids' bikes for your younger guests?"

Head bobbing, Jazz bounces on her toes. "Please."

"That would be great," I say.

Allen looks back up at me. "Cute kid. Yours?"

"No." I give Jazz's ponytail a tug. "We're just friends."

Allen spends a few minutes showing us the different options for cruisers and fitting us for helmets. As I'm paying for the helmets, he asks how the renovations are going at the inn.

"Coming along," I say. "The demolition is complete, and we've begun to rebuild."

"I offer guided mountain bike tours, if you think that's something your guests might be interested in. Your concierge would handle the bookings, and I would provide the bikes and conduct the tours."

I mentally add concierge to the list of positions I need to fill. "I love this idea."

"Great!" Allen says and sends me on my way with a brochure of the various tours he offers.

Jazz and I walk back to the inn, hand in hand with our helmets tucked under our arms. Naomi, her silver Honda sedan idling on the curb, is waiting for us under the portico. "Where have you been?" Her tone is one of anger not concern.

Jazz inches closer to me as though afraid of her mother. "We went to get ice cream, remember? You gave us your permission."

"But you've been gone for hours. I drove down to the Dairy Deli, but you weren't there. And what's with the bike helmets?"

"We stopped in at Cycle Trail on the way back. I'm sorry if we worried you, Naomi. I would've told you where we were going, but I don't have your number. Why don't we remedy that now." I pull out my phone, and as she recites her number, I tap it into my contacts. I send her a text. "There. Now you have mine."

Naomi says, "I want Jazz to stay close to me for a few days. Until Derrick . . . never mind." She takes the helmet from Jazz and hands it to me. "Here." She motions her daughter toward the car. "Come on, Jazz, we need to get to the grocery store."

"But I wanna go bike riding with Stella."

I quickly explain to Naomi about the bikes. "Allen should be here any minute with the truck. Jazz can hang out with me until he comes."

"Not today. She's coming with me," Naomi says, taking her daughter by the hand.

Jazz looks at me over her shoulder as Naomi drags her to the car. "Maybe we can go bike riding tomorrow."

I wink at the little girl. "It's a date."

Naomi opens the back door of her Honda and buckles her daughter into her car seat. "Your hair looks ridiculous like that," she says, yanking the elastic out of Jazz's hair.

Jazz cries out, "Ouch! That hurt, Mommy. And I like my hair like that."

As they drive off, Jazz, staring at me through the window, has tears streaming down her cheeks.

Having my heart stolen by a six-year-old kid was not what I had in mind when I decided to move to Virginia.

SIXTEEN

I'm shocked, and more than a little irritated, to find Naomi working at the computer in the manager's office early the following morning. She walked out on me a month ago with no indication of ever coming back. Does she seriously think she can resume her job as though nothing happened? On the other hand, it's my bad for not straightening her out about her job responsibilities yesterday.

Jazz is curled up in a chair in the corner watching a movie on Naomi's iPad. When she sees me in the doorway, she jumps up and hurries over to me, wrapping her arms around my waist. "Did you see, Stella? The bikes came!"

I pat her spongy mass of hair. "I know, Jazzy. I was here when Mr. Farmer delivered them. He brought several for you to try out."

In a begging tone, she asks, "Can we go for a ride now? Please . . ."

"I have a meeting in a few minutes. But I was thinking we could ride down to the lake later. We could even have a picnic. If your mommy says it's okay." I look over at Naomi who's watching us with keen interest. "I promise we won't leave the farm."

117

"That's fine," Naomi says, and returns her attention to the computer.

I kneel down in front of Jazz and speak to her in a soft voice. "What're you watching on your iPad?"

"*Frozen.*"

"Very cool." I tuck her hair behind one ear. "Why don't you finish watching it while I talk business with your mommy?"

Biting down on her lip, she returns to her chair in the corner.

I cross the room to the desk, but I don't sit down. Naomi's in my chair. To take a seat opposite her would be to hand over my authority to her. "Since workspace is at a minimum around here, we're going to have to share this office."

With a huff, as though annoyed at being disturbed, she tears her eyes away from the screen and turns toward me. "How is that possible with only one computer?"

Now that I own a laptop, I could easily work from the cottage. But I sense she's testing me, and I can't let her win. "We'll have to find a way."

Tapping on the desk with a red-lacquered fingernail, she says, "This is the general manager's office and I'm the general manager."

My mouth falls open. So, she *does* think she can waltz back in here after a month's absence. Is it audacity? Or has she lost complete touch with reality?

"You've been gone for three weeks, Naomi. The renovations are now in full swing. I'm organizing the contractors, and I'm making the decisions. I am the new GM."

She pins me against the far wall with her death glare. "That's not what Billy wanted."

I glare back at her. "That's exactly what Billy wanted. He left specific instructions in his will."

"He was too sick to make such important decisions. He was not of sound mind."

Pot calling kettle, I think. "I can either get Brian Powers over here to explain the situation to you, or we can work this out ourselves."

She leans back in the chair, examining her fingernails. "Why don't we share the job? There's enough work for two GMs."

Despite my racing heart, I manage to keep my voice even. "That's not happening. I'll tell you what I have in mind. Then you can decide whether you want to stay."

Cocking her head to the side, she says, "Fine, Stella. What do you have in mind?"

"There will be plenty of other positions to fill when we get closer to reopening. We can discuss which one you're better suited for later. As of now, I've hired a chef and groundskeeper. I—"

She sits up in her chair. "What happened to Bernard?"

"He pulled a gun on me, and I fired him."

"Ha. A gun loaded with snake shot."

"A gun is a weapon." I plant both hands on the desk and lean toward her. "As I was saying, Naomi, we have a groundskeeper and a chef. What we need most right now is a marketing director to develop campaigns for the reopening. You'll be useful in the role, since you're already aware of what marketing we've done in the past."

"Fine. I'll be the marketing director." As she spins around to face the computer, she mumbles, "For now."

I straighten. "Did you get my text about the meeting?" I've summoned all members of my team for our first official meeting in the carriage house lounge at nine.

"I'm not really into meetings," she says with a smirk on her lip.

I bang my fist on the desk. "Then I suggest you *get* into them. You'll either do things my way, Naomi, or—"

She bolts out of her chair. "Or what, Stella?"

"Or you can leave. Believe me, it's no skin off my back if you do." I glance at the wall clock. "You have an hour to pull together whatever information you can regarding prior publicity campaigns."

Turning away from her, I march out of the office, wiggling my fingers at Jazz as I pass her chair. The fresh morning air clears my head, taking the sizzle out of my anger, as I cross the grounds to the carriage house.

When I find Cecily arranging pots and pans she brought from home in the cabinets, I ask, "What do you think? Does the kitchen work for you?"

"It has a gas stove. Which, for me, is the most important thing. I can make do with the rest." Cecily studies my face. "What's wrong?"

"I have a nightmare on my hands." I tell her about Naomi taking care of Billy when he was ill, and how she walked out on me the day after my arrival, and her sudden return yesterday. "Powers asked me to give her the benefit of the doubt. He feels like we owe her that much. If she doesn't straighten up, I'll let him deal with her."

Cecily sets a utensil holder on the counter and fills it with ladles and spoons and spatulas. "I don't get it. Were Naomi and Billy romantically involved?"

I shake my head. "Not unless she was cheating on her husband. As best I can tell, she and Billy were just good friends. I feel sorry for her kid. She has the most adorable daughter, Cecily. Wait until you see her."

"And they're living here, in the carriage house?"

I point at the ceiling. "There are two suites upstairs. While you're technically sharing the kitchen with her, your work takes priority. Whatever you do, don't let her tell you otherwise."

I'm caught off guard when Naomi arrives five minutes early for our meeting. She speaks to Jack as though they're old friends and introduces herself with a warm smile to Cecily and Katherine. She's pleasant and polite, not at all the same person I encountered in the office an hour ago. Maybe she's had a change of heart.

While everyone is finding their seats, Naomi settles Jazz with a coloring book and a box of crayons in the chair beside her.

At the head of the table, I say, "I apologize for the short notice. But today seemed like a good time to hold our first official meeting now that Cecily and Katherine are officially onboard. In order to reopen as planned in early September, we must all work hard, as individuals and as a team. We are the dream team. Every idea, no matter how big or how small, will be considered. My vision is to restore Hope Springs Farm to its pinnacle of glory of the sixties and seventies. There is no obstacle we can't conquer, if we work together. Thanks to Jack and his hardworking crew, we're off to an excellent start."

The others join me in giving Jack a round of applause.

I continue, "Going forward, we'll meet every Monday at nine o'clock. This room will serve as our hub of activity. I realize it's not ideal, but it's the best we've got right now." I hand a stack of stapled printed copies to Cecily on my right. "Take one and pass the rest, please. This is a list of the vendors I'm working with and what we've accomplished to date. Please review it in your spare time and let me know if you have questions or concerns. I'd like for each of you to speak for a minute about what you hope to achieve in the coming week."

Volunteering to go first, Naomi recites her marketing report as though she's been preparing it for weeks. She describes in detail the campaigns she's run in the past and offers suggestions on ways to expand going forward. Her goal for this week is to create a list with the names of potential graphic designers as well as the local and state media outlets she'd like to pitch our reopening campaign. She's professional and asks intelligent questions of the others when they make their reports.

Cecily talks about developing her menus and Katherine is

knee-deep, literally, in laying mulch. Jack's eyes travel the table, speaking to everyone in turn as he brings us up to speed on the progress of the renovations. When he gets to me, his gaze doesn't meet mine. He's either angry or upset or disgusted over my drunken behavior on Friday night. It's best for us to keep our distance. He must think so as well, because he flees the carriage house as soon as I adjourn the meeting.

The others are gathering their things when Cecily leans in close to me. "I hate to say it, but I like Naomi."

"She definitely put on a professional show. Maybe I'm wrong about her," I say, even though I know I'm not. Naomi is after my job. Game on.

When Naomi and Jazz start toward the door, I call them back. "The office is all yours today, Naomi. I have some things I need to check on around here. Why don't I take Jazz with me? I'll bring her back to you this afternoon after our bike ride and picnic."

Palms pressed together, Jazz says, "Can I please, Mommy?"

"Of course, darling." Naomi kisses the top of her daughter's head, as though she's the most loving mother in the world. "You be sweet for Stella now, you hear?"

"Okay, Mommy."

Jazz and I stand together in the doorway, watching her mother walk away. "So, kiddo, are you ready to go check out those bikes?"

"Yes!" Jazz breaks free of me and twirls her way down the sidewalk. I catch up with her, and we race each other to the main building. She easily wins and I'm completely winded. Aside from yard work, I can't remember the last time I exercised. *Not good, Stella. You need to get into shape.*

Fastening on our helmets, we try out all the bikes, riding them back and forth on the road between the main building and the barn. Because they all perform about the same, our decision comes down to color. Jazz chooses pink and I pick baby blue.

"Are you ready to go?" I ask. "I have a surprise for you."

Her face lights up. "What kinda surprise?"

"You'll see. Follow me." I ride off down the sidewalk leading toward the lake, glancing back periodically to check on Jazz. Opal is waiting for us on her park bench with her supply satchel and Igloo cooler at her feet.

When Jazz sees Opal, she squeals and jumps off her bike, letting it fall to the grass. She hurries over to the old woman, jumping into her lap and wrapping her arms around her neck. "I've missed you, Opal!"

Opal smooths her hair back and kisses her forehead. "And I've missed you, child."

I clear my throat. "I hate to be the bad guy here, but Jazz, this is no way to treat your bicycle."

She brings her fingers to her lips. "Oops. Sorry, Stella." Sliding off Opal's lap, she walks the bike back to the sidewalk and parks it with the kickstand.

Jazz returns to the park bench. "Where's your bike, Opal? Aren't you gonna ride with us?"

"I'm sorry, sweet pea. I didn't bring my bike today. My bones are feeling a bit creaky. I thought we'd have some fun with these." From her supply satchel at her feet, Opal produces a bucket of sidewalk chalk. "I know a secret place with plenty of concrete for you to color."

Jazz wrinkles her nose. "Where?"

"Come with me." Opal grimaces as she slowly rises to her feet.

I've never seen her move so slowly, and as she leads us down to the lake, I ask, "Are you in pain?"

"Not much. Just my old bones acting up."

"Is it arthritis?"

She shrugs. "I'm not sure what it is. I'll feel better in a day or so."

Bypassing the summer house, we walk along the edge of the

lake to a large concrete pad with faint lines from an old shuffle-board game. She hands Jazz the bucket. "Color away."

Seated on the ground, leaning against the trunk of a nearby tree, Opal watches while I draw flowers and rainbows and Jazz creates houses with windows and roofs and streams of smoke billowing from chimneys. I'm not blessed with my mother's artistic talent, and my illustrations aren't much better than the six-year-old's. When we grow bored, we draw a tower of squares and play hopscotch until we're all three hungry for lunch.

Returning to the park bench, we spread out Opal's red-and-white checkered blanket and sink our teeth into the gourmet peanut butter and jelly sandwiches she purchased at the Local Market. Opal opens a bottle of Chardonnay and fills a plastic cup half full. She produces a second plastic cup and holds the bottle out to me. "Would you care for some wine?"

"No thanks. Day drinking for me always leads to a nap. And I have some phone calls I need to make this afternoon."

"I don't usually drink during the day either. I'm searching for inspiration."

When she looks over at her easel, which is set up in its usual spot under the tree, I notice for the first time the canvas is blank. "What happened to the painting of the spring house you were working on?"

"I grew tired of it. I've painted all the scenes around here dozens of times. I need new material."

Finished with her sandwich and bored with grown-up talk, Jazz leaves the blanket and begins cartwheeling and somersaulting across the grass.

I stretch out on the blanket with my hands behind my head and face to the sun. "Naomi is after my job." In a low voice, I tell Opal about finding Naomi at my desk and the snow job she did at the meeting this morning.

"Watch out for her. She's a conniving one. I worry about that poor child."

Shielding my eyes from the sun, I look over at Jazz, who has stopped tumbling and is making a dandelion chain.

"Isn't she the sweetest thing? Just as pretty as a picture." Opal removes her phone from her pocket, and zooming in on the child, she begins snapping pictures.

"Has Naomi disappeared before?"

"A time or two," Opal says. "But never for this long."

I roll over on my side, propping myself on my elbow. "There's something more about Naomi you're not telling me. What is it, Opal?"

"That falls under the category of one of those things you'll have to figure out for yourself."

"Ugh." I crawl to my knees and begin gathering up our trash. "I'm tired of everyone keeping secrets from me."

"What secrets are people keeping from you, Stella?"

I look up to see Naomi looming over me. How long has she been standing there? I didn't hear her approach. Opal appears as surprised as I am to see her.

I stand to face her. "I've told you before, Naomi. You shouldn't sneak up on people."

She stares me down. "And you shouldn't wander off with my daughter. I've been looking everywhere for you."

"Here we are, in plain sight." My arms shoot out from my sides. "You'd have to be blind not to see us. I promised we wouldn't leave the farm."

"True, but you neglected to tell me you were meeting her." She gestures at Opal. "She's a batty old bittie, and I don't want her around my daughter."

My blood boils. "You are way out of line, Naomi. Opal is my friend. And you don't get to talk about her that way. Besides, she loves Jazz."

Opal says, "Don't let her get to you, Stella. She's not worth it."

"Let's go, Jasmine," Naomi bellows, her loving mother act from earlier now forgotten.

"But, Mom! Why can't I stay here with Stella and Opal?"

"Because I said so." Clasping Jazz's wrist, Naomi drags her daughter up the sidewalk.

I help Opal to her feet, and we watch Naomi and Jazz disappear around the corner of the cottage.

"Have you ever met Naomi's husband?" I ask.

"Briefly, once or twice. He seems okay. I don't know how he puts up with her." Opal kicks up the kickstand on the child's bike and begins walking it up the hill.

"Leave the bike, Opal. I'll get it later."

"I'm fine. A little walk will loosen my joints."

I grab my bike and hurry after her. "What does Naomi have against you?"

"Depends on the day. Naomi is not a nice person. She's a user. She takes what she wants and leaves carnage in her wake. The sooner you figure that out, the better off you'll be."

SEVENTEEN

For the next few days, as much as it saddens me, I avoid spending time with Jazz. I'm a trigger for Naomi's anger, and I'm concerned that Jazz finds our heated exchanges disturbing. Poor kid doesn't need any more confusion in her life when she's already having to cope with her parents' recent separation. But every time I stop by the office to check on Naomi's progress, it breaks my heart to see Jazz in the corner chair watching movies on her mother's iPad. It's summertime. She's a six-year-old kid. She should be swimming and riding bikes and playing with her friends. On Thursday, I ask Opal to drive me to Target and we load up on crafts—Play-Doh and a Spirograph Kit and a Disney Princess Activity Tote. When I give Jazz the plastic Target bag, she looks at me with pleading eyes and I can't resist. I spend the next couple of hours playing with her on the floor.

Every time I ask to see Naomi's list of media outlets and potential graphic designers, she makes up an excuse as to why it's not ready. Finally, on Friday morning, I lose my patience. "This is serious, Naomi. We should've already hired a graphic designer and be networking with the media." I hold out my hand. "Show me what you've got so far."

She clicks her mouse and a blank sheet of paper spits out of the printer. "Here you go."

I'm aware of little ears listening, but I'm too angry to care. "You've been sitting behind this computer all week, and all you have to show for it is a blank sheet of paper."

"Pretty much, yep."

I ball up the paper and toss it in the trash. "This is unacceptable."

"I'm sorry, Stella. I'm dealing with some personal issues at the moment."

"I'm not paying you to deal with your personal issues." As the words leave my mouth, it crosses my mind that Naomi is my employee and I'm being unsympathetic to her situation. A growing number of disgruntled employees are suing their employers for lesser grievances these days. I could argue that she just returned from a month's leave of absence. But her attorney would counter that it was unpaid. Or was it? Brian is currently handling our accounting. Is it possible he's been paying her all along? Best if I back off and play it safe. "Look, Naomi. I'm sorry for what you're going through, but my primary concern is getting this job done."

"Just give me until Monday."

I don't want to give her another hour, but I don't have much choice. "You have the weekend, but I want to see your report at our meeting on Monday morning."

When I turn away from the desk, I see Jazz's hands are over her ears, blocking out the sound of our raised voices. On my way out of the office, I tickled her until she begs for mercy.

I'm certain Naomi won't have her list ready on Monday, and I question how much past exposure she has to marketing campaigns. I go straight to the cottage, brew a pot of coffee, and spend the rest of the day at the kitchen table, working on my laptop. I take pages of notes as I research graphic designers and media outlets. While I'd like to work toward having our own in-house marketing department, I ultimately conclude, in light of our time crunch, that we're better off hiring a full-service marketing agency for now.

Around four o'clock, there's a knock at my door, and I'm curious to see Brian on my front porch. While I've spoken to him on the phone several times, I haven't seen him since our initial meeting with Jack weeks ago. Brian is wearing long shorts and a knit collared shirt, as though straight off the golf course. What could be so important to warrant a visit from him on a Friday afternoon?

"Afternoon, Stella. I apologize for showing up uninvited, but I wondered if I might have a word with you."

"Of course. Come in." I step out of the way and motion him to the sofa. "Can I get you some coffee or tea?"

"I'm fine. But thanks." He waits until I'm seated in the chair next to him before broaching the subject. "I understand you're having some problems with Naomi."

The bottom drops out of my stomach. Has Naomi already hired a lawyer? "How'd you know?"

"There are eyes and ears all around you." The mischief in his blue eyes puts me at ease.

"Opal told you."

"Only because she's concerned." He repositions his body, making himself comfortable. "First of all, Jack has been giving me weekly updates and I'm pleased by your progress thus far. It's remarkable."

"Thank you for the compliment. Everything seems to be coming along."

"I realize I haven't been around much these past few weeks," Brian says. "I didn't want to hover over you while you were settling into your job."

I don't know what to say, so I smile.

"As for Naomi, I've just come from having a word with her. I made it clear, in no uncertain terms, that you are both the general manager of the inn and owner of Hope Springs Farm, and if she can't figure out a way to work with you, she'll need to seek employment elsewhere."

Relief rushes over me. "I appreciate your support, but I'm not sure it'll make much of a difference. She's a difficult person. Coincidentally, did you pay her during her recent leave of absence?"

Brian lets out a sigh. "Yes, because—"

"You owe her for taking care of Billy. I understand. From a legal standpoint, if things don't work out, what grounds do I need to have in order to fire her without worrying about a lawsuit?"

"You could fire her right now for insubordination. But, as a favor to me, I hope you'll give her one more chance. If she screws up again, or the two of you simply can't get along, I'll support you if you decide to let her go. Although, because I have history with her, I need to be the one to handle the termination. Understood?"

"Understood."

He plants his hands on his thighs. "Now. On a positive note. Would you like to go over to the main building with me to check out the progress?"

I jump to my feet. "Yes! I've been waiting all week to do that very thing. I try to stay out of their way while Jack's crew is working."

"That's smart," Brian says. "A watched pot never boils."

The point he makes brings on a smile. But when we conduct our walk-through, from top floor down to the lobby, I'm discouraged by what we find. My unwatched pot may never reach the boiling point. I admit to Brian, "Now that the demolition is over, I expected them to have made better headway this week."

"A lot is happening behind the scenes at this stage. But don't worry, Stella. Everything will come together soon."

"I hope you're right, otherwise we'll never make our deadline."

I say goodbye to Brian at the door, locking it behind him. When I turn around, Naomi is standing in front of me. My heart leaps out of my chest, and I jump back ten feet. "For the last time, Naomi, stop sneaking up on me!"

She steps toward me. "Thanks for ratting me out to Brian."

Hand against pounding heart, I say, "I didn't rat you out. That's not my style."

She continues walking toward me, backing me up against the door. "If you have a problem with me, come to me directly."

I lift my chin high. "We did that this morning, remember? I look past her, down the empty hallway to the reception area. "Where's Jazz?"

"Stop playing parent to my daughter."

"Well someone needs to, because you're doing a sucky job of it."

Naomi balls her fists at her sides, and I worry she might hit me. "Jazz is none of your concern."

"She is when she's living on my property."

I brace myself for the impact of her fist on my face, but instead of punching me, she sneers. "That's the thing, though. The property isn't really yours."

"Oh really? Whose is it, then?"

She opens her mouth to speak and closes it again.

"Go ahead, Naomi. Say whatever it is you need to say."

"It's not my place."

While she thinks she knows something, I no longer believe anything she says. "According to Brian, the farm, including the inn, belongs to me. If you have grounds to contest ownership, you should take it up with Brian."

"Maybe I will." She's so close to me I can smell her minty gum. But there's something else on her breath as well. Is it alcohol?

"Have you been drinking?"

"So, what if I have?" She spins on her heels and storms off.

"Where's Jazz, Naomi?" I call to her retreating back. When she doesn't answer me, I add, "You shouldn't leave her alone, Naomi. Bernard has been causing some problems around here."

I don't see either Naomi or Jazz again until late the following afternoon. I'm practicing my driving when I spot Jazz alone down by the lake. Slamming on the brakes, I get out of the car and call her name. When she sees me, she runs over and I lift her off her feet, spinning her around.

I set her down. "What're you doing out here alone, kiddo?"

She sticks her thumb in her mouth, talking around it. "Mommy told me to go outside and play."

"All by yourself?"

She nods, and with finger still in mouth, she says, "She's drunk."

Alarm bells go off in my head. So, I was right yesterday. Naomi had been drinking. And what does a six-year-old even know about being drunk. "What makes you think that, Jazzy?"

"That's what Daddy says when she drinks the stinky yellow stuff in the tall bottle."

Uh-oh. Not good.

Her lips make a popping noise when she pulls her thumb out of her mouth. "I like it when you call me Jazzy."

"Then I'll call you that all the time. Say, Jazzy, how about that promised trip to the library? I need to return a book, and we can pick out a few for you while we're there."

She grins. "Can we go in Billy's Jeep?"

I don't know why the mention of Billy's name surprises me. Of course, she knew Billy. Is it extortion to pry information from a six-year-old?

"Sorry, kiddo, but we'll have to walk. I'm just learning to drive. I don't have my license yet."

"Bummer," she says with a pout.

"I'll tell you what. You can ride with me to take the Jeep back to the cottage. But first we need to let your mom know where we're going." I thumb off a quick text to Naomi. *Found Jazz wondering around the property alone. I'm taking her with me to the library.*

I don't wait for Naomi's approval. She can get angry all she wants. I'm looking out for *her* child's best interests.

Parking beside the cottage, we go inside for my purse and library book. As an afterthought, I grab a canvas tote bag out of the coat closet for our books. The tote is leftover swag from an old Jimmy Buffet concert with a parrot on the front. Jazz smiles when she sees it and insists on carrying it.

We head off, hands clasped and arms swinging, toward town. "Tell me about Billy," I say. "What was he like?"

"Billy was nice. And funny. He made up silly songs and played them for me on his guitar. He liked to watch SpongeBob and eat licorice." She sticks out her tongue. "Yuck."

I laugh. "I agree. Yuck is right."

"And Billy loved to read." Her eyes shine with unshed tears. "I wish he were here now. He could help me learn to read."

I stop at the next corner and lean down to face her. "Have you asked your mommy to help you with your reading?"

Her lip quivers. "Yes. But she's always too busy."

"Well then, Jazzy, how about if I help you?" Whatever Naomi has against me, she'll have to get over it, because I can't avoid this kid any longer. She needs me in her life. I realize in a jolt of clarity that I need her as well.

Jazz buries her face in my belly. "Thank you, Stella."

We stand on the corner with me stroking her hair and her sniffling into my shirt while cars zoom past us. When she finally stops crying, we continue on to the library. Rose Mitchell has the day off, but her much younger coworker, Candice Moss, takes an immediate liking to Jazz. While I peruse the new release shelf for adults, Candice accompanies Jazz to the children's section where they load up our tote with age-appropriate books.

Jazz has apparently shared her frustration in learning to read with Candice, because when they return to the checkout counter, while Candice is scanning our books, she says to Jazz, "You'll learn to read soon enough, sweetheart. Try not to worry so much about the words and just enjoy the characters and their stories." Candice directs her attention to me. "One of my girlfriends is an elementary school teacher." She jots a name and number on an index card and gives it to me. "She has free time on her hands this summer if you're interested in hiring a tutor."

"Thank you. We'll keep that in mind." I slip the card in my purse, even though I can't see Naomi being receptive to a suggestion from me that she hire a reading tutor for her daughter.

Jazz tries to carry the tote bag, but it's too heavy for her and drags on the ground. I take it from her, and as we retrace our steps, she lists the titles of all the books Candice picked out for her.

"Will you read me one when we get home?" she asks.

"Of course." Naomi has yet to respond to my text, and I have no clue what's in store for us back at the farm. If luck is on our side, Naomi is taking a nap and will wake refreshed and sober and in a good mood for a change.

Jazz pauses in front of a diner, and we peek through the window. The diner has a retro theme with robin's egg blue walls, a black-and-white checkerboard floor, and red leather booths and stools. I observe Jazz watching the families with small children. I recognize the same longing from my own face when I was that age.

I nudge her. "I don't know about you, but it's dinnertime and I'm hungry. Wanna get some food?"

She looks up at me. "Do you think Mommy will get mad?"

"Not if we bring her a burger."

"Good idea," Jazz says and barges through the door of the diner.

I send a quick text to Naomi, letting her know we're grabbing dinner at Lucky's Diner and will bring her takeout. When I enter the restaurant, Jazz has claimed the only two available stools at the counter and is chatting up the waitress, a young woman named Mel whose uniform dress is the same color as the walls.

When I slide onto the stool beside her, Jazz announces, "I'm having a hot dog, french fries, and a chocolate milkshake."

Pen poised over order pad, Mel asks me, "Is that okay with you, Mom? It's kinda late in the day for chocolate."

"Sure! Why not? It's Saturday. And summertime." I wink at Jazz. "I'll have what she's having, please. And put in an order for a cheeseburger platter to go."

I underestimate the effect of caffeine and sugar on a six-year-old. Jazz finishes her hot dog and shake, and immediately begins spinning the barstool at top speed. As soon as Naomi's take-out order is ready, I pay the bill and drag Jazz out of the restaurant before she breaks something. She skips all the way back to the farm, and when we reach the front lawn, she cartwheels up the hill to the portico.

At the carriage house, I plant Jazz at the table in the lounge with her books while I go up to check on her mother. Naomi has still not responded to my texts, and I feel certain she's passed out drunk.

I knock on the door. "Naomi, it's Stella. Jazz and I brought you some dinner from Lucky's Diner. Their food's pretty good. Jazz and I already ate. We thought we'd give you some time to yourself."

My words are met with silence. I bang harder. "Seriously, Naomi. You're scaring me. I'll use my master key if you don't let me in."

When there's still no answer, I remove the set of keys from

my purse and insert the master key into the lock. "You leave me no choice. I'm coming in." Naomi is lying butt naked on her stomach with her face buried in the pillow. I set the Styrofoam container on the bedside table and give her arm a poke. "Wake up, Naomi. Jazz is downstairs. You don't want her to see you like this." Nothing. I shake her harder. "This isn't funny, Naomi. I'm calling an ambulance."

Naomi raises a hand, swatting at me, and muffled words come from the pillow. Naomi's alive. That's all I need to know. Her phone is lying on the mattress beside her. I plug it into the charger on the bedside table. So that she doesn't turn this around on me, I text her from her own phone. I want her to know I've seen her drunken, naked butt. *This is Stella. I'm standing beside your bed, and you are passed out cold. Jazz will spend the night with me.*

I lock the door behind me and return to Jazz. "Your mommy is sleeping so soundly I hate to wake her up. What say we have a sleepover at my cottage?"

"Yay!" She punches the air, and then her smile fades. "But won't Mommy get mad?"

"She knows where you are. Come on." I scrape her books into a pile and stuff them in the tote.

It's still early by my standards, but Jazz yawns, her sugar buzz wearing off, as we walk back to the cottage. I change into my pajamas and give Jazz my favorite *I heart New York* T-shirt to sleep in. Even though it falls way below her knees, she looks adorable in it. I clean her face with a washcloth, twist her curls into two braids, and show her how to finger brush her teeth. We get cozy in my queen-size bed with a few of the library books, but we make it through only two before she dozes off.

Jazz dances in her sleep. Literally. I receive ballet kicks to the abdomen and slaps in the face from flying hands. I lie awake for hours, worrying about this innocent child. Her mother has obvious emotional and substance abuse problems. Where is her father? Surely, he wants to spend time with his daughter. Does he even know where Jazz is? Has Naomi worked out visitation with him? If what Jazz says is true, he's aware of his wife's drinking problem. Is that one of the reasons for their separation?

I manage a few hours of sleep, but I'm wide awake again when the first streams of light peek through the wooden blinds. I go out to the porch to watch the sunrise. On the bench beside the front door, I find Jazz's car seat and a folded note—a short message scrawled on guest stationery with the inn's logo embossed at the top.

I'm seeking help for emotional problems. Please take care of my child while I'm gone.

I drop to the bench beside the door. Why would a mother leave her child with a woman she barely knows? Heck, Naomi doesn't even appear to like me. She certainly doesn't trust me. Taking Jazz on outings is one thing. I'm a decent babysitter at best. But I'm definitely not a parent. I know nothing about nutrition or discipline or time management. Never mind my professional commitments. I have important meetings scheduled for every morning this week. I wonder again about Jazz's father. This whole situation is seriously messed up. I'm in way over my head here.

EIGHTEEN

I'm still sitting on the bench an hour later when Jazz comes to find me. She crawls into my lap. "I'm hungry. Can we get some breakfast?" Her breath is surprisingly sour for such a sweet kid.

I kiss the top of her head. "Sure. Let's go see what I have in the kitchen." She giggles when I toss her over my shoulder like a sack of potatoes and carry her inside. I set her down and open the refrigerator. A lone carton of strawberry yogurt sits on the middle shelf of an otherwise empty refrigerator. "Yogurt?"

She turns up her nose. "I like the kind of yogurt you drink."

"Right. A smoothie." I slam the door shut. "I'll bet Cecily has some goodies down at the carriage house. Wanna go see?"

"Sure!" she says and dashes out the back door.

As we cut across the lawn, I send a group text to Brian and Opal. *We have a situation. Come to the farm ASAP.* I hold my breath, hoping to see Naomi's silver Honda parked at the carriage house, but of course it's gone. When we enter the foyer, I'm surprised and relieved when Jazz doesn't ask to see her mother. Instead, we go straight to the kitchen.

"Come on, kiddo. You can help me cook." Lifting Jazz onto

the counter, I remove eggs and bacon, butter and milk from the refrigerator.

When I was old enough to be left home alone, I often had to fend for myself for dinner. New York is the take-out capital of the world. But I quickly put on weight from eating rich food every night. Out of necessity, I taught myself to cook. Nothing fancy. Mostly simple foods.

We make plans for the day while I fry bacon and whip her up a cheese omelet. "So, Jazzy, do you know how to swim?"

She bobs her head. "I'm a good swimmer. But I didn't bring my bathing suit."

Where does one shop for kid's clothes? "Maybe we'll go on a hike instead."

Jazz swings her legs, kicking the counter beneath her. "But I want to go swimming."

Still no mention of her mother.

"Okay. We'll see."

I plant Jazz at the table with her breakfast. My stomach is too nervous to think about eating. I'm struggling to open the sliding glass doors when Opal and Brian arrive together.

"What's so urgent?" Brian wears a day's growth on his face, and the hair on the back of his head is flattened from his pillow.

I shake my head, finger pressed to lips and eyes on Jazz. "Eat up, Jazzy, while us grown-ups step outside for a moment."

I motion Brian and Opal out the glass doors to the small terrace. "Naomi's gone again," I say, and show them her note. I tell them about Naomi being drunk yesterday evening. "I didn't bargain for this when I moved to Virginia, Brian."

"I realize that. But the situation is somewhat . . ." He hesitates as though searching for the right word. "Sensitive."

A flash of anger pulses through my body. "Why do you let Naomi walk all over you like this? And why did she take care of Billy when he was sick? Who was he to her?"

Opal stares at Brian with what I interpret as pleading in her olive eyes. I sense she's ready to break, to tell me what I want to know, but Brian shakes his head at her.

The *we conspiracy* again. "Look, I have a right to know whatever it is that you two are keeping from me. On Friday afternoon, Naomi told me this property isn't really mine. What did she mean by that? I'm gonna scream, if you say it's one of those things I'll have to figure out for myself."

"Then I won't say it," Brian says in a sympathetic tone.

I stare back and forth between them. I'm wasting my time. These two may never tell me what I want to know. I look through the window at Jazz, who's finished her breakfast and is now twirling around the room. "It's not that I don't care about Jazz. I truly love her. But I know nothing about parenting. I'm worried I might break her or something. We need to find her father. I've never met him. I have no idea who he is and where he lives."

"I'll see if I can get in touch with Derrick," Brian says. "But for reasons I'm not yet ready to explain, Jazz is better off here with you."

Opal's fingers brush against my arm. "And you're not going to break her, sweetheart. She adores you. It might do her good to be away from her mama for a while."

"Are you aware Naomi has a drinking problem?" I watch closely for their response. Surprise and confusion cross their faces.

"She's certainly never missed work because of it," Brian says. "Perhaps this is a recent development. She's had a difficult few years."

"I've never seen any evidence of it," Opal says. "Good for her for getting help."

"If she's actually getting help," I say. "I wouldn't put it past Naomi to be in the Caribbean sipping a pina colada right now. How long do you think she'll be gone? And what will happen to Jazz if she never comes back?"

"Why don't we take it one day at a time," Brian says.

Shoulders slumped, I stare at the ground. "Being without a driver's license will present some challenges."

"I will help you in any way," Opal says.

"Same goes for me," Brian adds. "All you have to do is ask."

Jazz is overjoyed when I inform her that her mother has gone out of town, and she'll be staying with me for a while. Opal helps us move Jazz's things to the cottage. She has only a few articles of clothing, most of which need laundering.

"Mommy only let me bring what would fit in my suitcase," Jazz explains.

Opal takes us to run errands. At Target, I send Jazz into the dressing room with an armful of dresses, shorts, and tops. She looks cute in everything, so I buy most of it. We locate flip-flops and tennis shoes in her size, and she picks out a tie-dyed bikini in shades of blues and reds and yellows. As an afterthought, we stop by the sporting goods department for inflatable floats and two pairs of goggles. We pile a second basket high with healthy options from the grocery section.

Opal is visibly exhausted by the time we unpack our purchases at the cottage. "You've outdone yourself, Opal. Go home and rest."

She doesn't argue. "I can come back in the morning to help with Jazz."

"That would be great. I have a staff meeting at nine and the decorators from Richmond will be here at ten. Jazz will be much happier outside with you than stuck in the office with adults talking business."

"We'll have a jolly old time." She pats Jazz's head. "I'll be here at eight."

I discover a gas grill in the attached toolshed behind the

cottage and grill chicken breasts for sandwiches for lunch. Afterward, we put on our bathing suits, blow up our floats, and take them down to the lake. Positioning her goggles over her eyes, Jazz jumps off the pier and swims around in circles like a little tadpole. While she dives for fish, I stretch out on one of the floats with my face tilted to the warm sun. When she exhausts herself, Jazz climbs onto her raft and bobs in the water alongside me.

After a few minutes, she says, "You know what the farm needs?"

"What does the farm need, Jazzy?"

"A swimming pool."

"Hmm." I pretend to consider her idea, although I've long since decided to incorporate an outdoor pool into the spa facility. "You know, you're right. We do need a pool. I'll get to work on it right away." I manage to roll over onto my stomach without falling off. "Tell me about your daddy, Jazz. What's he like?"

Jazz scrunches up her face. "He's boring. All he does is watch football and fight with Mommy."

"The fighting must have been scary for you."

"I don't wanna talk about it," she says, looking away from me.

"I understand, sweetheart." I finger a tear off her cheek. "But, if you ever do feel like talking about it, you can come to me."

She nods, her chin quivering.

We swim for nearly two hours. Then, changing into dry clothes, we go for a trail walk in the farm's wooded area.

Our evening is uneventful. I make pasta with red sauce for dinner, and after tucking Jazz in around eight, I stay up late doing laundry. Exhausted, I finally climb into bed a few minutes before midnight. If Jazz kicks me in my sleep, I'm not aware of it.

The ringing of my phone wakes me the following morning. I answer, my voice groggy from sleep. It's Opal, calling to say she's sick and won't be able to watch Jazz after all. "I'm so sorry, Stella. I know you were counting on me, but I think I may have the flu."

"But it's not flu season." I don't say what I'm thinking—that a more serious medical condition is causing her fatigue and achiness. "I think you should go see your doctor."

"I'll be fine," she says, but even Opal sounds unconvinced.

The bedside table clock catches my attention. I forgot to set my alarm, and it's already ten minutes past eight.

"I'll check on you this afternoon," I say to Opal. "In the meantime, get some rest."

I shake Jazz awake. "We overslept, sweetie. I have a meeting at nine. We need to hurry."

I'm frazzled by the time I get both of us dressed and fed and over to the carriage house. My team has already started our meeting when we arrive ten minutes late. I settle Jazz in the corner of the room with a coloring book and crayons and join the others at the table.

I don't think Jazz is listening, but I lower my voice just in case. "I'm so sorry. Who knew that taking care of a kid was such hard work."

"Where's Naomi?" Cecily asks.

"She had to go out of town unexpectedly. Jazz is staying with me for a while. I feel sorry for the poor kid. I have back-to-back meetings all week long. How am I supposed to keep her entertained? Naomi didn't think to leave us her iPad."

"I may have a solution for you." Katherine pulls out a pink flyer and pushes it toward me. "I ran into my across-the-street neighbor on my way to the farm this morning. She's an adorable sixteen-year-old with a ton of energy. She's hosting a backyard camp for little girls this week. She still has a couple of openings and asked if I knew anyone who might be interested."

I scan the flyer. The camp runs every day this week from nine until two. Lunch is included, and the cost is a hundred dollars. "This sounds perfect, but how do we know this girl is responsible?"

Katherine points to a list of names at the bottom of the flyer.

"There are three counselors, actually. Leigh is my neighbor I mentioned. I don't know her all that well, but I've met her parents. They seem nice enough. Why don't you give her a call? You can put her through the inquisition."

"I'll do that. Continue the meeting without me. I'll be right back." Rising from the table, I take my phone and the flyer into the kitchen.

Leigh answers on the first ring. I explain who I am, and she tells me a little about the camp. "We have ten other little girls ranging in age from five to eight," she says, and I can hear the children squealing in the background. "We've planned crafts and games and other outdoor activities. She'll have a blast. I promise. This is my second year doing this camp. If it makes you feel better, my mother is on standby if we need an adult. I'm a certified lifeguard and one of the other counselors is a volunteer EMT."

"That seals the deal," I say. "I'll bring Jazz over right away."

"Awesome. We have plenty of sunscreen but be sure she brings her bathing suit."

I return to the lounge. "I owe you one for this, Katherine. Your neighbor knows more about kids than I do. Unfortunately, I'm going to have to leave now in order to walk her over and be back before the decorators arrive."

"You stay here," Katherine says, already on her feet. "I'll take Jazz in my truck. I don't have much to report today anyway. I'm working on a comprehensive landscape plan. I'll have it ready for you next week."

"You're a lifesaver."

Jazz is ecstatic when I tell her about the camp, and she practically drags Katherine out the door. "Don't forget to stop by the cottage for your bathing suit," I call after them.

Cecily waits for them to leave before asking, "What are you not telling us about Naomi's impromptu trip?"

I debate how much to say. But I'm likely to need their support and understanding in the weeks ahead if Naomi stays gone a long time. "Naomi got pass-out drunk on Saturday, and Jazz spent the night with me. On Sunday morning, I found Jazz's car seat and a note from Naomi on my front porch. She claims she's getting help for emotional problems. I have no idea when's she's coming back."

I risk a glance at Jack, who hasn't said a word since I arrived. Is that sympathy I see in his expression? I open a file folder in front of me. "Anyway, let's move on with business."

The week flies by. I meet with all our major vendors, but as the various components of the project begin to take shape, I'm faced with making an overwhelming number of decisions. I come to the conclusion that I am not a detail-oriented person and look to the professionals to provide input.

Jazz adores camp. She has girl crushes on her counselors and talks nonstop about her new friends. Based on a tip from one of the other moms, I sign Jazz up for a bible school and day camp at the local YMCA for later in the summer. For the coming weeks, I schedule private lessons with Jazz's ballet instructor and sessions with Ellen, the reading tutor Candice from the library told me about.

We receive no word from Naomi. When Powers calls me Wednesday afternoon, he says, "According to his coworker, Derrick will be out on vacation for the next two weeks. No one in the office seems to know where he's gone. At least they're not saying. They know who I am and understand my association with Derrick's estranged wife."

"Thanks for the update."

Jazz is tired in the afternoons when she comes home from

camp. She's content to chill out in the cottage, watching a movie in the living room while I work at the kitchen table. Late Friday afternoon, we're in our respective places when we have our first disagreement.

Jazz calls to me from the sofa, "Can we go out to dinner, Stella?"

"Not tonight, kiddo. I'm exhausted."

I hear a thud, followed by the pitter-patter of little feet on the floor. She appears in the doorway. "What're we gonna eat, then?"

I glance at the stove clock. It's almost six o'clock. Time to think about dinner even though I'm not the slightest bit hungry. What is it with growing kids? They're in constant need of food—frequent snacks and three square meals a day. I don't need to check the refrigerator. There's nothing meal-worthy in there. I should've asked Cecily or Katherine to drive me to the store. Life is so much easier in New York, where you can get anywhere either on foot or by subway, bus, or Uber.

"Why don't we order a pizza?" I suggest.

She stomps her foot. "I don't like pizza!"

I smile at her, even though she's trying my patience. "Of course you do. Everyone loves pizza."

She folds her arms and pouts. "Not me! I hate pizza! I want to go out to dinner."

Her petulance pushes me over the edge. What an ungrateful brat. I've been catering to her every whim all week, and she's not even my kid. I raise an eyebrow at her. "We don't use the word *hate* in this house. And since you dislike pizza so much, I'll eat a bowl of cereal and you can fix your own dinner."

Jazz storms out of the room, and seconds later, I hear the bedroom door slam.

I work for another hour, and when I go check on her, she's sound asleep. I plan to fix grilled cheeses for dinner, and I debate whether to wake her to eat, but I decide she needs her rest. When

I lean down to kiss her cheek, I see that her pillow is wet with tears. Guilt hits me like a ton of bricks, and I punish myself by skipping dinner altogether. I wake up with a rumbling belly on Saturday morning. Jazz wakes up with a fever.

NINETEEN

Jazz's skin is hot to the touch, even though she's shivering from chills. I wrap the comforter tight around her. "Where does it hurt, Jazzy?"

Through chattering teeth, she says, "Everywhere. I want my mommy."

"I know you do, sweetheart. But I'm going to take good care of you."

I force a smile to hide my concern. I have no clue what to do. Google will tell me. Grabbing my laptop, I search for *treating a child with a fever*. One prominent medical website says medication isn't needed for an otherwise healthy child, which I have to assume Jazz is since I don't know her medical history. Another website says, for a fever below 102, to make sure the child gets lots of rest and drinks plenty of fluids. I don't have a thermometer, and no way to get one without walking to the store. Surely there's something I can do right now. I read on. If the child is uncomfortable, give her Tylenol or Advil. Yes! I have Advil.

I retrieve my bottle from the medicine cabinet in the bathroom. My heart sinks when I read the label. It says for ages twelve and younger to call a doctor. What to do? I can't call Opal. She's still sick. I text Cecily and Katherine, to see if either of them is available to run to the store. Both respond immediately that they are out of town for the weekend. I consider calling Jack and Brian, but I'm not that desperate yet. I cut an Advil tablet in half, nearly severing my finger in the process. When Jazz refuses to swallow it, I pound it with my hardback library book, breaking it into pieces and mixing the pieces with a tablespoon of peanut butter. The kid who loves peanut butter turns up her nose, but at my insistence, she gives the spoon a lick. Thirty minutes later, she's back to normal, begging me to take her swimming in the lake.

"No way, kiddo. You're sick. Just because your fever is gone, it doesn't mean you're completely recovered."

"Yes, it does," she says, planting a hand on her hip. "I get fevers all the time."

So, she's not an otherwise healthy child. "What does your mommy do when you get sick?"

"She gives me medicine. Please! If we can't go swimming, can we at least go for a bike ride?"

I think about my nearly empty refrigerator. What am I going to feed this kid? She skipped dinner last night. Isn't she hungry? Why isn't she asking for food?

"I'll make a deal with you, Jazzy. If you'll walk with me to the market, we'll pack a picnic and go for a short bike ride."

"Deal," she says and gives her fanny a sassy shake.

Jazz and I stroll to the store. To avoid contaminating the other customers, we purchase only the bare necessities, including a bottle of children's Advil and a digital thermometer. At home, after putting away the other groceries, I throw together a simple picnic of ham sandwiches, apple slices, and chocolate chip cookies.

When I ordered forty bikes from Allen—twenty for adults and twenty for kids—he gave Jazz and me our two favorites for free. We ride our bikes down to the lake and set up our picnic in the shade of Opal's tree. Even though she insists that she feels fine, Jazz hardly touches her lunch, and instead of dancing or tumbling across the grass, she lies beside me on the blanket while I read to her.

Sprinkles drive us back to the cottage, and a heavier rain sets in for the afternoon. Jazz and I camp out on the sofa with a bowl of popcorn for a movie marathon.

Her fever returns around dinnertime—a thermometer reading of 102—and she chokes down the grape-flavored Advil liquid.

I reheat the homemade chicken soup I bought at the market, but she refuses to eat it. "Let's put your pajamas on and get you into bed."

"No! I want to stay with you." And so we cuddle under my comforter on the sofa, watching yet another movie.

When Jazz drifts off, I carry her to bed. She still feels warm to the touch, but according to the dosage instruction, I can't give her more medicine for at least another four hours. I change into my pajamas and crawl into bed beside her with my library book. I doze off around nine. Jazz wakes me two hours later when she projectile vomits all over the bed. She's crying hysterically, and I don't need a thermometer to tell me she's burning up with fever. I lift her off the bed and carry her into the bathroom, setting her down on the marble floor in front of the toilet.

Rocking back and forth on her knees, her hands pressed against her head, she wails, "It hurts so bad."

"What hurts, sweetheart?"

"My head."

"Hang on. We're gonna get you some help," I say as I clean her face and hands with a washcloth. My mind races. *What to do?* But there is only one thing I can do. I need to take her to the hospital. "Stay right here by the toilet, Jazzy, in case you get sick again. I'll be right back."

Jazz's pajamas were spared, but mine are covered in puke.

Changing into jeans and a clean T-shirt, I strip the bed linens and take the bundle to the laundry closet in the kitchen. Not bothering with the car seat, which is sitting in the middle of the living room floor from when Katherine brought Jazz home from camp on Friday, I wrap her in a fleece blanket, grab my purse, and carry her out to Billy's Jeep. Buckling Jazz into the back seat, I climb behind the wheel and speed off, careening around the corner of the main building.

Although I've never driven on public roads before, I've ridden in plenty of cars, and I'm on autopilot as I cruise down Main Street. I ask Siri to direct me to the nearest hospital, but Jazz is sobbing too loud for me to hear.

"I need you to stop crying, Jazz," I say in a stern voice. "I can't hear the directions."

She lowers the volume a decibel. When we arrive at the hospital five minutes later, as I'm getting her out of the car, she pukes all down my back. I can feel the warm dampness from my saturated T-shirt against my skin.

The emergency room is packed with people of all ages in varying degrees of Saturday night drunkenness seeking medical attention. Fortunately, there is no one waiting at the check-in desk.

"I have a sick child," I say to the receptionist. "She needs to see a doctor."

The young woman's beautiful face is distorted with meanness. "Is she *your* child?" I interpret the insinuation in her tone to mean she has a problem with mixed race couples.

Anger pulses through my body. *Is she kidding me? So what if she's my child and her father is black?* "She is *not* my child. I'm taking care of her while her mother's away."

"Are you listed on the child's HIPAA form?"

This has not occurred to me in my rush to get Jazz help. "Her parents had to go out of town unexpectedly on a family emergency. I have no idea how to get in touch with them."

She smacks her hand down on the counter, palm up. "Insurance card."

Jazz is getting heavy. I look around for a place to put her down, but all the chairs in the waiting room are occupied. "I don't have that either. Her mother forgot to leave it with me."

The receptionist rolls her eyes. "Naturally." She picks up a clipboard and thrusts it toward me. "Fill these out. The doctor will decide whether to treat her."

An older man with a sweet face gives me his chair. Balancing the limp child on my lap, I scribble Jazz's first and last names on the top form. Those are the only two blanks I can fill out. I know Jazz's favorite color is pink. I know she loves ladybugs but is terrified of spiders. I know she can't hold a tune but dances like an angel. But I don't know any pertinent information that will get her seen by a doctor.

I can hardly think. My throat swells. Tears of both fear and anger are close to the surface. I'm terrified something is seriously wrong with this child, but I'm also furious with Naomi for putting me in this position. She doesn't deserve to be a mother, especially to a kid as awesome as Jazz.

Fumbling in my purse for my phone, I click on Brian's number. He answers on the second ring, his voice alert despite the late hour. "Stella, is something wrong?"

"Jazz is really sick. We're at the emergency room. The receptionist is asking for her insurance card, which Naomi neglected to leave. And because of the privacy laws, they may not let me talk to the doctor about her condition."

"Jazz was born in that hospital," Brian says. "They should have her insurance information in their system."

"I'm sure they do. The receptionist is being a . . ." I catch myself. "She's being uncooperative."

"Can you get her direct dial phone number for me?"

My gaze travels to the check-in desk where the receptionist is sharing a laugh with a coworker. "Sure. Give me a minute. I'll text it to you," I say, and end the call.

When I stand up, Jazz moans. "It's okay, baby." I kiss her head. "We're gonna see the doctor soon."

Returning to the check-in counter, I say to the receptionist, "My attorney would like a word with you. I need your direct dial number, so he can call you."

The color drains from her face. When she stalls, I say, "Now!"

When she tells me the number, I one-thumb text it to Brian. Seconds later, the phone on the desk beside her rings and she lifts the receiver to her ear. She listens for a minute. "Yes, sir. I understand, sir." Her fingers fly across the keyboard. "Yes, sir. I have her patient information right here. Yes, sir. I'll make sure she's seen right away."

The nurse snarls at me as she hangs up the phone. "Have a seat. They'll call you back in a minute."

We've no sooner gotten situated again when a nurse wearing blue scrubs and a pleasant smile calls Jazz's name. I gather up the child and my purse and follow her through to the examining rooms. The nurse, who tells me her name is Maggie, closes the door behind us. As I'm settling Jazz on the bed, she fires off questions, most of which I can answer. "Has she been sick recently? When did she last eat? How long as she been running a fever? Has she complained of a sore throat?"

I give her a brief rundown of the past sixteen hours while she checks Jazz's vitals. Her temperature is 104, which seems alarmingly high to me, but Maggie seems unconcerned.

"The doctor will be in to see you soon," she says and leaves the room.

Jazz starts crying again, not the same loud bawling from earlier but a soft whimper. "What is it, sweetheart? Can I get something for you?"

"I want my mommy."

Of course, she does. Every kid wants their mom when they're

sick. "I know you don't feel well. But the doctor is gonna make you all better."

Dr. Boyd Taylor is about my age and kinda cute with blond hair, a baby face, and a platinum wedding band on his ring finger. As he's reading Jazz's chart, he sniffs and turns up his nose.

"Sorry. I'm wearing puke perfume, courtesy of my little friend here."

He smiles. "I know the fragrance well. I'm sure there's an extra hospital gown lying around here somewhere. I'll see if I can find you one."

After listening to Jazz's heart and lungs, Dr. Taylor looks in her ears, nose, and throat. "It's probably just a summer virus, but we'll run some tests."

Our examining room becomes a hubbub of activity. One nurse brings Jazz ibuprofen while another one delivers hospital gowns for us both. I remove my soiled T-shirt, tossing it into the trash can, and put on the gown, tying the extra fabric around my waist. When Maggie comes to draw blood, Jazz freaks out, and the nurse has to call in reinforcements to hold her down while she inserts the IV. After they leave, it takes me thirty minutes to calm Jazz down. I lie next to her on the bed, her little body a ball of fire. She tosses and turns before falling into a restless sleep.

It's nearing morning when Dr. Taylor returns with disturbing news. "Jazz's white blood count is alarmingly high. We're running more tests to rule out the possibility of meningitis."

The hairs on the back of my neck stand to attention. "Meningitis? But isn't that serious?"

He gives a solemn nod. "It can be."

TWENTY

Our morning in the emergency room is nothing short of hell on earth. The nurses wheel Jazz away for tests. They won't let me go with her, and when she returns, she's inconsolable. She sobs and throws fists and rakes her hands through her hair, screaming, "Make it stop!"

Jazz's fever spikes to 105, and when she has a seizure, I go into full panic mode. I threaten to air ambulance her to a major hospital, and even though I suspect she doesn't have her phone with her, I leave repeated desperate voice messages for Naomi.

Brian and I are in constant communication. He does his best to find Naomi. At the inn, he hacks into her email program on the office computer and discovers past correspondence with psychiatric hospitals and substance abuse programs. He speaks to the head administrators at all the facilities, explaining the urgency of the situation. None of them have seen or heard from Naomi.

My stomach does an acrobatic dive when the doctor enters the room wearing a face mask. "We've confirmed that Jazz has bacterial meningitis. While not as contagious as viral meningitis, you should still wear this." He hands me a mask identical to the one he's wearing. "This is serious, Miss Boor. If I were you, I'd locate her parents."

"Trust me, Doctor, we're doing everything we can to find them."

He doesn't tell me what I already know. I've been sleeping with the kid. I've already been exposed. I take the mask from him anyway. "You're gonna transfer her, right? To a better-equipped hospital?"

The doctor goes rigid. "We have a pediatric ICU, which makes us plenty *equipped* to handle her case here. While we are one of the smaller hospitals in the state, we serve many neighboring towns." He leaves the room before I can argue.

I google bacterial meningitis. What I learn causes me to hyperventilate. Not only is there a chance she could die, the effects from the disease can be long term if she survives.

Gulping in deep breaths, I click on Brian's number.

"The news is bad, Brian. She has bacterial meningitis. We need to find Naomi."

Brian lets out a loud sigh. "I have a friend in the police department. I'll give him a call."

As soon as I hang up, a team of nurses dressed in full surgical garb—booties, masks, gloves, and caps—arrives to transport Jazz. Her room on the pediatric floor is a fishbowl with floor-to-ceiling windows looking out at the nurses' station. Aside from the hospital bed and a host of medical equipment, there's a small desk, lounge chair, and bathroom complete with shower. With a sinking feeling, I realize this will be my home for the foreseeable future.

For the next few hours, Jazz thrashes about on the bed, muttering nonsense in her fever delirium. Nurses—wearing yellow isolation gowns, plastic gloves, and masks—bustle in and out, monitoring her vitals and injecting fluids into her IV. How do they cope with the heartache of tending sick children every day while remaining so positive and cheerful? To be sure, there's a special place reserved for them in heaven.

Midafternoon, Jazz's regular pediatrician stops by to examine her. In her fifties, Dr. Flowers is attractive with salt-and-pepper hair and a gentle bedside manner. She speaks to Jazz in a comforting tone as she moves her stethoscope around the child's chest. With glassy eyes, Jazz smiles up at the doctor as though she trusts her.

When I ask the doctor when the fever might go down, she asks, "Who did you say you were again?"

"I didn't say." Using Brian's legal jargon, I add, "I'm acting as Jazz's personal representative in her parents' absence."

"Unless you're identified on the HIPPA forms, by law, I'm not at liberty to discuss Jazz's medical condition with you."

Here we go with the privacy laws again. "Look, Dr. Flowers, Naomi had to go out of town at the spur of the moment, and she left Jazz in my care. I have no idea where Naomi is and no way of getting in touch with either Naomi or her husband. That is not my fault, and it's certainly not Jazz's." I flash my phone at her. "Would you like to speak with my attorney?"

Dr. Flowers takes in my vomit-matted hair and hospital gown. "That won't be necessary."

Jazz and I have a long road ahead of us, and I need the doctor on my side. I lower my tone. "I promise, we're doing everything we can to find Jazz's parents. But, until we do, you're stuck with me. I adore this kid. I only want what's best for her. I will do whatever it takes to get Jazz well."

Dr. Flowers straightens, and giving Jazz's head a pat, she says, "You hang in there, kiddo. We're gonna make you all better soon." She takes me by the arm and leads me out of the room. "While we are hitting Jazz hard with antibiotics, it could still take days to lower her temperature. We're also giving her meds to hopefully avoid any more seizures and to make her comfortable so she can rest. Our primary concern at the moment is avoiding the long list of potential complications."

"Right. I read about those online." Despite my discussion with Dr. Taylor, I'm not convinced Jazz is in the right hospital. "I'm going to be honest with you, Doctor, and I expect the same in return."

Dr. Flowers gives me an affirmative nod.

"I'm from New York, the home of some of the best medical centers in the country. Do you feel the staff here is equipped to handle this case? I'm committed to getting Jazz the best possible treatment, even if that means transferring her to a larger facility."

The doctor's posture relaxes and her lips part in a smile. "That is a fair question. And I respect your line of thinking. As of now, I feel that Jazz is in very good hands. I will be checking in on her several times a day and monitoring her progress with the doctors on staff. If my opinion changes, you'll be the first to know. I'll give you my cell number. If you have any concerns at all, I want you to call or text me immediately, night or day."

"Don't worry. I will."

After we exchange phone numbers, the doctor moves down the hall to visit another patient, and I return to Jazz who is finally resting peacefully. Exhaustion hits me like a wrecking ball. Reclining the lounge chair, I close my eyes and immediately fall asleep.

I'm dreaming of needles and nurses in hazmat suits when someone nudges me awake. I'm surprised to see Jack standing over me with a backpack slung over his shoulder.

Rubbing my eyes, I bring my chair to the sit-up position. "Jack. What're you doing here?"

"Brian asked me to check on you. He wanted to come to the hospital himself, but he's down at the police station filling out a missing person's report."

I mentally roll my eyes. Being a parent is a privilege Naomi does not deserve.

I snatch a disposable mask from the box on the desk beside me. "You should wear this."

He waves off the mask. "I'll take my chances. I want Jazz to see my friendly face."

I smile. I like his style. When I stand to face him, he gets a whiff of my vomit hair. Eyeing my hospital gown, he says, "I can tell you've had a rough time of it. Go home and get cleaned up. I'll sit with Jazz while you're gone."

My gaze travels to the sleeping child. "No way! I'm not leaving her."

Jack places a hand on my arm. "Who knows how long you'll be here, Stella. But you won't be of any use to Jazz if you get sick. Taking care of yourself is a priority. Be sure to grab plenty of clothes for both you and Jazz. And any toys or stuffed animals that might make her feel more at home."

His concern touches me. "You sound like the voice of experience. Do you have kids, Jack?"

"Nope. No kids. Let's talk about how you got here. Did you drive without a license?"

"Yep. I drove Billy's Jeep. It was the middle of the night, and Jazz was burning up with fever. I didn't think, Jack. I acted. This town really needs Uber."

He laughs. "Believe it or not, we actually have a few Uber drivers. You just have to catch them when they're on duty. Do you want to call Cecily or Katherine to take you home?"

"No. After the day I've had, breaking the law is the least of my concerns."

"How much longer before you can get your license?"

"Technically, I can take the test at the end of the month. But I need to learn to parallel park first."

I drive slowly and carefully on my way back to the farm, holding my breath when a patrol car pulls up beside me on Main Street. What's the worst he can do? Give me a ticket for driving without a license? Brian can get me out of it. When the light turns green and the patrol car drives off, I exhale a sigh of relief.

At home, I throw the soiled comforter from my bed into the washing machine while I shower, dress, and pack. In addition to my clothes and toiletries, I add Jazz's two pairs of pajamas and her favorite stuffed bear. When the drier buzzes, I grab the comforter and the tote with the books from the library and return to the hospital.

What I find in Jazz's room brings a smile to my face. Jack has dimmed the lights and pulled the lounge chair close to the bed. Classical music plays softly from a Bluetooth speaker on the bed table while he reads to a sleeping Jazz from the June issue of *Sports Illustrated*.

Leaving my suitcase beside the door, I enter the room. Peering over his shoulder, I see he's reading an article highlighting predictions for the upcoming Wimbledon tournament. "Jazz is a big fan of tennis," I say.

"That's what she told me." He closes the magazine and smiles up at me. "You look refreshed."

"I feel, and smell, much better. Thank you." I drag the desk chair to the side of the bed opposite him. "You're an old pro at this. Soft music, dim lighting." I gesture first at the speaker and then the overhead lights.

Jack stares down at the magazine in his lap. "I've spent my share of time in this hospital."

He told me earlier that he doesn't have children. "With sick parents?" I ask.

He shakes his head. "My wife. She died of cancer three years ago."

"Oh, Jack. I'm so sorry. I had no idea." I think back to all the references I've made to his wife. What an idiot I am.

His hazel eyes are warm. "You had no way of knowing."

"What kind of can—" I stop myself. "I'm sorry. That's none of my business. It's just . . . you're so young. I assume your wife was as well."

"Jenna was only thirty. She had stage four melanoma. Fortunately, she didn't suffer long."

His demeanor exudes such sadness. He obviously loved her very much. While I want to know more about Jenna, I sense this is not the right time to ask.

Jack stuffs his magazine in his backpack. "Would you like me to leave the speaker?"

"That would be awesome." In a teasing tone, I add, "Maybe the *Sports Illustrated* as well."

He laughs and gives me a quick tutorial on how to connect the speaker to my phone. "Did you get something to eat while you were out?"

I shake my head. "I was in too much of a hurry to get back to Jazz."

"You need to eat. Do you want to run down to the cafeteria before I leave? The food's actually pretty good. You can't go wrong with the salad bar."

"I'm fine, but thanks."

"You're not fine," he says. "When's the last time you ate?"

When I think back on what I've eaten over the weekend, I feel a pang of guilt for allowing Jazz to go to bed without dinner on Friday night. She was already sick, and I didn't know it. "I had a bowl of chicken soup for dinner last night."

Jack gets to his feet. "If you won't go to the cafeteria, I'll bring the cafeteria to you."

"Jack, seriously, don't go to the trouble."

He walks toward the door. "If you don't tell me what you want, you'll have to settle for what I bring you."

"In that case, I'd like a salad with mixed greens, sliced chicken, lots of toppings, and balsamic vinaigrette."

"Thatta girl. One healthy salad coming up."

Through the window, I watch him disappear down the hall. *Now there's the Jack I met my first week in town.*

TWENTY-ONE

Following Jack's lead, I play her favorite ballet music and read her library books over and over. I order her an iPad and have it shipped directly to the hospital, so she'll have it when she feels up to watching movies.

Katherine drops by on Monday afternoon to show me her landscape blueprint. I meet her in the ICU waiting room down the hall so as not to disturb Jazz. We're the only ones in the waiting room, and we spread the plans out on the coffee table in front of us. After we study the plans, we talk for a few minutes about budget and schedule.

"Great work," I say finally. "I applaud your innovative use of Virginia's native plants. I realize a lot of the planting will have to wait until fall but go ahead and put whatever you can in motion now."

A beaming Katherine rolls up her plans, returning them to a cardboard tube for safe storage. "How are you holding up, Stella?"

"I'm okay. Exhausted, but nervous energy is keeping me going. I'll feel better once the police locate Jazz's parents."

"Is there anything I can do for you?"

I walk her to the elevator. "There's not much anyone can do for now. Prayers are appreciated."

Katherine gives me a warm smile. "That goes without saying."

On Tuesday morning, Cecily brings blueberry muffins still warm from the oven. "I'm on my way to the library. Can I pick up some books for you and Jazz?"

"That would be great! I've memorized the ones we currently have," I say and give her the tote bag of Jazz's books to return to the library.

Jack comes every day at dinnertime, bringing takeout for both of us from one of the restaurants on Main Street. He stays most nights until past nine o'clock. We sit on the same side of the bed, talking in hushed tones, not only about the renovations but about our past lives. I tell him the bazaar circumstances of how I came to be in Hope Springs, including my *we conspiracy* suspicions, and he speaks openly about his wife's death.

It takes the police until Wednesday to locate Naomi and Derrick. Brian comes to the hospital to deliver the news. I meet him in the lounge, and he leads me over to the bank of windows. "Naomi is at an alcohol rehabilitation facility in Arizona. She left her car in a monthly rental parking lot instead of one of the lots at the Roanoke airport. Which is why it took the police so long to track her down."

"Wow," I say. "She obviously didn't want to be found. Why Arizona?"

"Apparently, this particular program is regarded as one of the top in the country. I spoke with the head administrator at length. According to him, Naomi is beginning to show improvement, and he feels the news of her daughter's illness might impede her progress."

"Forgive me for sounding callous, but I don't really care about Naomi's progress."

Brian smiles. "Between you and me, I don't either."

This rare show of emotion makes me warm to Brian a little more. "What about Jazz's father?"

"He's fly-fishing in Montana."

My chin drops to my chest, and I stare at him from under furrowed eyebrows. "Seriously?"

"Seriously," Brian repeats. "According to his coworkers, Derrick is hiding from his wife. He made them promise not to divulge his whereabouts to anyone. They finally broke under pressure from the police."

"So, all this time they knew where he was?"

Brian's face is grim. "Afraid so."

"Please tell me Derrick is on a plane headed back to Virginia."

He slowly shakes his head. "I asked the police not to tell him about Jazz's illness just yet. You'll find this difficult to understand, Stella. But you have to trust my decision. I've known Naomi a long time. There are things about her past I'm not yet ready to reveal to you. If I thought for a minute that Derrick could provide value to this situation, I would personally pay for a private plane to bring him home. For the time being, Jazz is much better off in your hands."

I collapse against the window. "And when does that time change, Brian?"

"I say we give it twenty-four more hours. If Jazz doesn't turn the corner, then we'll send for Naomi."

"Sounds like you're worried too, that Jazz doesn't appear to be getting any better. All she does is sleep. The big-city girl in me thinks we should move her to a major hospital."

"And the small-town boy in me doesn't disagree. But Jennette Flowers is an old friend. She promised to let me know if and when we get to that point."

I push off the window. "If she's not better in twenty-four more hours, we're moving her."

I'm halfway across the waiting room when I remember to ask

him about Opal. I retraced my steps. "By the way, have you seen Opal? Do you know how she's feeling?"

His lips grow thin. "Definitely not a hundred percent. She can't seem to beat this virus."

"Has she seen her doctor yet?"

"Nope. She's a stubborn one."

I shake my head. "The last thing we need is for her to end up in the hospital."

When I return to Jazz's room, I recline the lounge chair and close my eyes. Even though I haven't slept much since Saturday night, I force myself to rest periodically. For Jazz's sake, I'm trying to take care of myself.

My mind replays my conversation with Brian. He's definitely holding out on me. Something is fishy about the situation with Derrick. He's Jazz's father. How could he not add *value* to this situation? Unless he's a total deadbeat. Or he's not her father. Even so, he's still her stepfather.

This situation with Naomi and Derrick is screwed up. Despite what I said to Brian about Naomi, I'm all for her getting the help she needs. But she didn't just fly out to Arizona on a whim. She took the time to plan her trip. She should've taken the time to make certain her daughter would be properly looked after while she was gone. At the bare minimum, she should've left a set of instructions. Name and contact information for Jazz's doctors. What to do if she gets sick? Who to call in an emergency? While she had no way of knowing her daughter would become ill, isn't it a parent's responsibility to always be prepared for the unexpected? I know my parents were when I was a kid.

What makes some people better parents than others? While taking care of Jazz for two weeks doesn't make me a mother, it has given me a healthy dosage of parenting. I've thought a lot about my mothers over the past few days, and I've been tempted to call them no fewer than a hundred times. Every kid finds fault in their parents at some point in their lives. My parents were excellent providers. But they let their friends and careers take priority over me. I'm glad they lead fulfilled lives. They've been good role models in that regard. But them lying to me about my father being a sperm donor is wrong. So what if I blocked their numbers. Hannah knows where to find me. If she wanted to make things right between us, she would've come to Virginia weeks ago. Once I get Jazz well, I'm going to find out the truth about her relationship with my father. Once I get Jazz well, I'm going to find out the truth about a lot of things.

On Wednesday evening, I've just finished giving Jazz a sponge bath and changing her hospital gown, when Jack arrives with two cheeseburger platters from Lucky's Diner. He sets the Styrofoam containers on the desk and goes to stand beside the bed. "Any change?" he asks, his face full of compassion as he stares down at the patient.

"None. And I'm getting frustrated." I tell Jack what I learned from Brian about Naomi and Derrick.

"That is seriously messed up."

"Tell me about it," I say. "I've been sitting here for most of the afternoon wondering how some people don't deserve to be parents."

In our respective chairs—Jack always lets me have the comfortable one—we talk for a while about what his crew accomplished today at the inn.

I find him easy to talk to, and before I can stop myself, the words escape my mouth. "I'm glad we're friends again."

He casts a sideways glance at me. "I never thought otherwise."

I shrug. "We started out on the right path, but I feel like I disappointed you when I came home drunk from happy hour with Katherine and Cecily."

His face goes dark. "I don't judge people, Stella."

"I didn't mean that. Exactly." I pick at a loose thread on the fabricated hole in my jeans. "I'm hypersensitive to what people around here think of me. Because of my age and my sudden appearance in Hope Springs. Because I'm Billy Jameson's daughter. Everyone who knew him, loved him. There's no way I can measure up."

Jack's face softens. "You measure up just fine, Stella. Billy would've been proud of the way you're handling the renovations with such confidence and determination."

"Anyway, my point is, I'm glad things are no longer awkward between us."

"I prefer to think of our relationship as complicated." He angles his body toward me. "The truth is, Stella, when we first met, I was feeling more for you than friendship, and it freaked me out. I ran away with my tail between my legs." His gaze shifts to Jazz. "Times like these remind us of how fragile life is. I've been reflecting a lot on my life this week, thinking about where I've come from and where I'm headed. Until now, I've been afraid to love again, but Jazz's illness, and seeing you taking such excellent care of her, has made me realize that any life worth living is full of risks. Look at the risk you took in leaving behind your life in New York and moving to a small mountain town where you know no one."

I snicker. "That's probably not the best comparison. I didn't have much going for me in New York to leave behind."

He smiles. "I don't believe that."

"It's true," I mumble.

"There's something between us, Stella. I feel it, and I think you feel it as well. Once we get Jazz through this, I'm going to ask you out on a date. Will you say yes?"

I like the sound of *we*. It's nice to have a partner in her recovery. *Yes* is on the tip of my tongue when one of the monitors on the wall behind Jazz's bed buzzes. Another one starts rapidly beeping. Alarms go off and nurses swarm the room, asking us to leave.

I'm already on my feet, but I remain glued to the floor.

"Come on, Stella. We're in the way." Taking me by the hand, Jack drags me out of the room and down the hall. I'm relieved to find the waiting room empty.

"I'm so scared, Jack. What if we lose her?" I turn to him, and he embraces me. His body against mine feels right. I'm safe in his arms. How I wish he had the power to heal Jazz.

He whispers into my hair, "She's a tough kid, Stella. She's gonna pull through."

I press my face to his chest, praying to God not to take her. Long minutes pass—I don't know how many—before I finally pull away. "We need to call Brian. Will you do it? I'm afraid I might cry."

"Of course." Jack's call is brief, and when he hangs up, he says, "Brian is on the way."

We walk together to the window and watch the sun begin its descent below the mountains. "It's going to be a long night," I say, and even though I don't want him to leave me, I add, "You should go home."

"No way. The only place I'm going is to the cafeteria for some coffee. Would you like some?"

"Yes! Please."

Jack leaves me alone with my thoughts, but I can't bear to think about what might be happening to Jazz. I need to talk to someone. I need my mom.

I unblock Hannah's number. Marnie is the maternal one, the parent I always go to when I'm sick or sad or in trouble. But Hannah is the closest to this situation. She's the one I need at this moment in time. But when she answers on the third ring, I hear laughter and loud talking in the background.

"Mom?"

"Oh, Stella, it's wonderful to hear your voice," she says as though I'm a long-lost friend, not her daughter.

"You're at a party. We'll talk some other time." *Like never.*

"No! Wait! Let me step outside."

The laughter fades, replaced by busy street noises. I'm stunned at the revelation that I don't miss New York one bit.

"What's going on?" Hannah asks. She knows I didn't call to chat.

"There's this kid. She's six years old, a talented little ballerina. And . . . well . . . I've fallen in love with her. And she's sick, and I'm scared she might die." No longer able to hold back the tears, I sob, "Her mother is in rehab. She left Jazz in my care."

"The child's name is Jazz?" I hear curiosity in Hannah's voice, but there's another emotion as well.

"Yes," I say, sniffling.

"Is it short for Jasmine?" she asks, and this time with a note of suspicion in her tone.

"What else would it be short for? But enough about her name. She has bacterial meningitis."

"That's very serious," Hannah says, as though I don't already know this. "Is she in the hospital?"

This conversation is going nowhere. "Of course, she's in the hospital. I just told you she might die."

"In Hope Springs?"

I stop crying. "You know where I am, Mom. I'm sorry. I made a mistake in calling you." I hang up on her. I don't block her number again, but she doesn't call back.

I mean nothing to my parents. All I've ever been to them is a showpiece for their friends.

Jack returns with three coffees and Brian on his heels.

"We should call Naomi," I say to Brian. "She deserves to know."

"Naomi deserves nothing." His face is set in an angry scowl, but when he sees my shock at his response, he softens. "Let's find out what's going on with Jazz, and then we'll decide whether to notify Naomi. What can she do from Arizona anyway?"

Long hours pass with no word from the doctors and nurses inside the intensive care unit. The three of us take turns pacing the floor. We bite fingernails and stare at our phones. Jack returns to the cafeteria twice for more coffee, and we make countless trips to the restrooms. Around eleven o'clock, an exasperated Brian bursts into the ICU, demanding answers. Dr. Flowers sends him away, but at least we know Jazz is still alive.

Finally, at almost one in the morning, Flowers emerges through the double doors. None of us gets up to greet her. We're all too paralyzed with fear to move. I can't read her expression. I want to believe that's relief I see on her face.

She sits down heavily in the chair opposite us. "It was touch and go for a while, but she's finally stable, and we're giving her a new antibiotic."

I spring to my feet. "I'm done with this situation, Dr. Flowers. We're moving her to Richmond."

Flowers stands to face me. "I understand your frustration, Stella. But this medicine appears to be working. Jazz is awake. She's asking for you."

TWENTY-TWO

Jazz's health improves with each passing day. Although she continues to run a fever and tire easily. While she doesn't appear to have any permanent damage, the doctors warn she's not yet out of the woods.

Keeping Jazz entertained is a challenge. She plays games and watches movies on her new iPad and works the activity books—puzzles as well as hidden picture ones—I buy for her in the lobby gift shop. Cecily visits with more library books and a picnic basket of baked goodies, and Katherine brings a lovely bouquet of flowers she cut from her own yard. Jack continues with his nightly visits, but now he arrives with dinner for three. On Saturday, he sits with Jazz while I go home to do our laundry.

On Sunday morning, when Jazz asks if her mother knows she's sick, I have my answer prepared. "No, sweetheart. Mr. Brian and I decided not to tell her. Your mommy is sick too, but in a different way."

She furrows her little brow. "What do you mean? Does she have many-gi-tus, too?"

"Not meningitis," I say, pronouncing every syllable. "You

know how your mommy sometimes drinks the gold stuff in the tall bottle that smells bad?"

Her upper lip curls. "Wine. She gets drunk a lot."

"That's because something, deep down inside of her, is making her unhappy. And the doctors are helping her figure out what that is so she'll feel better."

"I know what it is. She misses Billy."

Oh really? That kind of grief for someone who's only a friend? "Jazz, do you know how long your parents have been married?"

She holds her hands out, palms up, as if to say she doesn't have a clue.

"Of course you don't," I say, mussing her hair. She's a six-year-old kid. I'll need to pose my questions to a more reliable source.

By the time Dr. Flowers releases Jazz midday on Monday, we are both eager to go home. An orderly pushes Jazz's wheelchair to the main entrance where they wait while I go to the parking lot for Billy's Jeep. I've been tempting fate by driving without a license. I have two weeks to go until my sixty days is up. I've yet to learn how to parallel park, and my driving coach is still under the weather.

I'm unlocking the Jeep when I spot Brian hurrying across the lot. I call his name. Slowing his pace, he makes a detour toward me.

"Jazz is finally being released. We're on our way home. I'll tell her you stopped by. Maybe you can visit at the cottage."

He rakes his hands through his salt-and-pepper hair. "I'm thrilled for both of you. But I'm not here to see Jazz. I came with Opal. I finally convinced her to see her doctor late last week. He ran some tests. It appears as though she may have leukemia."

I deflate, as though I've been punched in the gut, and I collapse against the Jeep. "Poor Opal. I'm so sorry, Brian. How's she handling the news?"

"It hasn't sunk in yet. She just found out this morning. I brought her in for more tests."

"Please tell her I'm thinking about her, and I'll be in to see her in a couple of days, as soon as I get Jazz settled."

"I'll tell her," Brian says. "I'm sure she'd appreciate a text."

I give Brian's arm a squeeze. "Hang in there."

I drive around to the main entrance and help the orderly load Jazz into the Jeep. On the way back to the farm, I think about Opal. How scary for her to be facing such a serious medical crisis at her age. At least she has her wonderful son to take care of her. I've grown to love Opal. Her quirkiness brings joy to my life. I would hate to lose her when we're becoming friends.

Jack brings a large pie from Ruby's Italian Pizzeria for dinner, and we sit at the table like a family. Jazz, her appetite not fully recovered, takes only a few bites of one slice. She yawns and lays her head on the table. She showered as soon as we got home from the hospital and is already in her pajamas.

"I'll put her to bed while you clean up," Jack says lifting the little girl into his arms.

He's gone for a while, and by the time he returns, I've finished putting away the leftovers and loading the dishwasher.

"Jazz perked up when I tucked her in," he says. "She begged me to read her a bedtime story. I ended up reading three."

"Is she asleep now?"

"Oh yeah! Out cold." He begins opening and closing cabinets. "Would you care for a glass of wine?"

"I would love one, but I don't have any."

Locating two wine glasses, he sets them on the counter and walks to the back door. "I brought a bottle with me, but I left it in the car. I didn't want to upset Jazz. You know, because of her mother's drinking problem and all."

I smile at him. "Thank you for being sensitive to her feelings."

Jack has been my rock this past week. I've grown accustomed to sharing everything with him. I told him about my conversation with Jazz regarding her mother's whereabouts, and when he returns with the wine, while he's opening the bottle and filling the glasses, I tell him about Opal having leukemia.

"I'm sorry to hear that. But Opal is a strong woman. If anyone can beat it, she can."

"I hope you're right."

Jack and I take our wine into the living room and sit close together on the sofa. "It's nice to be home," I say, tucking my feet beneath me.

He places an arm on the cushion behind my head. "It's good to have you alone. Can we go on our date soon?"

I smile over at him. "That depends. Do you know any responsible babysitters?"

He laughs. "A sitter for the sitter. I can't think of anyone off the top of my head, but I'll ask around."

"Cecily might be willing to keep Jazz, if I can drag her away from Lyle long enough."

He takes my wine glass from me and sets it on the coffee table beside his. "I can't wait until our date to do this." Cupping my head, he draws me close and kisses me, his lips soft and gentle against mine. My stomach tumbles and heat radiates through my body. Our lips part and tongues meet. He tastes like pizza and wine and something deliciously sweet that I identify as lust. I yearn to rip off his clothes and straddle him naked. But the mature me—the one evolving from the responsibilities of managing a multi-million-dollar renovation project and nursing a critically ill child—controls this impulse.

I jump to my feet and run a hand down my shorts, straightening them. "I'm sorry, Jack. I can't risk having Jazz walk in on us."

He stands to face me. "I understand about Jazz. And I respect that. But, did you not feel the attraction between us just now? Because I'm pretty sure the earth just moved."

I laugh out loud. "Yes! I felt it."

"Then why are you pushing me away when we have a chance at something special?"

I place my hand on his cheek. "I'm not pushing you away. This week . . . having you by my side during Jazz's crisis . . . I want that kind of close relationship in my life. Someone I can count on. Someone I can grow with. But I'm the queen of screwing up relationships, Jack. I have the track record to prove it. If it's okay with you, I'd like to take things slow."

Relief crosses his face. "I'm willing to take things slow as long as you promise to be honest with me. But I sense there's something more. Something else holding you back."

I cross the room to the bookshelves. My eyes roam my father's collection of books and memorabilia. I've combed through everything once. What if I missed something? What if there's an important clue here about my family?

I turn my back to the bookshelves. "You're right. Something else is holding me back. I need to figure out who I am before I commit to a relationship."

For the rest of the week, I work out of the cottage kitchen. When Cecily and Kathryn stop by with updates on their various projects, I make them sanitize their hands with Purell and wear surgical masks to avoid spreading germs. Jack brings dinner most nights, except on Wednesday when I cook my mother's baked ziti recipe. At night, after he leaves and Jazz is in bed, with Billy on my earpods, I meticulously comb through the bookcases, looking for clues to my family history. When I find nothing, I quietly scour the bedroom so as not to wake a sleeping Jazz. Tucked inside a Bible in the bedside table drawer, I discover an unframed photograph of Hannah and Billy at a party. His arms are around her waist, and she's gazing into his eyes, two young people very much in love at what appears to be a college band party. Hannah was twenty-four when she gave birth to me. I hug the photograph to my chest. Does this mean I'm a product of a long-lasting relationship and not a one-night stand? On the other hand, if they once meant something to each other, why prevent me from being a part of my father's life? I return the photo, a reminder of my mother's betrayal, to the drawer.

Earlier in the week, when I called the doctor's office to schedule Jazz's two-week follow-up, the nurse made the appointment and then advised me to let Jazz determine when to resume her normal activities. By Friday, she is feeling much better and hasn't had a fever since leaving the hospital. When she begs to go for her first session with the reading tutor, I reluctantly agree.

Carrie Anderson lives in an adorable house two blocks from the inn. Considering her petite size and childlike manner, I sense she and Jazz are a good match and that Jazz will blossom under her tutelage.

Carrie leans down to speak to Jazz at eye level. "After we read awhile, if it's okay with Stella, I'd like to take you to story time at the library and then to the pharmacy for lunch."

The Hope Springs Pharmacy on Main Street has the original 1960s-era soda counter. I've heard plenty about it, but I've yet to eat there.

Jazz clasps her hands. "Can I please, Stella?"

I smile. "As long as you promise not to overdo it."

Carrie winks at me. "I'll keep an eye on her. Okay if I drop her back at the inn around one?"

"That would be great."

I'm grateful to have the morning free, a first since Jazz got sick. I hurry back to the inn for my bicycle and ride all the way to the hospital to see Opal. It's a warm day, and I'm sweating by the time I get there. After asking the elderly volunteer at the information desk for Opal's room number, I stop by the lobby gift shop for flowers.

When I arrive at Opal's room, a nurse informs me she's too

sick for visitors. I've spoken to Brian nearly every day this week, but he never mentioned her condition was so dire. I leave the flowers with the nurse and take the elevator down to the lobby.

———

Jack takes Jazz and me into the mountains for a picnic on Saturday, and on Sunday, we go fly-fishing. I struggle to get the hang of casting, but Jazz is a natural. She catches three trout to add to Jack's two. I hook one but fail to reel it in.

"Can't we stay a little longer?" Jazz begs when it's time to go home.

I hip-bump her on the way to the car. "Not today, Jazzy. If we're lucky, Jack will bring us fishing another day. After I've had a chance to practice casting."

"I'll set you up with a rig, so you can practice down at the lake," Jack says to me, and to Jazz, "When we get back to the cottage, you can help me clean the fish."

This brings the smile to Jazz's face. Her feelings for him are nothing short of adoration.

The fish is seasoned perfectly, and I insist he give Cecily his recipe for our menu. We're like a small family gathered around the pine table. Our threesome feels right, like we belong together, and I have to remind myself that Jazz is not my child. Nor is Jack my husband. It's been a perfect weekend, and I'm sad to see it come to an end.

Late that night, I'm alone in the living room, listening to Billy's music when I finally find my first clue—lyrics from a song written about Jasmine.

Jasmine, sweet as a summer blossom,
Wherever you go,
Whoever you're with,
You'll always be in my heart,

My Jasmine, my love.

I google the song title. According to Wikipedia, the song was released in 1991, twenty-three years before Jazz was born. I would guess Naomi is in her late thirties, definitely no older than forty. Which means Naomi would've been eleven at the time. Which means Naomi named her child after one of Billy's past lovers. Why would she do that?

The clue doesn't provide answers. It only creates more questions.

TWENTY-THREE

The two weeks leading to the Fourth of July pass in a frenzy of activity. When I take Jazz for her follow-up appointment, Dr. Flowers is pleased with her progress and cautiously optimistic there will be no permanent damage. Jazz goes for ballet lessons on Tuesday and Thursday afternoons and to her reading tutor on Monday, Wednesday, and Friday mornings. In her free time, I arrange playdates with her new friends from the day camp. Jack teaches me to parallel park, and when the time comes, I go for my driving test. I pass with flying colors. Being able to drive opens up a whole new world of opportunity for Jazz and me to explore. We visit Natural Bridge and feed the animals as we drive through the Virginia Safari Park. I go to the hospital every chance I get, but the nurses refuse to let me see Opal. When I question Brian about her restricted visitation, he says they are taking things one day at a time and promises I can see Opal soon. Katherine sends bouquets of fresh flowers to brighten her room, and I drop off magazines and books and plastic containers of Cecily's edibles.

The inn begins to take shape. The decorators select paint colors and order miles of carpet, fabric, and wall coverings.

Plumbers set fixtures in the guest bathrooms and the tile contractor lays marble and ceramic tile on walls, floors, and in the showers. Electricians update wiring, HVAC guys install all new heating and cooling systems, and large teams of sheet rockers put up drywall. Despite all this progress, Jack claims we're running behind schedule. When he comes to the cottage for dinner at night, he's visibly stressed, but he never complains.

Jack invites Jazz and me to go with him to a friend's Fourth of July party. "There will be families with kids of all ages," he says, his face bright with excitement. "Jazz will have a blast. Wait until you see this spread of land, Stella. Hands down, Jason has the best view overlooking Hope Springs. He hires professionals to shoot off fireworks from a vacant field he leases on the outskirts of town. The best fireworks you've ever seen."

"Ha. Even better than New York?"

He laughs. "I wouldn't know. I've never been to New York on the Fourth of July."

Jazz and I choose our outfits with care. I decide on a navy-and-white striped sundress, and for Jazz, we find a pair of blue shorts printed with white stars at Target. She wears them over her bathing suit with a white T-shirt and red ribbons in her braided pigtails. We accessorize our ensembles with red, white, and blue star necklaces ordered from Amazon.

We arrive at the party promptly at four, just as the games are about to begin. They have three-legged races, egg tosses, and a scavenger hunt. I meet too many of Jack's friends to remember their names. They all beg for details of the renovations, and we're more than happy to oblige. When the games end, the kids go swimming in the pool while the adults sip blueberry lemonade margaritas in lounge chairs nearby.

"Thanks for bringing me here, Jack. I'm having so much fun. Does this count as our first date?"

"No way," he says, vehemently shaking his head. "Being

surrounded by screaming kids is not what I had in mind for our first date."

I cast him a sideways glance. "Oh really. What did you have in mind?"

"You and me alone together at my house. I'll cook you a fabulous meal, and then I plan to seduce you. I've been a patient man, Stella. But that patience is running out."

Jack and I rarely find time alone, but when we do, the flames burn hot.

"Ooh. An actual invitation to your house? I was beginning to think you live in a tent in the woods somewhere."

"Ha ha. Aren't you the funny one?" he says in a playful tone.

I stick my tongue out at him. "Seriously, though, Cecily volunteered to babysit. She even offered to spend the night if we want her to."

"We definitely want her to." He leans in close to me, planting little kisses on my neck. "I can hardly wait."

I brush my lips against his cheek. "Me either."

When a uniformed server rings a brass handbell, announcing dinner, kids make a mass exodus from the pool. Wrapping Jazz in a towel, we join the lines forming at the banquet tables. The food offerings include traditional cookout fare—hot dogs and hamburgers and grilled chicken breasts—but there are also some tasty salads with summer-fresh fruits and vegetables. We load up our plates and claim one of many picnic blankets spread out on the vast lawn.

Jazz is taking her first bite of her hot dog when a little girl about her age asks Jazz to join the small group of kids on a nearby blanket. She looks to me for permission and I say, "Of course, sweetheart. Go! Have fun!"

Taking her plate with her, Jazz runs off with the little girl, but she returns five minutes later, her golden eyes glistening with tears.

She snuggles up close to me, and I ask, "What's wrong, Jazzy?"

"Do you know when my mommy's coming home? Has the doctor fixed her yet?"

"No, honey, I'm sorry. I don't know." I lift Jazz onto my lap. "Are you missing her?"

"Sorta. But I like being with you more. It just that . . . well . . . I'm the only black kid here."

Alarm bells sound in my head. Jazz doesn't usually notice such things. "While that may be true, the rest of us are jealous your skin is prettier than ours."

"You're just saying that, Stella. Can we go home now? I don't belong here."

My eyes meet Jack's over the top of her head. "Says who?"

"That boy over there."

I follow her finger to a boy of about nine or ten with dark curly hair. He's cutting up, making the other kids laugh by acting obnoxious.

"What does he know? Talking like a big shot makes him feel important, especially when he's picking on kids who are different from him. Same thing used to happen to me all the time when I was a kid. Wanna know what I did?"

She nods her head. "What?"

"I ignored them. It drives mean kids crazy. And it makes them look like fools in front of their friends."

She pushes off of me, so she can see my face. "Really?"

"Really. Wanna give it a shot? We'll be right here if you need us."

"I guess." She butt-scoots to the edge of the blanket. With a quick swipe of the eyes and an uncertain glance back at us, she returns to her friends.

Jack and I watch as the scene at the neighboring blanket unfolds. When the mean kid starts to taunt Jazz again, she stares him down with chin high. After a while, the boy gives up and directs his attention on another poor kid.

Jack takes my hand, bringing it to his lips. "You're really good with her."

"Bullies are all the same. I encountered my share of them when I was growing up. Kids thought I was a freak, being raised by lesbian mothers before same-sex couples were a thing."

"I imagine that was difficult for you," he says, his face pinched in concern.

"It was lonely at times, but I learned to stand up for myself."

I stretch my legs out in front of me, my sandaled feet crossed. As the sun dips below the mountains, the sky fades from orange to black. Stars come out, twinkling in a cloudless sky, and a gentle breeze delivers the scent of roses from a nearby garden. I yearn to freeze this moment in time. While I'm curious to learn more about my family's past, I fear that what I discover will ruin everything I've gained since coming to Hope Springs. I never thought I could be this happy. I've fallen head over heels for an incredible man and an awesome kid.

Uniformed servers light tiki torches, hand out sparklers, and cut a ginormous sheet cake decorated like the American flag. The crowd cheers when the first fireworks light up the sky with bursts of blues and reds and whites.

Jack fingers a lock of my hair. "You're a million miles away. What're you thinking?"

"About past Fourths of July."

"And how did you typically spend them?"

"With my parents, watching fireworks from different venues around the city while celebrating my birthday."

"Wait. What?" Jack sits up straight. "Are you saying today is your birthday?"

"Yep. I'm thirty years old today."

He laughs, shaking his head. "You are full of surprises, Stella Boor. Why didn't you say something?"

"I just did."

"You know what I mean."

"Because I didn't want you to feel obligated to get me a gift. Having the same birthday as our nation has its perks. The evening has been perfect."

"Not quite." Jack leaves the blanket and disappears into the dark, returning a minute later with a square piece of cake, a sparkler hissing in the middle. He drops to his knees, presenting the cake to me, and sings *"Happy Birthday"* loudly and embarrassingly off-key. The rest of the guests join in, and Jazz rushes over.

"I didn't know today was your birthday," she says, knocking me over as she crawls on top of me.

"I was hoping not to make it a big deal." I cross my eyes at Jack. "But someone let the cat out of the bag."

Snatching the sparkler, Jazz dances graceful ballet moves around our blanket while Jack and I share the cake.

I'm disappointed to see the evening come to an end. It's past ten o'clock when we thank our hosts and load Jazz into Jack's pickup truck. On the way back to town, she chatters on about the new friends she made. She's keyed up from the excitement of the party. Getting her to bed will be a challenge.

At the inn, when we round the corner from the main building, I notice a black sedan parked behind Billy's Jeep. "Are you expecting someone?" Jack asks.

I shake my head. "I have no idea who that could be. Especially at this hour." But as we draw closer, I see a figure sitting on the bench on the front porch. I would recognize the elegant slope of her neck anywhere. "That's my mother."

Jack jerks his head toward me. "Which one?"

"Hannah. My birth mother. The one with all the answers."

He parks in front of the cottage, and I slide out of the truck.

Hannah gets to her feet. She looks movie-star glamorous in white high-waisted jeans and a blue-and-white cropped top with puffy sleeves. She's still wearing her brimmed hat even though the sun set hours ago.

"Darling, it's so good to see you." She holds out her arms to embrace me, but when I don't move toward her, she lets them drop to her sides.

"What're you doing here?"

"I came to wish you a happy birthday."

I snort. "You could've texted or called."

Jack goes to the porch to introduce himself while I help Jazz out of her car seat. When I set her on the ground, she darts up the steps to my mother. "I'm Jazz. Who are you?"

"I'm Hannah. Stella's mother." Mom leans over to get a good look at the child. "I understand you've been sick, Jazz. I'm glad to see you're feeling better."

"I'm all better," Jazz says. "We went to a party tonight. They had tons of fireworks."

"Sounds like fun," Mom says.

I unlock the cottage and the four of us file inside.

Mom circles the room. "Lester Stokes, the caretaker back then, lived here when I was coming along." She pauses in front of Billy's framed collection of ticket stubs, poking a finger at the glass. "I went to that concert with him—Billy Joel in Philadelphia in 1984." She points again and again. "And Bruce Springsteen in 1985 and ZZ Top in 1987." She moves on to Led Zeppelin's bomber jacket. "I remember when Billy bought this. He wanted to wear it, if you can believe that. I told him the point was to preserve it."

This insider's knowledge of my father's life is what I've been desperate for since I arrived in Hope Springs. But, instead of being fascinated, I'm irritated. If only she'd told me about my father years ago, I could've heard all the stories from him.

"It's late, Mom. I need to get Jazz to bed. Where are you staying?"

"Good question. I wasn't aware the inn was under construction." She sits down on the sofa, giving the cushion a firm pat. "This will do."

The cottage is small enough with Jazz and me living here. I don't need my mother sucking up oxygen. I'm glad I took the time to clean Naomi's suite after she left. "You can stay in the carriage house."

Jack rests a hand on my shoulder. "Why don't I help Jazz into her pajamas while you take your mom over there now?"

"That would be great. Thank you." I turn to Jazz, wagging my finger at her. "Brush your teeth. I'll be back to tuck you in."

I open the front door, motioning my mother outside. With an exasperated sigh, she slowly gets to her feet. As she walks past me, I hold out my hand. "Give me your keys. I'll drive over."

She drops the keys in my hand. "When did you learn to drive?"

"I got my license last week." On the way over to the carriage house, I ask, "How long are you planning to stay?"

"As long as it takes to sort out a few things."

"You'll have to fend for yourself. Between Jazz and the renovations, I don't have time to entertain you."

"Forgive me for intruding on your life, Stella. I finally worked up the nerve to come down here, and this is the thanks I get? Don't you want to know about your father and me?"

I grip the steering wheel. "Why does everything have to be on your terms? You should've told me about Billy a long time ago. Of course I want to know about my father. But I'm too tired to face ghosts tonight. And I don't want to spoil a perfectly good birthday."

"I understand," she says. "Can we go for brunch tomorrow?"

"We'll see."

At the carriage house, I remove two large suitcases from the trunk and drag them up the stairs to her suite. One is undoubtedly full of art supplies, which means she's planning to stay indefinitely.

I unlock the door and hand her the key to her room. "I'll lock the downstairs door behind me. We had to fire the old groundskeeper. And we've had some trouble with Bernard lurking around. Although we haven't seen him in weeks, we still need to be careful."

She shakes her head as though in disbelief. "Bernard was here when I was a kid. He gave me the creeps, even back then."

TWENTY-FOUR

I let Jazz sleep late on Sunday morning. I'm sitting on the back porch drinking coffee, mentally rehearsing what I'll say to my mother, when Jack comes around the corner from the side of the house.

"I was checking on a few things in the inn and thought I'd stop by," he says.

I eye the disposable coffee cup in his hand. "Can I offer you a refill?"

"Thanks, but I've already had my caffeine limit." He gestures at the empty rocker beside me. "May I? I don't want to intrude on your quiet time."

"Please! I'm grateful for the interruption. I was just thinking about the conversation I need to have with my mother."

"About that . . . several of the families you met last night are going tubing on the river. Why don't I take Jazz with me so you can have some time alone with Hannah?"

I give him my best sulky pout. "I'd rather go tubing with you guys."

"And we'd love to have you. I just thought . . ."

"No, you're right. I should talk to her in private." I sip my coffee. "This anger I feel toward my mom really scares me, Jack."

"Anger is a complicated emotion. For the longest time, I was angry at God for taking my wife from me. If you let it, anger will eat away at your soul. You're better off if you can find a way to forgive her."

"But how do I do that?"

"By keeping an open mind. I'm sure she has a legitimate reason for not telling you about your father. Try to understand why she made those choices. If you feel yourself getting angry, it's better to walk away than say something you'll later regret."

On the sidewalk off in the distance, a figure comes into view. Mom is race-walking in running shorts and a tank top. "Speak of the devil."

Hannah waves when she sees us. "Yoo-hoo! I'm just out for my morning exercise. What time's brunch?"

I look at Jack. "When are you all going tubing?"

"Around eleven," he says.

"Let's meet here at eleven," I call out to her. "We'll walk to town, so wear comfortable shoes."

She gives me a thumbs-up and continues on the sidewalk toward the main building.

"This will give me a chance to go to the grocery store beforehand. I need to stock up for this week. I'm thinking I'll cook steaks on the grill tonight. If Mom and I are still speaking, I'll invite her to dinner. I'd love for you to join us."

"I'll bring some wine," he says, pushing himself out of the chair. "See you at eleven."

Thrilled at the prospect of going tubing, Jazz, coated in sunscreen and dressed in her bathing suit and cover-up, is waiting for Jack on the front porch when he arrives at eleven.

As I kiss them both goodbye, I warn him not to take his eyes off her and for her to listen to everything he says.

"Don't worry," Jack says. "She's in good hands."

"Stella's a worry fart," Jazz says with a snicker.

Hand on hip, I feign indignation. "First of all, the term is worry *wart*. And secondly, fart is an unladylike word for a prima ballerina."

"Sorry," she says with a wicked grin.

As I watch them drive off, I wonder if, when the time comes, I'll worry about my own children as much as I worry about Jazz. The notion of having Jack's children brings a smile to my face.

Mom arrives wearing a flowy floral-print sundress, Birkenstocks, and her sunhat. Without exchanging greetings, we start off toward town. At the front of the main building, she pauses to look through the front door window. "I'd love to see what they've done so far."

I'm not in the mood to give her a tour. "Maybe later," I say.

"You're hangry. We need to get you some food." When she tries to loop arms, I jerk mine away.

I'm not hangry. I'm angry. And I know I'm being rude, but I can't help myself.

"Tell me about Jack. He seems like a nice guy, although maybe a little old for you. Are you two in a relationship?"

"I'm not talking to you about Jack."

"Sorry." Her hands fly up. "Touchy subject."

"It's not a touchy subject, Mom. I'm just not going to discuss my boyfriend with *you*."

We walk the rest of the way down the drive in silence.

When we hit Main Street, she talks about what's changed and what hasn't since she was last in town. She pauses in front of the children's clothing shop. "This used to be a women's boutique. I shopped here all the time. They had the cutest things." Continuing down to the Pizzeria, she says, "This place is run down. Is the pizza still good?"

I shrug. "It's fine."

When she enters the pharmacy to have a look around, I remain on the sidewalk. Emerging, she says, "Nothing's changed here. Back in the day, they made an awesome root beer float."

"I wouldn't know about that. I haven't eaten there yet."

We cross the street to the coffee shop. "This used to be the corner market. We came here every morning for the newspaper."

"Who's we, Mom? Your parents? I know you don't have any siblings. At least that's what you've always told me. Then again, you're a proven liar. Do you have any brothers and sisters?" I don't give her a chance to respond. "You know what, I'm not really hungry. Let's just get some coffee." I burst through the door of Caffeine on the Corner, leaving her to follow me inside.

I had in mind to take her to Elmo's, the only decent restaurant in town, but I'm not in the mood to sit across the table from her, pretending to be nice.

We order our drinks at the counter—caffe mocha for me and black coffee for her—but neither of us ask for food.

Mom waits until we're seated at a table by the window before asking, "Why are you being so hostile, Stella? I intentionally postponed coming to Virginia to give you a chance to calm down."

"Calm down? I'm not a child. I'm not sulking because you won't let me have an ice cream cone before dinner. You told me my father was some random guy who donated his sperm for money, when he was actually this supercool, talented man. I mean, seriously, Mom. My father was Billy Jameson, lead singer for the Wild Hollers. You introduced me to their music. Other kids were listening to ABC singalongs and I was developing a fondness for classic rock music."

"It's complicated, Stella."

"It can't be *that* complicated, *Hannah*."

She opens her mouth to speak and closes it again. When she looks away, staring out the window, her eyes are wet with unshed tears. "I spent my summers here when I was growing up. My family rented one of the cottages. Have you seen Cottage Row? It's mostly hidden by trees now."

"Jack showed me the cottages," I say.

"Billy was the best friend I ever had." Her lips part in a smile as she slips into the past. "Every year for three months, we were inseparable. We shared all our secrets, hopes, and dreams. Our summers were magical. There was always something to do on the farm, outdoor activities and festivities at the inn. We were both devastated when I returned to Richmond in August. When it came time for us to go to college, Billy and I applied to the same schools, so we could be together all the time. We were in our third year at UVA when he confessed that he was in love with me, that he'd always been in love with me. By that time, his band, the original members of the Wild Hollers, had begun to build a reputation for themselves, playing fraternity parties and sorority formals."

I settle back in my chair, thinking about the photograph I found in the nightstand. Sipping my coffee, I try to imagine their life together.

"Something changed in our relationship when Billy and I became lovers. We weren't good together as a couple. He was needy. And I wasn't ready to be tied down. At least not to him. That's around the time I started experimenting with my sexuality. But you know all about that."

"Right." My mothers have always spoken openly about their lesbian relationship. I've had my share of questions over the years, which they've been more than willing to answer.

"Me being gay was the one secret I couldn't bring myself to tell Billy. I knew he still loved me, and I didn't want to hurt him. But I also suspected he wouldn't understand." Mom blows on her coffee before taking a tentative sip. "Anyway, we grew apart after graduation when I went to New York for art school and he began touring with the band. And then Billy's brother died. Do you know about Ethan?"

I glare at her. "Only because I read about his plane crash in the newspaper." I've been doing what Jack suggested—trying to keep an open mind about the choices she made. But she's yet to give me a legitimate reason as to why she never told me about my father. "That's also how I found out about my paternal grandfather, Ethan Senior, and my grandmother, Janis. From the newspaper. Not from you."

"Ouch. I guess I deserve that."

"I'm just getting started. But go on. You finish first."

She sets down her mug. "I was distraught over Ethan's death. I'd grown up with him. Despite the two-years difference in our age, I considered him a friend. I flew down for his funeral. Billy was such a mess, I couldn't bring myself to leave him. I ended up staying for a week. We did our fair share of drinking. Which was not a good idea considering how emotionally fragile we were. My last night here was the hardest. We were both especially down, uncertain of our futures and clinging to the past. We turned to one another for comfort. One thing led to another, and—"

"You slept together. And I was conceived. This is worse than a cheap novel."

Mom leans across the table. Her voice is low and angry. "Watch your mouth, Stella. I'm sitting here pouring my heart out to you. The least you could do is try to understand."

"Oh, I'm trying, Mom. But so far, I'm not understanding. I totally get the part where you got knocked up by your old boyfriend. I'm guessing you were already in a relationship with Marnie at the time, and you decided to raise the baby together. Am I right?"

"Yes," she says. "If you'll let me finish, I'll explain."

I plant my elbows on the table. "Fine. Go ahead."

"When Billy found out I was pregnant, he begged me to marry him and move to Hope Springs. I finally confessed that I was gay, and when I told him I wanted to raise the baby with my partner, he sued me for custody."

My jaw hits the table. "What?"

"We had a nasty court battle that dragged on for a couple of years. My attorney was worried. This was before same-sex marriages were legal, and he thought Billy had a chance of winning." Mom pauses to catch her breath and slurp some coffee. "Did you read in the newspapers about Billy's parents dying close together so soon after Ethan's death?"

"Ethan Senior in 1992 and Janis in 1994," I say.

She cocks an eyebrow. "I'm impressed. You have done your homework. As you might imagine, losing his entire family within a matter of four years was hard on Billy. About a month after his mom died, he dropped the custody suit. He requested visitation and offered to pay child support, but I couldn't let him be a part of your life."

"Why not? I don't understand."

"Because I knew he'd fall in love with you. And I couldn't risk another custody suit."

As much as I hate to admit it, this makes sense. "What about your family? I've asked you so many times about my grandparents, my aunts and uncles and cousins. If I even have any. Why did you keep them from me? Or me from them? They may not even know I'm alive."

"They know you're alive. But that story is more difficult to explain. I don't even understand it myself, honestly." She stares down at her hands, folded on the table. "I take it you've met Opal?"

"Yes, of course. What does she have to do with anything?"

She pauses long enough for me to connect the dots. "Are you saying that Opal is—"

"Your grandmother."

Folding my arms over my stomach, I lean into the table.

"How is that possible? Brian is her son. You told me you don't have any siblings."

A lone tear spills over her left eyelid and trickles down her cheek.

"Another lie?"

She nods, biting on her lower lip to stop it from quivering.

"But your last name is Boor? Did you make that up too?"

She shakes her head. "Dewey Boor, my biological father, died from cancer when I was just an infant. My mother . . . Opal . . . married Robert Powers when Brian and I were still very young. Robert adopted us, but Boor is the name on my birth certificate."

This is way too much information for me to grasp at once, and I stand abruptly. "The custody suit was a legitimate reason to keep me from my father. But you robbed me of the chance to know my grandmother. I'm not sure I can ever forgive you for that." I start toward the door but turn back around. "By the way, in case you're interested, Opal has leukemia."

TWENTY-FIVE

Certain aspects of automobile ownership continue to escape me. Like being cognizant of how much gas I have in the tank. Back at the farm, when I start the engine, the low-gas light blinks on. Because I have to stop on the way to the hospital for gas, my mother beats me there. When I arrive, she and Brian are having a hushed but heated conversation outside of Opal's room. Brian is barring the door so Mom can't get in. As they stand face-to-face, the resemblance between brother and sister is so remarkable I'm surprised I never noticed it before. Long graceful limbs with the same handsome profile—high cheekbones and strong jawlines.

I feel like such a fool. I'm so over the lies. If not for Jazz and Jack, I'd pack up my things and leave Hope Springs forever. But where would I go? Certainly not back to New York. And why would I leave when I'm finally getting what I've always wanted? Family. Opal, my grandmother. Brian, my uncle. Because they didn't trust me to tell me the truth. And I can't build a relation-ship that isn't based on trust.

Mom's face is inches from her brother's. "You can't stop me from going in there, Brian."

His blue eyes are dark with anger. "I can and I will. She's too sick for visitors. Your drama is the last thing she needs."

Mom places her hand on her heart. "I won't upset her. I promise."

"Just seeing you will upset her."

Mom tugs on the sleeve of his white starched shirt. "Please! Just ask her if she wants to see me. I bet she'll say yes."

"I can't let you in, Hannah. Especially not today. She had a rough night, last night. But, if I have my way, you won't see her until she's fully recovered."

"What if she doesn't get well? I have a right to see my mother before she dies."

The muscles in Brian's face tighten. "She's not going to die. Not on my watch."

"Since when are you a doctor? Our mother has *leukemia*. She could totally die!" Her voice rises to a level loud enough to be heard through Opal's closed door.

I step between them. "What is wrong with the two of you? This is a hospital. And Opal can hear you."

Mom and Brian look at me, as though startled to see me.

"Let's take this conversation outside." Grabbing each of them by the arm, I march them down the hall to the elevator. On the way to the lobby, they stare at their feet, but I catch them sneaking glances at each other. Their hostility sucks up all the air, and when the doors open, we flee the elevator cart. Oblivious to others in the lobby, they immediately start bickering again, and I shepherd them through the revolving doors and down the sidewalk to the tranquil garden. Fortunately, no one is in the garden.

Mom stops in front of the water fountain and turns to her brother. "When did you and Mom move to Hope Springs?" she asks, her tone less angry.

"A very long time ago," Brian says. "After everything that happened with you, and when Opal's divorce from Dad was final, we decided we needed a change."

"What?" Mom says with furrowed brow. "I didn't know Mom and Dad divorced."

"That's your fault for not keeping in touch," Brian says.

"My fault." She thumbs her chest. "How can you say that after what you did to me? You turned our mother against me." Hannah's arm shoots out, finger pointed at me. "My daughter blames me for keeping her grandmother from her, when it's really *your* fault."

"That's all on you, Hannah. You're the one who chose to live an alternative lifestyle."

"I didn't choose to be gay, Brian."

He rolls his eyes. "Now you sound like the poster child for the LGBT community."

"What happened to you, big brother? You were always the kid rooting for the underdog. I would never have taken you for a homophobic."

The cords in Brian's neck stand out. "I am not a gay basher. I know plenty of gay people. And I consider every single one of them a friend."

Mom plants her hands on her hips. "Then explain why you took Billy's side against your gay sister."

"Because I agreed with him. Billy loved you. We both did. We knew the life you were choosing would be challenging, potentially full of heartache, not only for yourself but your child. We wanted you to have a more conventional life. A life Billy could provide." With outstretched arms, he adds, "Here in the mountains, with all this fresh air, at the inn you loved so much."

She looks away, staring off at some point in the distance. "Don't think for a second I didn't consider that when I got pregnant. But I chose Marnie. If I had to do it all over again, I would make the same choice." Hannah looks back at her brother. "Did you ever marry, Brian?"

"Nope. You ruined it for me. I could never trust a woman again after the way you destroyed Billy."

Mom tosses her hands in the air. "Why not blame all your problems on me?"

"If the shoe fits. I've been too busy taking care of *our* mother all this time while you've been off doing god knows what with your wife."

Mom points her finger at his nose. "See, you are a gay basher."

He brushes her hand away. "No, I'm not. You just bring out the worst in me. You always have."

"Here we go again. Everything is my fault."

With hands pressed against ears, I scream, "Please! Stop arguing! Instead of blaming each other, why not find a way to work past your differences?"

Mom's blue eyes fill. "There's no way I can forgive and forget. Too much water has flowed under the bridge." Tossing her bag over her shoulder, she runs off toward the parking lot.

I look up at Brian and he shrugs, but neither of us go after her. He drops to a Chippendale wooden bench, and I sit down next to him. Neither of us speaks for a long while. I replay the argument in my mind, checking off the questions I now have answers for and adding others to my list.

Finally, I break our silence. "Why didn't you tell me any of this before? You're my uncle. Opal is my grandmother. I have a right to know my family."

"You have no idea how difficult it's been for Opal and me to keep that knowledge from you. But Billy and I agreed you should hear both sides of the story. When I first came to see you in New York, my hope was that you would tell your mom about your inheritance, and she, in turn, would tell you about her past."

"Sorry. I was too angry to talk to her."

He chuckles. "My fondness for you grew when you made the decision to come to Virginia without consulting her. But that put me at a disadvantage. I knew all about you, but you didn't know my true identity."

"Is that why you kept your distance in the beginning?"

"Exactly." He angles his body toward me. "You see, Stella, I couldn't tell you what I don't know. I haven't talked to my sister in nearly three decades. I don't know why Hannah has stayed away all these years. Or why she never invited us to visit her in New York. Or why she refused to let Billy have visitation after he dropped the custody suit."

"She told me some of it earlier today. Why *did* Billy drop the custody suit?"

"Billy was angry and hurt when Hannah turned down his marriage proposal. He thought her being gay was a passing fancy. Growing up, Hannah was always the first to try something new and the first to get bored with it."

I think back to the different hobbies Mom has taken up over the years. Cooking. Yoga. Photography. None of them held her interest for long. "She's still like that with certain things. But not with Marnie. Their relationship is real and lasting."

"I'm glad to hear that," he says with a genuine smile. "Anyway, the custody suit was Billy's way of testing Hannah's resolve. When he realized she wasn't coming back to him, he dropped the suit, hoping she'd allow visitation. But Hannah shut us out. No matter what my sister tells you, she definitely pushed us away."

"Can you blame her? You ganged up on her with Billy. And she was worried he'd sue for custody again." I look away from Brian. "From what I've heard today, it doesn't sound like either of you made much effort to get in touch with the other."

"There's some truth to that. So many hurtful things had been said, we all retreated to our own corners to lick our wounds."

A thought suddenly occurs to me. "You were Billy's attorney. Did you represent him in the custody fight?"

Brian gives me a somber nod. "At the time, I thought I was doing the right thing. I thought I was protecting you."

A wave of sympathy for my mother washes over me. How hard it must have been for her family to turn on her. I get up from the bench and walk over to the fountain, dipping my hands in the cool water.

Brian joins me at the fountain. "Billy was my best friend, Stella. He talked about you often. He would've given anything to have had you in his life."

I pick up a pebble and drop it in the water. "If that's so, why didn't he try to contact me once I became an adult?"

"Because, by then, he was a very sick man. He didn't want to be a burden to you. And he didn't want you to remember him as being weak and frail." Hands on my shoulders, Brian turns me toward him. "Your father denied you the chance to know him, but he's giving you now the life that he loved so much."

"Who knows? If I'd been given the chance to know him, my presence in his life may have made a positive impact on his health. The one person I feel sorry for is Opal. I can't imagine how difficult all of this has been for her."

Brian removes his hands from my shoulders. "The mountain living is good for her. And she has her art. But she hasn't been truly happy since Hannah left. Until you came along. I've seen a renewed spark in her these past few weeks. I'm only sorry she got sick now, when she finally has the chance to know her grand-daughter."

"Me too." We turn away from the fountain and stroll toward the parking lot. When we reach Billy's Jeep, I ask, "Do the doctors think she'll beat the leukemia?"

Brian's face is grief-stricken. "They're giving her a fifty-fifty chance. The chemo has hit her hard. That's why they're keeping her in the hospital."

"Let me see her, Brian. I've missed having a grandmother for thirty years. Please don't keep me from her now."

He inhales a deep breath and lets it out slowly. "I thought I was doing the right thing in restricting her visitation. But what you said earlier about your father really hit home. You're right.

Your presence in Billy's life could have made a positive impact on his life. Who am I to stand in the way of you doing that for Opal?"

TWENTY-SIX

Back at the farm, exhausted from my dramatic morning, I fall fast asleep in the hammock Katherine recently installed between two trees in the small side lawn of the cottage. Jack and Jazz wake me when they return from tubing around five. While Jazz rides her bike on the road in front of the cottage, Jack crawls into the hammock with me, and I tell him everything I've learned today.

My conflicting emotions make my head spin. I'm angry with Mom one minute, and Brian and Billy the next. But Jack finds all of them at fault.

"They used you, an innocent child, as their pawn. They should've found a way to work it out. Instead, because of their petty vindictiveness, you were deprived of the opportunity to know your family."

"It's not that simple, Jack."

He hugs me close to him, kissing my head. "It seems pretty simple to me."

I'm beginning to see that the world according to Jack Snyder is simple. He believes in right and wrong and not a lot in between.

"I promised I'd wait until Opal's feeling better to visit, but I'm counting on her to tell me the unbiased truth."

"For your sake, I hope she does," Jack says in a skeptical tone.

When we move inside to start dinner, I text Mom, inviting her to join us. When she declines, I say to Jack, "I hate the idea of her being alone."

"After what she's been through today, I imagine she needs some time to herself."

Removing the meat from the refrigerator, I say, "I bought an extra steak. Should I take her a plate?"

"She's a grown woman, Stella. She has a car. Let her fend for herself." He takes the steaks from me and begins seasoning them. "I'm sorry if I sound harsh. But it's time someone looks out for your best interests for a change."

"You're too good to me, Jack Snyder."

"Because you deserve it, Stella Boor."

I hug him from behind, resting my head against his back. I appreciate Jack wanting to protect me. But this very thing, people wanting to protect me, has cost me the opportunity to know my family. Going forward, I will make my own decisions.

After dinner, Jack and I take Jazz on a ride in the golf cart—another one of Katherine's latest additions to the farm. When I spot Mom down by the lake, sitting on the pier with her legs swinging over the side and staring into the water as though in a trance, I ask, "Should we go check on her?"

"It's getting late. We should put Jazz to bed." Jack whips the golf cart around and heads in the opposite direction.

Despite my earlier resolve to make my own decisions, I don't argue with him. Because it is late, and Jazz is tired. And Mom and I both could use a cooling-off period.

I sleep in fits and rise early the following morning. When I take my coffee out to the porch, I'm surprised to see Mom's car is gone from the carriage house. Would she leave Hope Springs without saying goodbye? Would she go back to New York when there's so much unfinished business here?

An hour later, I'm helping Jazz gather her things for her first day of bible camp when I receive a call from Brian. He sounds out of breath, and I hear music from his car radio in the background.

"Have you seen your mother this morning?" he asks.

"No," I say, stuffing a change of clothes in Jazz's backpack. "Her car's not at the carriage house, though. I was wondering where she went."

"Hannah did exactly what I asked her not to. She came over to the hospital at the crack of dawn this morning and got Opal all worked up. I'm due in court in Roanoke in an hour. Mom is asking to see you. Is there any chance you can sit with her for a while this morning?"

"I would love that. I'll drop Jazz at camp at nine and head straight over."

Brian exhales loudly. "Thank you, Stella. I don't think she will, but if Hannah comes back to the hospital, don't let her near Opal. Call security if you have to."

"I understand."

I have a vision of a brawny security guard tossing Hannah out of the hospital on her butt. Fifteen minutes later, I'm relieved when I pass Mom's rental car coming up the driveway as Jazz and I are leaving the inn. Jazz, who has expressed hesitation in going to bible camp, is thrilled to find three of her friends from school have been assigned to her designated group. She's already forgotten me by the time I wave goodbye to her at the door.

Stopping in at Caffeine on the Corner, I order a mocha for me and a chocolate chip croissant and green tea for Opal. At the hospital, I'm pleased to find her looking remarkably well considering the poison pumping through her veins.

When she spots me in the doorway, she holds her hand out to me. "My sweet granddaughter. I'm so happy to see you."

Squeezing her hand, I lean down and kiss her cheek. Her skin is soft and warm beneath my lips. "I've been begging Brian to let me visit. He's quite the gatekeeper."

Opal presses her lips into a firm line. "He's overprotective is what he is."

"I'm mad at you for not telling me you're my grandmother. But you're the only one in this mess I forgive."

She grimaces. "Because you know my hands were tied."

"That, and because I already love you so much. Having you as a grandmother is a bonus."

Her eyes cloud over. "I do believe that's the nicest thing anyone's ever said to me."

I drop the bakery bag on her bed table and place the tea bag in the cup of hot water. "I brought you a croissant and some tea."

"Thank you, sweetheart. The food in this place sucks."

I giggle. "Opal, watch your language."

Once the tea has steeped for five minutes, I remove the bag and raise the head of her bed so she can drink it.

Opal tears off a piece of croissant and dips it in her tea. "I had a visitor this morning."

"That's what I hear. How did it go?"

"Not well, as I'm sure Brian told you."

"He didn't provide any details, except to say Mom upset you. I'm sorry, Opal."

"She blames me for everything. But that's my Hannah—pretty to look at on the outside but eaten up with bitterness on the inside."

"I don't want to upset you, Opal, or tire you out. But if you feel like talking, I'd love to hear your perspective."

"I've waited a long time for the chance to tell you my story."

I flash a stupid grin, all teeth and gums. "I still can't believe you're my grandmother. We have a special connection."

With a twinkle in her olive eyes, Opal says, "We met once before, you know? In New York City, a very long time ago. You were five years old at the time."

My eyes grow wide. "Was that you? In front of our apartment building?" My mind travels back a quarter of a century "You gave me an Indian arrowhead. You said it was from the Spring of Good Hope." I palm my forehead. "Wow. Now it all makes sense."

I still remember what my mother told me when I asked about the woman with the long gray braid. *She's just some crazy homeless person.* "Mom was so rude to you that day."

Opal shrugs as though it doesn't matter. "I should've told her I was coming. Hannah never liked surprises."

"That's no excuse. You were my grandmother." I sit back in the chair, sipping my mocha. "Did you ever try to see us again?"

"I couldn't. Hannah made it clear she didn't want me in her life." A faraway look settles on Opal's face. "I flew home to Richmond that same afternoon. The very next day, I put my house on the market and moved to Hope Springs to be near my child who *did* want me in his life. Moving turned out to be the best decision I ever made. Billy, who had always been like a second son to me, needed me too. He was so lost after his brother and parents died. And when he became ill, I helped nurse him. In some strange way, I felt I owed him. After all, it was my daughter who broke his heart."

I set my coffee on the bed table and lean in, elbows planted on knees. "Do you disapprove of Mom being gay?"

"Disapprove? No. I'm not one to pass judgment. But I admit I don't understand the younger generation. I'm old school in that regard. I was thrilled when Billy and Hannah started dating in college. Nothing would've made me happier than for the two of them to get married. Then out of the blue, she announces she's pregnant with his child and that she's gay. I found it all very confusing."

"And so you took Billy's side in the custody suit, hoping Mom would come to her senses?"

"I was caught in the middle, Stella. In the beginning, I admit I had my reservations about her sexuality. And yes, I hoped she would change her mind and marry Billy. Over time, I accepted her lifestyle. But it was too late. The damage had been done. Hannah had cut me out of her life."

A fit of coughing overcomes Opal. The nurse rushes into the room and coaches her until she stops. But the coughing leaves Opal exhausted, her face as white as the pillow beneath her head.

When the nurse leaves the room, I say, "You need to rest now, Opal. I'll be right here. Can I get anything for you?"

"You can read to me." She waves a gnarled hand at the small hardbound book on her table.

Picking up the collection of Walt Whitman's poems, I read out loud until Opal dozes off. I put the book down and study her peaceful face, memorizing her features in case I lose her. She sleeps for hours, which gives me a chance to sort through the chaos I brought upon my family by being born. I scrutinize the situation from their individual perspectives. Billy's. Brian's. Opal's. I save Mom's for last, and I try to put myself in a young Hannah's shoes. I imagine her confusion over her sexuality. Being unmarried and pregnant. Her hurt when everyone she loved turned their backs on her. I've experienced firsthand her rare and unconditional love for Marnie, which helps me understand the difficult decisions she made. But I can't get past one thing. When Opal reached out to her, when she surprised her with a visit to New York, Hannah treated her own mother like a stranger, a random homeless person on the street.

Opal sleeps on through lunchtime. I'm starving, but I don't dare leave for fear Mom will return. Fortunately, I don't have to pick Jazz up until three. Several of the younger bible camp counselors have organized an extended day program for a small group of kids. I want Opal to wake up, to tell me more about her life. Not about Hannah and Brian or even her second husband but about Opal's childhood and her husband, my grandfather, and how she became interested in art. But she's still sleeping when Brian arrives at two.

We step out into the hall to talk. Brian leans against the wall with his ankles crossed, reminding me of the first day we met outside my apartment in New York. "Did she say much about her visit from Hannah this morning?"

"Not really. We mostly talked about the past. She's a class act, your mom."

When Brian smiles, his blue eyes brighten with the love he feels for his mother. "She is that."

"I feel so guilty. I caused you all such heartache. If not for me, your family would still be united."

"Don't say things like that, Stella. Despite having to wait thirty years, we're thrilled to have you in our lives." He shifts his weight, recrossing his ankles. "Hannah and I have never gotten along. I was always the overprotective older brother. And believe me, she needed protecting. She was so damn beautiful and such a wild card. If not for the custody suit, something would've eventually driven us apart."

"Did you mean what you said yesterday? Is Mom the reason you never married?"

He chuckles. "Hannah pushes my buttons and makes me say things I don't mean. The truth is, I never found the right woman. I devoted my time to my career and my mother, and the years just slipped away. You might find that strange."

"I find that admirable, actually." I lift my gaze to the ceiling. "What's the saying? How a man treats his mother is a good indication of how he'll treat his wife. I hope I find a man like you one day."

"That's a very nice thing to say, Stella. I'm looking forward to getting to know my niece better."

I've never seen Brian wear his glasses before, but the black wayfarer-style frames make him seem more current, less old-mannish. "How long does Opal have to go through chemo?"

"She's three weeks in. So, she's only just getting started. Once she's feeling better, she'll continue as an outpatient. The initial treatment is intense. It's not uncommon for patients to be hospitalized during this phase."

"Can I see her again?"

"She'd like that. But keep in mind that shorter visits are best." We start down the hallway toward the elevator. "I had a lengthy phone conversation with the hospital administrator on my way back from Roanoke. He promises to put his staff on alert. Until further notice, my sister is not allowed in Mom's room. I hate to do that, but Opal's health is my primary concern."

"I understand." The elevator doors part, and I step inside. "Mom brought this one on herself."

TWENTY-SEVEN

I'm acutely aware of Mom's presence on the farm, even though we avoid each other as much as possible. When our cars pass on the driveway, we wave without stopping to speak. I see her walking early in the mornings and sitting by the lake in the evenings, and from my kitchen window, I have a clear view of her working at her easel under Opal's tree.

Hannah makes a positive first impression on Cecily and Katherine.

"I've never met a woman so accomplished," Katherine says, and Cecily adds, "She's a whiz in the kitchen."

She's a good faker, I think to myself. I've tasted Mom's food. Her cooking is mediocre at best. And what does a New Yorker know about gardening?

When Jack asks why she's still in Hope Springs, I answer, "Because she's up to something. My mom always has an agenda."

Every morning after dropping Jazz at bible camp, I go straight to the hospital to visit Opal. On Tuesday, I take her a basket of fruit, and on Wednesday, Cecily sends her homemade blueberry streusel loaf. I beg for details about Opal's past, and she tells me about growing up on a horse farm in Goochland, a rural area outside of Richmond.

Opal snickers. "I loved grooming and feeding the ponies, but I never cared much for riding."

She tells me about her husband, Dewey Boor, and how they met when she was at Sweetbriar and him at Jefferson College. "Dewey was originally from Richmond, but he loved Hope Springs. We planned to retire here one day." Her lips part in a woeful smile. "You might say I'm living his dream. As for my second husband, Robert, he was . . . as you young people say, my rebound person after Dewey died. He helped me through a difficult period, but when the honeymoon was over, I realized I'd made a mistake in marrying him. I don't know why it took me so long to get up the nerve to divorce him."

When I ask her about her art career, she says, "I don't remember a time when art wasn't a part of my life. Hannah is the same way. She started painting masterpieces before she entered kindergarten."

She talks about her home, a cottage on a wooded lot at the edge of town not far from the farm. And when I ask her how she spends her weekends, she says, "I teach art classes at an old folks' home on Saturdays, and Sundays are for church and chores."

Opal's health improves every day. I'm flattered when the nurses give me credit for her sudden rally. Her energy returns, and by Wednesday, she's pushing a walker around the third floor. Her appetite increases, and on Thursday, she sends me out for a hamburger from Lucky's Diner. That afternoon, her doctor pronounces her well enough to go home.

"Give her the day on Friday to get settled at home," Brian says, his polite way of asking me not to visit. "I've arranged caregivers to be with her around the clock for the next couple of weeks."

When Katherine invites Jazz to accompany her to the farmers

market on Saturday morning, I use the free time to go see my grandmother.

Window boxes bearing pink and white flowers adorn the windows of her yellow-framed Cape Cod-style cottage. Sharon, the caregiver, greets me at the front door and shows me into the living room. She's a pleasant-looking woman about Mom's age wearing a uniform top, printed with cartoon dogs, over her ample bust.

The home's interior rooms are painted in hues that remind me of the Caribbean—aqua and tangerine and chartreuse—and accented by furnishings in pops of baby blue, lilac, and fire-engine red. I find the mix of colors slightly nauseating, but the eclectic combination suits the aging artist perfectly.

Opal, seated in a comfortable armchair with a blanket across her lap, barely glances in my direction before returning her gaze to the small mirror in her hand.

I give the bouquet of sunflowers I purchased from the Local Market to Sharon, who takes them to the kitchen for water. I drag a green lacquered bamboo chair close to Opal and sit down. "What's up? Are you not feeling well today? You're usually happy to see me."

Placing the mirror facedown in her lap, she cups my cheek. "Of course I'm happy to see you, my darling. You're the light of my life. I never realized I was so vain, but I'm having a difficult time with this." She grabs a fistful of hair and tugs it loose from her scalp.

"Vain or not, it's a woman's prerogative to fret over her hair." I say this with a smile, despite the pain I feel in my heart for this woman I've grown to love so much. If only I could give her my own hair. A thought occurs to me. But there is something else I can do.

"You know, Opal, it might be less painful for you to shave your head."

"I thought about that." She hangs her head, staring at the tuft of hair in her lap. "Maybe it would be easier to get rid of it, instead of watching it come out in clumps."

I nudge her arm. "You're the hippest grandmother I know. You will totally rock your bald head."

"Humph! I'm not even sure what *hip* means. Will you do it, Stella? Will you shave my head?"

"No way. We need a professional." If her stringy gray hair is any indication, Opal hasn't been to a stylist in decades, and I haven't lived in Hope Springs long enough to need a trim. "Maybe we can go to Brian's barber," I joke.

Sharon enters the room with the vase full of sunflowers. "My daughter's a stylist. She's done this very thing for several of my clients."

Opal's head jerks up. "Get her over here before I lose my nerve."

"Do you think she's available?" I ask.

"Probably. She has the day off." Sharon calls her daughter who arrives within minutes.

"You caught me as I was leaving town for the weekend." Jennifer pulls electric hair clippers out of her canvas tote. "I understand we have a hair emergency."

My hand shoots up. "Me first."

Jennifer's face falls. "Oh, you poor dear. You're so young."

I drop my hand. "Sorry. I should've explained. I don't have cancer. I want you to shave my head as a show of solidarity to my grandmother. I can't let her have all the fun."

Opal wags her finger at me. "Don't you dare, Stella Boor! Only your mama would pull such a crazy stunt."

"All the more reason to do it. Who knows? Maybe my hair will grow back straight. I've always wanted straight hair." I sit down in my chair with my back to Jennifer.

"Are you sure?" Jennifer asks. "You have such lovely hair."

"I'm sure," I say. "But can you leave a little stubble?"

Setting her electric clippers on the coffee table, Jennifer

removes scissors and a comb from her bag and sets to work. I immediately regret my decision as she begins tugging and snipping on my hair. I want to scream for Jennifer to stop cutting, but it's too late. I'm merely grateful not to be sitting in front of a mirror.

Unable to watch, Opal turns her head away. "I'm not having any part of this."

"Don't be mad at me, Opal. Think of the fun we'll have shopping for hats." When I hear the sound of the trimmers, pressure builds in my chest and I have trouble breathing. *Chill, Stella. It's only hair. It will grow. Jack will think I've lost my mind.*

When Jennifer finishes, she hands me a mirror. A lump develops in my throat at the sight of my reflection. I look like Natalie Portman when she shaved her head for her role in *V for Vendetta*. Not only will Jack think I've lost my mind, he'll think I'm ugly. I fight back tears. I can't let Opal see my dismay.

"I feel liberated," I say, running my hand over the half-inch stubble. "Think of all the money I'll save on hair products." I hand Jennifer the mirror. "Opal's turn."

When Opal finally brings herself to look at me, she smiles, and a rush of relief washes over me. "You have a lovely-shaped skull, my darling."

Opal closes her eyes while Jennifer is shaving her head, and she refuses to look in the mirror when she's finished. She looks like a cancer patient, which makes me all the more glad I shaved mine.

I linger a long time after Jennifer leaves. I feel safe here with Opal. I'm terrified of venturing out into the world where everyone will stare at my bald head. We talk about everything except our hair, but I catch Opal sneaking glances at me. When Opal's eyelids begin to droop, I stand to go. "Get some rest, Opal. I'll see you tomorrow."

When I kiss the top of Opal's bald head, she pulls me in and holds me tight. "What you did for me today took real guts.

You're a special person, Stella. I'm proud to call you my grand-daughter, and I'm thrilled to have you in my life."

I don't even try to hold back the tears. Her words mean more to me than my hair ever did. I walk out of her house with my bald head held high.

Jazz is the first to see me when she barges through the door of the cottage. She stops short in the middle of the room, her golden eyes as round as her lips forming an O. "What happened to your hair?"

"Opal and I decided to get pixie cuts. What'd you think?"

"I love it!" Closing the distance between us, she pulls me down to her level and scrubs her small hands over my head. "It's so soft." Lifting my face, she pats my cheeks. "Can I get a pixie cut?"

I laugh out loud. "No, you may not." I sniff her breath. She smells like berries and chocolate. "What did you eat at the farmers market?"

"Some raspberries and granola with chunks of chocolate."

"Mm-hmm. I thought so." I cross my eyes at Katherine who's standing in the doorway.

Jazz makes a beeline toward the bedroom. "I'm gonna put on my bathing suit. Jack's outside. We're all going tubing on the river. Cecily and Katherine and their boyfriends are coming, too."

I cross the room to Katherine. "Jack's here?" I ask, looking past her.

She reads the uncertainty on my face. "You look adorable. He's gonna love it. You're a badass, Stella Boor. You know that, don't you?"

I know no such thing. I feel like a dumbass at the moment.

When Jack appears in the doorway, Katherine sidesteps him on her way out.

I run my hand over my cropped hair. "Did I ever mention I have an impulse control problem. Opal was having a tough time saying goodbye to her hair, and . . . well . . . it just seemed like the right thing to do at the time. Solidarity and all that."

Taking my face in his hands, he thumbs my cheek. "Now that all your crazy curly hair is gone, I can see how stunningly beautiful you are. You're truly remarkable, Stella. I've never loved you more than I do at this moment," he says, and crushes his lips against mine.

His kiss leaves me breathless. "Was that a declaration of love, Jack Snyder?"

"I've loved you from the first moment I set eyes on you." He kisses me again. This time with a passion that sets my entire body on fire. "If we don't have that date soon, I'm going to explode."

I press my body to his. "I know what you mean." I ache for him. I've never wanted a man like this before.

A tiny voice interrupts from the bedroom. "Hurry up, Stella! Put on your bathing suit! We're going tubing."

Jack pushes away, rearranging his shorts to hide his excitement. "That's it. I'm taking matters into my own hands. *I* will find a suitable babysitter. Mark your calendar. Next Friday night, we're going on a date."

TWENTY-EIGHT

J ack hits it off with Dean and Lyle, and after a
companionable day on the river, he invites our small
group over for a cookout. Jazz wears shorts, but I slip on
a flowery sundress, a touch of femininity to soften my
stark hairstyle.

Jack is waiting on his small front porch when we arrive. He's
told me a little about the arts and crafts-style house he bought
and renovated after his wife's death, but his descriptions didn't do
it justice.

I hand him the log of goat cheese and box of crackers I
picked up at the Local Market on the way over. "I love your
home. You didn't tell me it was so big."

He blushes. "Because it's way more than I need. But it was a
good investment. If I ever decide to sell, I stand to make a huge
profit."

I kiss his cheek. "This is your dream home. Why would you
ever want to sell it?"

"Because the house has so many idiosyncrasies—slanted
floors and bowed walls. Not everyone will find that appealing."

I take that *everyone* to mean me. "Maybe not, but I imagine most people find those features charming."

He gives us the tour of the downstairs—a small foyer with a dining room to the left and living room to the right leading to a renovated kitchen with a family room addition on the back. The decor is handsome without being overly masculine with walls painted a rich khaki color.

"There aren't many arts and crafts homes in Hope Springs," he explains. "I've always particularly admired this one. The elderly lady who lived here before really let the place go. About two months after Jenna died, the woman's family moved her to a nursing home and put the house on the market. I snatched it up, even though it needed a ton of work. The project was a welcome distraction during those dark days. I've done all the work myself."

"You're kidding? All of it?"

"Every last bit. I built the kitchen cabinets and updated the electrical and plumbing. A couple of my guys helped with some of the more labor-intensive projects. But mostly, it was all me."

"I'm seriously impressed, Jack. The house really showcases your expertise as a builder."

He beams. "I'm glad you approve."

The other two couples arrive at the same time, their arms laden with food and drink. Katherine hands Jack a bouquet of zinnias and a bag of fresh tomatoes, purchases from the farmers market, and Cecily offers a tray of mini cheesecakes for dessert.

Our easy camaraderie from earlier continues throughout the evening. Jazz dances around the bluestone patio while the guys cook burgers on the grill and the girls set seven places at the rectangular umbrellaed table. During dinner, Jazz is visibly bored with grown-up talk, and when she falls asleep in my lap soon after she's finished eating, Jack carries her upstairs to his guest bedroom.

Our guests linger until nearly ten o'clock. After we say good-night to the foursome at the door, Jack dims the lights and turns on soft jazz music. Taking me in his arms, we dance in small circles in the center of the living room.

"Your *G.I. Jane* hairstyle is really turning me on. I could hardly take my eyes off of you all night."

My cheeks warm. "I may have noticed."

"I'm not sure I can make it until our date next weekend."

I nestle my face in his neck. "Tell me about our date. Do you have anything special planned?"

He lets out a groan. "Do you need to ask? We're going to have sex."

I laugh. "That's it? Just sex?"

"Not *just*, Stella. Sex will be the highlight. We'll have it more than once in multiple positions."

I nibble at his ear. "What will we do for food?"

"Food is not high up on the agenda. But, if you insist on eating, we'll order a pizza. Or I'll make you an omelet." He glances toward the stairs. "Jazz is sound asleep. How about we have a quickie now?"

I draw away to look at him. "A quickie? We've waited this long, and you want to ruin it by having a quickie?"

"Damn straight," he says with a maniacal grin.

"No!" I slap his chest. "We are not having a quickie. Besides, Jazz could wake up any minute. She's in a strange place and she might be scared. I want to hear her if she calls me."

As if on cue, Jazz's faint voice drifts down from above. "See. I told you."

"I'm consumed by lust." He follows me to the stairs. "In the best interest of my health, I may have to refrain from seeing you until our date."

Over my shoulder, as I climb the stairs, I toss back at him, "We work together, remember?"

"Right. In that case you better get used to this," he says, and grabs a handful of my butt.

I let out a squeal and dart to the top of the stairs.

Down the hall in the guest bedroom, Jazz is sitting up in bed with tears streaming down her face. "Oh, honey." I rush over to her, taking her in my arms. "What's wrong?"

She sniffles. "I'm scared. When I woke up, I didn't know where I was. I thought you'd left me."

"No, sweetheart. I would never leave you. Are you ready to go home?"

She nods, chewing on her lower lip.

When Jack tries to pick her up, Jazz reaches for me instead, clinging to me like a baby koala on the way out to the car. After buckling her into her car seat, Jack kisses me goodnight, which ends up being more than a peck on the lips. When I feel eyes on us from the car, I reluctantly push him away.

On the way home, Jazz asks, "Are you and Jack getting married?

"I don't know, Jazzy. Maybe one day. But we only just met. We're still getting to know each other. Why do you ask?"

"I was wondering what would happen to me if you do." In a hopeful voice, she adds, "You could adopt me and be my new mommy and daddy."

"You already have a mommy and daddy," I say to her reflection in the rearview mirror.

"But what if they never come back?"

"They'll come back," I say with more conviction than I feel.

Derrick has yet to reach out to me, even though he was due back from his fishing trip weeks ago. And I've heard nothing from Naomi in the six weeks she's been gone. I have no clue when or if she's coming back.

As much as I love Jazz, I'm not sure I'm ready to be a full-time parent. The truth is, I'm as sexually frustrated as Jack. I've finally fallen in love with the right man, and we can't find any time to be alone. What if Naomi doesn't ever come back? I can't . . . I won't turn Jazz over to child services to be placed in a foster home. I've never discussed it with Jack. Would he be willing to raise a child that's not his? The situation causes me considerable anxiety, and I try my best not to think about it. But with each passing day with no word from Naomi, my concern mounts.

———

The counselors at last week's bible camp got the kids excited about attending Sunday school, and Jazz is up bright and early the following morning, raring to go. After breakfast, we throw on casual dresses and set out on foot toward town. We're halfway down the driveway when we see Naomi's silver Honda speeding toward us. Naomi jumps out of the car, and when she drops to her knees to embrace her daughter, Jazz hides behind my legs.

Naomi stands to face me. "Stella."

I nod at her. "Naomi."

"What happened to your hair?"

"Opal has leukemia," I say by way of explanation about my shaved head.

"Oh. That's too bad," she says in a manner that tells me she doesn't care one way or another about Opal's leukemia.

"How was Arizona?" I want her to know that I know where she's been and what she's been doing.

"Arizona was exactly what the doctor ordered. I feel like my old self again. Thank you for taking care of my child. I see you've succeeded in turning her against me, but that was a risk I had to take to get the help I needed."

I hold my tongue. I won't say all the things I need to say to this woman in front of Jazz. "We're on our way to Sunday school. Why don't you get settled? I'll bring Jazz over afterward. Coincidentally, my mom's visiting for a few days. She's been staying in your suite. You'll have to take the other one."

"But . . ." She starts to protest and then clamps her lips shut.

I'm sure she's thinking about the cleaning necessary to make

223

the other suite habitable. But that's not my problem. Jazz and I stroll off hand in hand down the driveway.

Jazz's cheerful mood from earlier has disappeared, and she walks in silence to church. I should try to lift her spirits, but I can't think of a single positive thing to say about her mother's sudden return.

I drop Jazz at her classroom, grab a coffee from the fellowship hall, and find my way into a bible study geared for my age group. People stare, but no one comments on my bald head.

Jazz and I agreed we'd only go to Sunday school, but when I pick her up from her classroom, she begs me to take her to church. I recognize the stall tactic, and I go along with her without an argument. It would've been nice for Naomi to give us advance notice of her return, not only so I could prepare Jazz but so I could prepare myself.

On the way back to the farm, we stop in at the pharmacy and order grilled cheeses and chocolate shakes for lunch. Jazz, wearing the biggest mope face ever, doesn't touch her food.

"Come on, Jazz, is it that bad?" I ask, taking a bite of my sandwich.

Her eyes fill with tears. "Why can't I live with you? You make me food, and we do fun stuff together, and I'm never scared."

A chill travels my spine. "Are you scared when you're with your mom?"

Jazz nods as fat tears trickle down her cheeks.

Is this child in danger? Is Naomi abusive? Damn it! I wanna know where Derrick is in all this. "What does your mommy do that scares you?"

"She yells at me a lot, and sometimes when she's sleeping, I can't wake her up."

"So . . ." I set my sandwich down on the plate and reach for Jazz's hand. "Remember when I told you that your mom was sick inside, and she went away to get help so she'd feel better?"

"I remember," she says, staring up at me with big round eyes.

224

"Well, the doctor sent her home because she's better." I have no idea if this is true. Is a six-year-old too young to have a cell phone? "I don't think you'll be scared anymore, but if you ever are, I want you to come find me. I'm usually at the cottage or in the main building. And there's always a security man on patrol. You know, the guys we always wave at in the white truck with the blue lights on top?"

"Martin," she says.

"That's right. Martin is one of them. But there are a couple of others. If you ever need help, you flag one of them down. Okay?"

"Okay."

I nudge her with my arm. "You're not going to let that perfectly good chocolate milkshake go to waste, are you?"

She brings the straw to her lips, but she takes only a sip.

I try everything I can think of, but I can't get her to eat. Finally, I give up and pay the bill, and we walk back to the farm in silence.

While I pack her things in her suitcase, Jazz sits on the end of the bed with her arms hugging her belly as though it aches. It's nearly two o'clock by the time I walk Jazz over to the carriage house.

My heart sinks when Naomi swings open the door to her suite. A sheen of perspiration covers her face, and there's a wild gleam in her eyes. I look past her into the room. Clothes are strewn across the floor and beds are unmade. She's far from being well. How can I possibly leave this child alone with her?

I tighten my grip on Jazz's hand. "Maybe it would be better if Jazz stays with me for a few more days. At least until you get settled."

Naomi swipes her forehead with the back of her hand. "Don't be ridiculous. We'll be perfectly fine. Come on in, sweetheart." She steps out of the way so Jazz can enter. "Let me finish cleaning the room, and we'll go out for some fresh air."

What has she been doing for the past three hours? I wonder.

Jazz removes her iPad from her suitcase and sits down on the edge of the mattress.

"Where'd you get that?" Naomi asks.

"Stella bought it for me when I was in the hospital," Jazz answers without looking at her mother.

Naomi's gaze shifts to me. "The hospital?"

"You've been gone a long time. We should talk. In private." Brushing past Naomi, I kneel down in front of Jazz. "Your mommy and I are going downstairs for a minute. Will you be okay up here by yourself?"

"Whatever," she says, and I can tell she doesn't want me to go.

I follow Naomi down the stairs. When we reach the lounge, she turns to face me. "My child was in the hospital? How dare you keep that from me."

"That's so ridiculous, it's laughable. You're a narcissistic bitch, Naomi, who doesn't deserve to have a kid as awesome as Jazz. Did you ever once consider my feelings? No! You just assumed I would be willing to take care of your daughter. Lucky for you, I adore Jazz. Otherwise I would've reported you to social services."

There's fear in her voice when she asks, "But you didn't, did you?"

"Not yet. But I will if you give me reason to. It took the police forty-eight hours to locate you when Jazz came down with bacterial meningitis." Naomi appears grief-stricken. "That's right, Naomi. Bacterial meningitis. We had quite a time of it. I thought we might lose her."

"I don't understand. Why wasn't I notified?"

"I suggest you ask your doctor in Arizona that question. He didn't want to disrupt your therapy. Don't get me wrong. I applaud you for seeking help. It's your manner of going about it that I have a problem with. And where is your husband in all of this? Oh, that's right. I forgot. He's fly-fishing in Montana. Except that he's been back from his little trip for weeks now."

Naomi tenses. "You still don't know, do you, Stella?"

I stop pacing and turn to face her. "Know what, Naomi?"

"You're pathetic."

"No! You're the pathetic one."

Out of the corner of my eye, I catch a glimpse of movement in the entryway. My mother's blonde head as she's exiting the front door. How much did she hear?

I step toward Naomi, getting close to her face. "I'm warning you, nothing better happen to that little girl up there," I say, pointing at the ceiling.

"Or else what, Stella?"

"Or else you'll have to answer to me." It's a stupid thing to say, but the only thing I can think of in the moment. Naomi isn't afraid of me. She isn't afraid of anyone, because everyone around here always caters to her needs.

I storm out of the carriage house, and with tears blurring my vision, I stride down to the lake. Dark clouds are building in over the mountain range. Is it supposed to storm? I don't remember hearing the forecast.

I don't see Mom, sitting on the pier, until I nearly trip over her. "Jeez, Mom," I say, gripping her shoulder as I prevent myself from falling.

Craning her neck to look at me, she asks, "What on earth did you do to your hair? Wait. Let me guess. This has something to do with Opal's leukemia. What exactly were you trying to prove by shaving your head?"

"I wasn't trying to prove anything. I was trying to show Opal how much I love her." I start back in the direction I came.

"You're not only pathetic, Stella, you're a fool," she says to my retreating back.

I spin around. "So, you *were* eavesdropping."

"Somebody has to save you from yourself. It certainly won't be my brother or my mother."

"What's that supposed to mean? And why am I a fool?"

Tucking her long legs beneath her, she gracefully rises to her feet. "Being here has brought back so many wonderful memories of summers past. Jasmine used to grow wild along the side of our cottage. Billy loved that sweet smell. He said it was soft and delicate like me."

The song lyrics come crashing back to me.

> *Jasmine, sweet as a summer blossom,*
> *Wherever you go,*
> *Whoever you're with,*
> *You'll always be in my heart,*
> *My Jasmine, my love.*

My voice is barely audible. "*You're* Jasmine."

Mom's face is grim. "I am . . . I was . . . Whatever."

Thoughts race through my mind. None of them make much sense. "I don't understand. Why would Naomi name her child after Billy's old lover?"

Mom shrugs. "Your guess is as good as mine."

"I'm sure it's a coincidence. Naomi's married to Derrick. He's Jazz's father."

"Stella, please. I can't believe you haven't figured this out yet. I knew the minute I saw Jazz. She has Billy's eyes. Billy is Jazz's father."

I shake my head to clear it, to allow this revelation to sink in. "Are you saying Jazz is my half sister?"

"It appears so."

The possibility has always been there, lurking at the corners of my mind, but I was too afraid to hope for fear of the letdown if it proved not to be true. I'm so tired of the secrets and the lies. I glare at Mom. "Why are you still here?"

"I keep asking myself the same question. I figure I'll know when it's time to leave."

"No one wants you here, Mom. Do us all a favor. Come

down off your weed cloud and get on the next plane back to New York."

I start off again toward the cottage, but Mom grabs me by the arm, holding me back. "Please, Stella. I want to work things out, not only with you but with Brian and Opal."

"I remember that day in New York, Mom, when we saw Opal on the street. She came all that way to see us, and you were so rude to her. Your own mother? I don't blame Opal if she never forgives you."

"You wouldn't understand this, Stella, having never experienced that kind of betrayal. When my family turned their backs on me, I cut them out of my heart and my mind. I admit I was hard on Opal. She tried to make things right. At least in the beginning. But Brian taking Billy's side hurt me to the core." Mom's chin quivers, and she pauses for a minute to collect herself. "Our stepfather, Robert, was a lousy husband and father. He spent much of his time on the golf course, and there were often rumors about other women. As a result, Brian was extremely overprotective of our mother and me. He always had my back. Until he didn't. Until he turned on me."

Mom's admission tugs at my heartstrings. "I imagine that was difficult for you."

"I want to put the past behind me and make things right. Unfortunately, neither Opal nor Brian will see me. Will you talk to them for me, Stella?"

Anger pulses through me. "No way! You're on your own here, Mom. You all have used me as a pawn against one another long enough."

TWENTY-NINE

I click on Brian's number as I'm marching back to the cottage. When he answers on the second ring, I blurt, "Why didn't you tell me Jazz is my half sister?"

He lets out a sigh. "How'd you find out?"

"I'll tell you how I *didn't* find out. From you. *You* should've told me, *Uncle* Brian. Instead, I had to hear it from my mother, who claims she realized it the first time she saw Jazz."

"Then why didn't *she* tell you? Hannah should've told you about your father a long time ago."

"I won't argue with that." I burst through the door of the cottage, but the small living room is confining, and I leave again. Ignoring the pitch-black sky, I head up toward the barn.

"It doesn't matter who did or didn't tell me. The point is, I've been taking care of her all this time, and I should've known. By the way, Naomi's back. She's staying in the carriage house. Jazz is with her."

"How does Naomi seem?"

I search for the right word. "Frazzled."

"Hmm. Not good, considering she just got out of rehab."

When the first raindrops begin to fall, I duck my head and

keep walking. "I feel sorry for Jazz. She admitted she's scared when she's with her mother."

"Do you think Naomi is physically abusing Jazz?"

"I honestly don't know. Jazz told me that Naomi yells at her a lot, and sometimes when Naomi's sleeping, Jazz can't wake her up. But I was afraid to flat out ask Jazz if her mother hits her."

"Do you want me to come to the farm, Stella? You sound like you could use a friend."

"Friend? I hoped we could be friends, Brian. But now I'm not so sure. Friends are honest with each other. You've been anything but."

"I haven't been dishonest with you, Stella. I've been following Billy's wishes. I worried this would happen. I warned him I was too close to the situation. I tried to convince him to let one of my law partners handle his estate, but he would hear nothing of it."

I experience a new wave of anger, this time directed at Billy. The rest of them may have used me as a pawn, but Billy manipulated me. "Whatever. I can't talk about this anymore. I gotta go." I reach the barn and turn around, heading back to the cottage.

"Wait! Before you hang up, I want to thank you for what you did yesterday. Shaving your hair. . . that's something Billy would've done."

"Really? Because Opal says it's something Mom would've done."

He laughs. "Maybe. But for different reasons. Hannah would've done it for the thrill. Or to get attention. Billy would've done it for the show of love."

I don't know how to respond, so I say nothing, the sound of my heavy breathing filling the line.

"I have something for you," Brian says. "Something Billy asked me to give you when the time was right. Can I drop it off? I won't stay long."

I'm intrigued, but I'm not in the mood to see Brian. "Not today. Maybe tomorrow. Call me."

I end the call and click on Jack's number. When I hear his voice, I fight back the tears. "Something's happened, and I really need to see you. Can you come over?"

"I'll be there in ten."

I'm relieved when he doesn't ask questions. I need to see his reaction when I tell him Jazz is my sister.

I'm nearing the cottage when the skies open up, and even though the rain pounds hard against my head and shoulders, I walk the rest of the way.

Five minutes later, I'm standing inside the door, water dripping off my clothes and pooling onto the floor at my feet, when Jack arrives.

"Stella. What is it? You're scaring me."

"Billy is Jazz's father. She's my half sister."

I watch his face closely as disbelief transitions into confusion and then into that aha expression when everything makes sense. "You didn't know, did you?"

He narrows his eyes. "How would I have known?"

"You knew Billy."

"But not that well. How did *you* find out?"

"According to my mother, it's quite apparent. Jazz has Billy's eyes. Amber eyes are rare. Did you never notice them?"

He thinks about this a minute. "I can't say that I did."

The air conditioner kicks on, blowing cold air from the vent above my head. I begin to shake uncontrollably.

"You're freezing. We need to get you into some dry clothes." Jack disappears into the bedroom.

While he's gone, I strip off all my clothes, dropping them in a wet mound at my feet. When he returns, I'm completely naked. He moves toward me with my bathrobe, but I snatch the garment from his hands and hurl it across the room. This is not how I imagined our first time together, but I can wait no longer. I'm all over Jack as I peel off his clothes. He takes me in his arms and kisses me. His skin warms me, and my shivers subside. He swoops me off my feet and carries me to the bed.

Our hands press against flesh as we paw at one another, desperate to get closer, to become one. When he enters me, his body consumes me, and I become whole. I've been on a long journey, working my way toward this man. I wasn't born for Hannah or Billy. I was born to be with Jack. Our lovemaking is exquisite, raw passion coupled with our tender feelings for one another. We climax together, but he remains inside of me.

"I'm absolutely certain I felt the earth move," he says, burying his face in my neck.

I laugh. "That was thunder." I push his head up so I can see his face. "Did you mean what you said when you first saw my hair?"

"About me loving you?" He kisses the tip of my nose. "Of course I meant it. I love you with my whole heart."

"And I love you too, Jack Snyder. I've never said that to a guy before. I've never been in love before. Please, don't break my heart."

"You have nothing to worry about. I will treasure your beautiful heart."

As the storm rages outside, peace settles over me inside the cottage. We spend the rest of the afternoon and evening in bed, exploring each other's bodies and sharing our deepest secrets. Around eight o'clock, when hunger gets the best of us, we're forced to think about food. We're rummaging through the contents of the refrigerator, me in my robe and Jack in his boxers, when there's a loud knocking at the door.

The worst of the storm, the thunder and lightning, has moved on, but rain continues to fall in sheets. "I wonder who's out in this weather," I say, wrapping my robe tighter as I cross the living room to the door.

A wild-eyed and dripping-wet Naomi barges in. "Please tell me Jazz is with you."

Cold dread travels my spine. "I haven't seen Jazz since I left the carriage house hours ago." I catch a whiff of alcohol and notice her bloodshot eyes. "You've been drinking."

She wrings her hands. "It's Cecily's fault for leaving a bottle of wine in the refrigerator. The day has been so stressful. Facing ghosts, and Jazz has been difficult, complaining that she'd rather be with you. I just needed something to take the edge off."

By facing ghosts, I assume she means Billy. But I don't go there. I'm not her shrink. "So, you got drunk and lost your child in the worst storm of the summer."

"I had a glass of wine while I reheated some mac and cheese and another while Jazz ate. They wouldn't let me have my phone in rehab, so I was catching up on the news. Jazz went up to our room to get her iPad. But she never came back."

I sense movement behind me, and Jack is at my side. "How much time passed before you went to check on her?

Naomi's eyes fall to the floor. "As long as it took me to finish the bottle of wine. I found Jazz's iPad in our room."

My hands itch to throttle her neck. "Have you checked with my mom? Maybe she's seen Jazz."

"I went there first. The door was ajar, so I let myself in. Her suite's empty, and her clothes are gone. I assume she left town. You don't think she kidnapped Jazz, do you?"

With a stab of guilt, I remember my last conversation with her. *No one wants you here, Mom. Do us all a favor. Come down off your weed cloud and get on the next plane back to New York.*

"Don't be ridiculous." Even though it's not out of the realm of possibilities, it would be extreme, even for my crazy mother. "Did you call Derrick?"

"Yes. He hasn't seen her."

"Did you check all the closets and under the beds?" Jack asks.

Still staring at the floor, Naomi nods. "She's not in the carriage house."

When I fear my legs might give way, I lean into Jack. "Something's wrong. Jazz would be too afraid to go out in the storm alone."

Jack places a reassuring hand on the small of my back. "Think hard, Naomi. How long has Jazz been missing? Thirty minutes? An hour?"

"At least an hour," she mumbles.

"We need to get on it." He retrieves our cell phones from the bedroom, handing me mine. "See if you can get through to your on-duty security officer while I contact the police."

Jack and I spring into action while Naomi stands by watching us. My first call isn't to Martin but to my mom. When the call goes straight to voicemail, I leave an urgent message and follow up with a text, asking her to get in touch with me ASAP.

Martin reports that he hasn't seen Jazz, or signs of anything out of the ordinary, but he promises to call in reinforcements.

Our calls concluded, Jack and I retreat to the bedroom, and we're finishing getting dressed when three patrol cars, with two officers in each, arrive ten minutes later.

The air in my living room quickly becomes stifling with so many bodies pressed tight. Officer Kennedy—an imposing man, tall and bald—takes charge, asking Naomi the pertinent questions. Where was Jazz last seen? And what was she wearing.

To her credit, Naomi leaves nothing out when she walks him through the events of the evening. But she can't remember what Jazz was wearing and can't find a picture of her daughter on her phone to show him.

I lock eyes with Naomi. "When I left Jazz with you earlier, she was still wearing her dress from church. Did she change clothes after that?"

Naomi hugs herself. "Not that I'm aware of."

I turn to Kennedy who's taking notes on an iPad. "The dress was sleeveless, blue-and-white seersucker with red flowers embroidered on the fabric."

I whip out my phone and scroll through my pictures.

Kennedy gives me his cell number, and I text him three of the clearest images of Jazz.

"Should you issue an Amber alert?" Jack asks.

Kennedy shakes his head. "Not unless we have reason to believe the child has been abducted. Where is the child's father?"

"Her father is dead, and my soon-to-be ex-husband says he hasn't seen her. But you should verify this." Naomi provides Derrick's contact information.

Kennedy points at Naomi. "You need to go back to the carriage house in case your daughter returns." He gestures at the only female officer in the room. "Officer Stevenson will go with you."

To me, Kennedy says, "I want you to call your friends, family, and neighbors, and organize a search party. We need all hands on deck. It's nasty out tonight, and we have a lot of ground to cover."

As the others are dispersing, I pull Kennedy aside. "In the interest of full disclosure, I should tell you that my mother was staying in the other suite in the carriage house. We had a bit of a disagreement earlier. According to Naomi, her room has been cleared out. If she left town, she didn't say goodbye. She would never intentionally hurt anyone. But this might be some kind of sick prank to get back at me." I give him Mom's cell number and provide a physical description of her and the rental car she's driving.

I call Katherine, Cecily, and Brian while Jack contacts his two most trusted workmen. Everyone arrives within thirty minutes. The men help the police search the grounds while Cecily, Katherine, and I cover the inside of the main building. We start on the top floor and work our way down. The process is tedious. There are tools and building materials stacked up in nearly every room. We're combing through the main floor when Brian calls with an update.

"The police located your Mom, who swears she knows

nothing of Jazz's whereabouts. She was at the airport in Roanoke, waiting for a flight to New York. Her flight was canceled due to the storm. She's headed back to Hope Springs now."

"I'm relieved, and I'm not. I was hoping for some strange reason that Jazz was with her. How's the search coming on your end?"

"We're scouring the grounds. We've checked the obvious places, the barn and summer house and the site for the new storage building. So far, we've seen no sign of her. I'll stay in touch."

When we finish at the main building, we head over to the carriage house. Mom is seated at the table with Naomi and Officer Stevenson. We don't speak, and our eyes don't meet. In the kitchen, Cecily makes a fresh pot of coffee while Katherine and I throw together a plate of cheeses and crackers. We're serving our snacks to the others when Officer Stevenson receives the message that Bernard is holding Jazz hostage in one of the cottages on Cottage Row.

My vision blurs with red hot fury. "I'm gonna kill him."

I take off toward the cottages with the others on my heels. The rain has finally stopped, but the ground is muddy, and more than once, I nearly lose my footing. We find the other members of the search party, officers and civilians, hiding behind a stand of trees a hundred feet away from the furthest cottage.

I ask Kennedy, "Are you certain it's Bernard? And that he has Jazz with him?"

"Yes, ma'am. One of my men spotted them through the window. Bernard fired at him, so we know he's armed. We're trying to communicate with him, to find out his demands, but he either doesn't have his cell phone with him or he's ignoring our calls."

Before he can stop me, I make a dash toward the cottage. Kennedy runs after me. "Hey! What do you think you're doing?"

"I'm going to talk some sense into that crazy old kook."

He grabs my arm, but I shrug him off. When I near the cottage, I crouch down in front of the porch. "Here, wear this." Kennedy tosses a bulletproof vest at me with one hand as he unholsters his revolver with the other.

"Bernard!" I call out. "It's Stella. We need to talk. This is between you and me. Let Jazz go."

Bernard responds by throwing his boot through the window. It tumbles across the wooden porch floor toward us.

Jack appears at my side. "Stella, are you crazy? Let the police handle this."

"Too late now." Cupping my hands around my mouth, I yell, "If it's money you want, Bernard, just tell me how much."

Bernard's voice booms out from within. "You ain't nothing like your father, Stella. He would never have fired me. He was a good man."

Kennedy whispers to me, "Don't argue with him."

"You're right, Bernard. Billy was a good man. And I know he was your friend. Did you know that Jazz is his daughter?" I can't see my sister, but I imagine the surprise on her sweet face at hearing this news. I hate for her to find out this way. I wanted to tell her myself.

"You're lying," Bernard hollers.

"Look at her eyes!"

"Well, I'll be damned," Bernard says, his voice now muffled.

"Let her go, Bernard, and I'll make sure you get the help you need."

"I'm too old for prison," Bernard yells.

"No one said anything about prison," Kennedy responds.

"Please, Bernard," I beg. "I just found out today that Jazz is my little sister. Give us a chance to be a family. Billy arranged for me to come to Hope Springs so that Jazz and I could be together." Although I don't know for certain if this is true, I'd be willing to bet this is what my father had in mind.

After an excruciating long moment of silence ensues, we hear, "Aw, heck. Get on outta here."

The pitter-patter of little feet against hardwood floors is followed by the screeching of the front door opening. Jazz is in my arms and, together with Jack, we run away from the cottage, back into the woods.

THIRTY

We watch from behind the trees as Bernard is taken away in handcuffs. One of the officers who brings him out of the cottage reports that Bernard's gun is unloaded. For the first time, I feel sorry for the old man, and I beg Kennedy to look out for him.

"Trust me," Kennedy says, "he'll be well taken care of. As soon as possible, we'll commit him to a state facility for the mentally ill."

With the exception of Brian, the other members of the search party take off for home. It's late on a Sunday night, and everyone has to be at work early in the morning.

Jazz clings to me, arms choking my neck and legs gripping my waist, as Brian, Jack, and I make our way back to the carriage house. Naomi is waiting for us at the door. She murmurs apologies as she smothers Jazz with kisses, but Jazz keeps her face buried in my chest.

"She'll spend the night with me," I say matter-of-factly, and Naomi doesn't dare argue. I'm no longer the stranger from New York. And I'm not just the older sister either. I've earned my stripes. I've proven myself reliable. I nursed her through her illness and took care of her while her mother was in rehab. And Jazz trusts me. For good reason, she doesn't feel the same way about her mother.

Behind Naomi, I notice my mom and Brian standing three feet apart in the foyer. They're not talking, and their eyes are bouncing around the room, as though looking for an escape. I've never seen my mother so vulnerable. I was wrong to suspect her of taking Jazz.

I whisper to Jazz, "Sweetheart, will you go to Jack for a minute while I talk to my mother?"

Nodding, she holds her tiny arms out to Jack.

As I approach my mom, Brian steps away to give us privacy. "Did you get rebooked on a flight for tomorrow?"

"A very early flight, departing at 5:20 a.m. Needless to say, you won't see me again."

"I hate for us to part on bad terms, Mom. The things I said earlier were uncalled for, and I'm sorry."

She smiles. "You were right. It is time for me to go home. I need to get back to Marnie. She grounds me. I don't do well when I'm away from her for too long."

I think about reliable Marnie, how she's always the one keeping everyone in line. "Maybe you can both come down for the grand reopening. Hopefully, Opal will be feeling better by then, and you can spend some time together."

"That's a nice idea." Mom opens her arms, and I step into them. Her floral fragrance is familiar, reminding me of the times she comforted me through scraped knees, bad test grades, and friend problems. No matter where I live, she'll always be my mother.

She pulls away. "This is a special place, Stella. I have no doubt but what you'll be happy here." Tears well in her eyes as she gestures for Brian to join us. "Take care of my girl. Thank you for giving her the opportunity to know her family. I was wrong in keeping her from you."

Brian gives her a half hug. "What say we try to forget the past and focus on the future?"

"I would like that very much." When she can no longer hold back the tears, she excuses herself and dashes up the stairs.

Brian removes a flash drive from his pocket and hands it to me. "Billy asked me to give you this. I probably should've given it to you weeks ago. I tried my best to do right by you, Stella."

Standing on my tiptoes, I kiss his cheek. "I know, Uncle Brian. And I appreciate it."

"Billy worked hard on this video. He even ordered a fancy camera to tape it."

I smile. "I was wondering about that camera."

He hands me an adapter. "You'll need this in order to watch it on your computer. You'll undoubtedly have questions. Call me anytime day or night."

Brian claps Jack on the back and kisses the top of Jazz's head, but he doesn't speak to Naomi on his way out.

"We should get this kiddo to bed," I say to Jack, and to Naomi, "We'll talk tomorrow."

At the cottage, Jack offers to spend the night on the sofa, but I want to be alone when I watch my father's video. Jazz is too exhausted to notice the tangled sheets. Jack straightens the bedcovers while I help Jazz, the limp rag doll, out of her dress and into one of my T-shirts.

When I walk Jack to the door, he says, "I'll come back if you discover you don't want to be alone."

"We'll be fine." I give him a peck on the lips. "Thanks for everything, Jack. Having you to lean on means so much."

As soon as he's gone, I brew a cup of chamomile tea, change into my pajamas, and climb into bed with my laptop and earpods. I insert the flash drive into the computer. There's only one file and I click on it. The man whose face fills the screen has aged twenty years from the photos I've seen of him around the farm. Based on the time stamp in the upper right corner, Billy recorded this video only six months ago, when he was nearing the end of his life. He's gaunt and pale, his hair completely gray. But the golden-brown eyes are the same as Jazz's. He starts off by saying how much he regrets not having the chance to know me. Then his eyes cloud over as he disappears into the past. For ten minutes, maybe longer, he relives the days of his youth on the farm with Hannah.

"Your mother was a spectacular being—the face of an angel with the soul of a temptress. I've never loved anyone like I loved Hannah.

"For you to fully understand why I brought you here, Stella, I need to tell you about Naomi. Ours was a relationship of convenience. At least on my part. Naomi wanted more from me than I was willing to give. I insisted we keep our affair secret. I wasn't prepared to make that kind of commitment to her. But Naomi, as you may have discovered by now, has a mind of her own. She tried to trap me into marrying her by getting pregnant. When I refused, she quit her job and married the first guy who came along. She did everything in her power to make me jealous, including naming her daughter after the woman I talk about in my sleep. I've never told Naomi about Hannah or you. But I will before I die."

Billy pauses to take a sip of water. I recognize the glass from my kitchen.

"Six months after Jazz was born, Naomi came to see me, begging for her job back. She admitted things weren't going well in her marriage. How could I say no, when the arrangement gave me the opportunity to know my daughter?

"I'm grateful to Naomi for nursing me during my illness. But she is not mentally stable. Nor are her intentions honorable.

"I apologize for rambling. I easily lose my train of thought these days.

"I've used private investigators to keep tabs on you all these years, Stella. You're the best of Hannah and me. You're intelligent and independent. Your gusto for life and enthusiasm for the hospitality industry makes you the ideal person to run the inn. As for Jazz, I trust you've fallen in love with her by now. It's easy to do. I have faith that you'll take care of your baby sister in the event something happens to Naomi. Or in case Jazz needs you."

After the video ends, I sit in the dark for nearly an hour, wondering again how my life might've been different if I'd had the chance to know my father.

I email the file to Jack with a message for him to please watch it, and I fall asleep wondering what Billy thought might happen to Naomi.

I wake on Monday morning with golden eyes staring at me from inches away.

"Are we really sisters?" Jazz asks.

I hug her close to me. "Apparently so. What do you think about that?" I don't bother with the details. She's too young to understand about us being only half sisters. And, as far as I know, she believes Derrick is her biological father.

"I think it's way cool! Can I go to my dance lesson today?" She's temporarily forgotten about last night's incident. Ballet is far more important than Bernard. But I fully anticipate the after-effects of the kidnapping to be dramatic.

"Sure! If you want to." I toss back the covers. "But we need to get moving. We'll have to get your clothes from the carriage house."

"Do I have to see my mommy?" Jazz asks, sliding off the bed to her feet.

"We can't get your ballet shoes and leotard without seeing her. You can't hide from her, Jazz. She's your mommy."

"She's a bad mommy. I want *you* to be my mommy."

Hunching my shoulders, I hold my hands out by my sides, palms up. "How can I be your mommy when I'm your sister?"

Her chin quivers and eyes fill with tears. I kneel down in front of her. "Do you trust me, Jazzy?"

244

I'm relieved when she answers yes without hesitation. I would fully expect this kid to have trust issues.

"Then you're gonna have to trust me to make things right."

"But how?"

I touch the tip of my finger to the end of her nose. "I haven't figured that part out yet. But I'll come up with something."

My mind is as clear as the cloudless sky outside my window. My father entrusted his daughter to me. And I won't let him down.

We eat bowls of yogurt with fresh berries and granola for breakfast before heading over to the carriage house. Naomi is surprised to see us. "Jazz needs her ballet clothes," I say. "She has a lesson this morning."

Naomi stiffens. "I didn't authorize any lessons."

Jazz gives her mother a dirty look as she grabs the handle of her suitcase, which is parked in the same spot beside the door where she left it yesterday.

"I'm paying for the lessons, Naomi. You authorized me to make these decisions when you left Jazz in my care." I take the suitcase from Jazz, and we hurry down the stairs.

My weekly staff meeting is already underway in the lounge. I poke my head in the room to make certain there are no crises that need my attention. Jack is at the head of the table, looking fresh and ever so handsome in a white polo shirt and jeans.

He gives me a thumbs-up. "We've got everything covered."

I text Brian on the way to the car. *I have some questions. I'm on the way to the ballet studio. Can you meet me there?* I forward the studio's address to him.

Through an observation window, I'm watching Jazz perform a stunning pirouette when he arrives fifteen minutes later. "Wow," he says when he sees Jazz dance. "She's really good."

I smile. "Her instructor thinks she has real talent. Can you believe Naomi is against her taking lessons?"

"I'm afraid to ask. Why?"

"Because she wants Jazz to study biology, so she can become a doctor." I angle my body away from the window toward my uncle. "I'm exploring my options, Brian. Do I have grounds to sue for custody?"

"Yes," he says without hesitation, as though he's already given this considerable thought. "And based on Naomi's recent behavior, you might win. Is that what you want?"

"I want Jazz to feel safe and loved. She feels neither with Naomi. But a custody suit ruined this family once. I don't want that to happen again."

He rests a hand on my shoulder. "Whatever you decide, Stella, you have my full support."

"Thanks. That means a lot." We're both quiet for a minute while we watch Jazz. "I assume Billy provided for her in his will."

"Yes, but not in the same way as he provided for you. Billy left a trust designated for Jazz's care. She will be well taken care of for the rest of her life."

"I'm glad to hear it," I say. "By the way, how's Opal today?"

"Much better, thanks to you. She was in her backyard watering plants when I stopped by a few minutes ago."

I let out a little whoop. "That's the best news I've heard in a long time. I'll try to get by to see her tomorrow."

THIRTY-ONE

Despite the trauma of last night, Jazz dances beautifully, the best I've seen from her to date. She knows she performed well and talks excitedly about it on the way home. But the minute we arrive at the cottage, she goes silent.

I put the Jeep in park and turn around to look at her in the back seat. "I don't feel like working today. Why don't we go for a drive in the mountains? Maybe we'll come across a quaint little place to have lunch."

She gives me a small smile. Not exactly what I was hoping. But it's something.

I'm backing out of the parking space, when Jack appears in my rearview mirror. I roll down my window, and he sticks his head inside. "Where are you two lovelies headed?"

"For a drive in the mountains," I say. "Wanna come?"

Jazz claps her hands. "Please, Uncle Jack!"

A broad smile lights up his face. "You bet." He opens my door. "But move over. I'm driving. I'm not riding on winding mountain roads with a novice driver."

Scrambling over the center console, I buckle my seat belt as he takes off around the main building. Jazz falls asleep before we reach the town limits.

"Did you watch Billy's video?" I ask as we begin our first ascent.

Jack glances over at me, but I can't read his expression. "I did."

"And? What do you think?"

He returns his eyes to the road. "I think Billy went to extreme measures to protect Jazz. He had good reason to suspect trouble ahead with Naomi. He makes it clear how much he missed having you in his life. He obviously had faith in you."

"How could he, when he never really knew me? He only had reports from private investigators to go on."

"Maybe so, but you're his daughter. His and Hannah's."

"True." I brace myself against the dashboard as Jack takes a hairpin curve too fast for my liking. I wait until my heart stops pounding to ask, "Do you think Brian's been testing me? I have a hunch Billy authorized Brian to use the renovation project as a gauge, to see whether I measure up to Jameson standards."

"Can you blame him? You're awfully young for such an enormous responsibility. But you passed with flying colors. You're doing a remarkable job with the renovations, and you're taking excellent care of Jazz, much better than her mother."

When we come to a steep incline, Jack steps on the gas, and we ride for a while, each of us lost in our thoughts.

We're cruising along a straight stretch of highway when Jack breaks the silence. "I love you, Stella. Whether today or next week or a year from now, I'm gonna marry you."

Despite the fluttering in my belly, I pretend to be insulted. "You're awfully confident."

"Damn right, I'm confident. We have something special. You know that as well as I do."

I smile. "I do know that. There's nothing I want more than to be with you." My smile fades. "But how does Jazz fit into your vision of our happily ever after?"

"However she fits into your life, she fits into mine. I love that kid." He flashes me a grin. "And she loves me too. Did you hear her call me Uncle Jack earlier?"

I laugh. "I did hear that."

"If you want to try for custody, I'll raise her as my own," Jack says.

Warmth radiates throughout my body. "You're too good to me, Jack."

He takes my hand. "I'm just getting started," he says, bringing my fingers to his lips.

Craning my neck, I watch Jazz sleeping peacefully in her car seat. "I'm not ready to give up on Naomi just yet. For Jazz's sake, I feel compelled to give her one more chance to straighten out her life. As we work through the issues, though, Jazz will continue to live with me. It's not ideal, I know. I'd much rather be sharing my bed with you than a six-year-old."

"The two of you could live with me. I have enough empty bedrooms for all three of us to have our own." Jack winks at me. "Then we can sneak around at night after Jazz goes to bed."

The arrangement could work. His house is close enough to the farm. But I want to do what's best for my little sister. "As much as I relish the thought of living in your beautiful home, we need to remain at the cottage. Jazz feels safe there. The location is ideal. I only wish there was more than one bedroom."

"At some point you'll have to address that issue."

"How do you suggest we go about doing that?"

"Raise the roof. You could easily add a second floor with three bedrooms. You'd need an architect, of course."

"As it happens, I'm meeting with an architect next week about the summer house." I play-punch his arm. "You're full of good ideas. Having a builder boyfriend comes in handy."

"I want to be more than your boyfriend, Stella. I want to be your fiancé. I won't pressure you to get married until you're ready. But I need a commitment from you now." He unbuckles his seat belt and digs into his pocket. He produces a gray silicon wedding band. "This is the best I could do on short notice. We'll shop for a diamond together later."

I stare at the ring and back at him. "Are you seriously proposing right now, while you're driving on the highway?"

He grins. "At least it's a scenic route. What do you say, Stella? When the time is right, will you marry me?"

I take the plastic band from him and slip it on my ring finger. "Oh look!" I say with mock surprise. "It's a perfect fit!"

"I take that as a yes."

Leaning across the console, I lay my head on his shoulder. "Yes, Jack, I'd be honored to be your wife. When the time is right."

We drive for another twenty miles as we make plans for the future. We agree to keep our engagement a secret for now, to put some distance between last night's traumatic event and our happy announcement. We've known each other only a little over two months, and we want to take our time in getting to know each other better.

When Jazz finally wakes up, we grab sandwiches from a gourmet market in the next small town and have a picnic at an overlook park on our way back to Hope Springs. As we're pulling into the farm, I say, "I have something I need to take care of, Jack. Any chance you could watch Jazz for a few minutes?"

"Of course." He searches for Jazz in the rearview mirror. "Hey, kiddo, wanna walk through the main building with me? I'm pretty sure I can find a hard hat to fit over all that hair of yours."

She sticks her tongue out at him. "Funny, Uncle Jack."

He parks the Jeep beside the cottage and drops the key in my palm. "Cecily wanted me to tell you she's preparing a tasting menu for us to sample later this afternoon. She's even including some kid-friendly dishes for Jazz."

"Sounds like dinner to me," I say. "Maybe afterward, we can take Jazz for a swim in the lake." I say this for Jazz's benefit, and out of the corner of my eye, I watch for her reaction. She appears visibly relieved that, for the foreseeable future, she'll be with me.

Jack says, "I'll have to run home for my swim trunks, but count me in."

When Jack and Jazz head off toward the main building, I cut across the lawn to the carriage house. Naomi doesn't answer when I knock on the door of her suite, but I find Cecily sautéing mushrooms on the stove in the kitchen.

"Have you seen Naomi? Her car's out front, but she's not in her room."

Rolling out biscuit dough on the counter, Cecily says, "She left about an hour ago, but she didn't say where she was going."

I talk to Cecily for a minute about her plans for this afternoon's tasting before continuing my search for Naomi. I don't have to go far. I find her sitting on the ground, leaning back against Opal's tree. When I approach, she springs to her feet.

"Where's Jazz?" she asks, looking past me. "I've been waiting for you for hours. I thought you'd bring her back after her ballet lesson."

"She's up at the main building with Jack. I asked him to keep an eye on her while we talk. We're playing by my rules now, Naomi."

She rolls her eyes. "And what rules are those, Stella?"

"Jazz is going to continue living with me for the foreseeable future. She doesn't feel safe with you. Who can blame her after everything that's happened?"

Naomi looks down at her feet. "Can I visit her?"

"Of course. On Jazz's terms. It's up to you to earn back her trust. You'll have to find somewhere else to live, though. Jack will be starting renovations on the carriage house soon. As for your job, you can head up our marketing department. On a trial basis. If it doesn't work out, you'll have to find a job somewhere else. You have issues you need to work through, Naomi. Take this time for yourself, to sort out your life."

She glares at me. "And what if I don't play by your rules?"

"I'll sue you for custody of Jazz. Brian thinks I have a good chance of winning."

Naomi grunts. "I highly doubt that," she says, but I hear skepticism in her tone.

I hold up a finger. "There's one more rule. The most important one. In order to work at the inn and be allowed visitation with Jazz, you'll have to attend regular meetings at Alcoholics Anonymous. I'm happy to help you find a sponsor."

She spins around and stalks off.

I call after her, "If it were up to me, I'd kick you off my property right now and never let you come back. I'm giving you one more chance, Naomi. But only because you're Jazz's mother."

I don't wait for her response. I stroll off in the opposite direction toward the cottage. For the first time since coming to Hope Springs, I feel in control. I'm behind the wheel, and Billy is riding alongside me in the passenger seat. While I'm in charge of my own destiny, I trust Billy and Brian and Jack not to let me go off course.

In the bedroom at the cottage, I remove the photograph of Mom and Billy from the Bible in the nightstand and study it closely. I am the product of these two people, each talented in his and her own way. Managing the renovation project has enabled me to discover some of my own hidden talents. And I have a sneaking suspicion I'm just getting started. With my newly acquired confidence, I can accomplish anything I set my mind to. I have a vision for the future of the inn, and thanks to the Jameson fortune, I can make that dream a reality. Billy has entrusted me with his family's heritage and his beloved daughter. Regardless of the terms of the will, my little sister is the rightful co-owner of Hope Springs Farm. I will rebuild the inn bigger and better than before, not only for me but also for Jazz. During my first days in Virginia, my Uncle Brian encouraged me to dream big. And I aim to do just that.

Did you enjoy this title? Please consider leaving an honest review on GoodReads or your favorite online retailer.

SHOW ME THE WAY-EXCERPT

(HOPE SPRINGS SERIES #2)

Presley waits in her parked rental car across from the address she found on the torn envelope in her adoption folder. When she discovered the file in her mother's desk drawer late yesterday afternoon, she booked the next available flight to Virginia. What is she even doing here? She's not interested in medical history. A genetic testing website could determine if she possesses the dreaded breast cancer gene or whether she's at risk for Parkinson's or Alzheimer's. But Presley's test kit, purchased over a year ago from 23andMe, remains unopened in her bedside table drawer back in Nashville.

Kids on bikes and young mothers pushing baby strollers pass by, seemingly oblivious to the stranger in their midst. The neighborhood is Norman Rockwell picturesque, like one might expect in a small town called Hope Springs. Maple trees with brilliant orange leaves line the street. Pansies in yellows and purples border sidewalks leading to small front porches bearing displays of pumpkins and gourds and mums. Most of the houses are two-story brick colonials with well-tended lawns. But the white-washed brick and Wedgewood-blue front door make number 237 stand out from the rest on Hillside Drive.

Presley drums her fingers against the steering wheel. She's been here two hours. Should she leave and come back later? She checks the time on the dash. Five forty-three. She'll stay until six.

What does she want from the people she's waiting for? Another family? Because her mother . . . her adoptive mother, Renee, died two months ago and left her all alone in the world. That's not it. Presley isn't afraid of being alone. She has no siblings. She lost her beloved father to cancer when she was a young child. This inner sense of disconnect has nothing to do with Renee's death. Presley feels a calling, like there's someone else in the universe searching for her. She's not looking to disrupt anyone's life. She simply wants to know who her people are. To look into the faces of others and see something of herself.

All her life, Presley has been a square peg trying to fit into Renee's round hole. Renee was an overachiever, a producer with one of Nashville's top country music record labels. Renee prided herself on being a hard-ass and faulted Presley for being soft. Presley prefers to think of herself as easygoing and good-natured. Renee's death was permission granted for her to find her round hole.

When a burgundy minivan rounds the corner at the far end of the street, Presley sits up straight in her seat. She glimpses the attractive middle-aged blonde behind the wheel when the van pulls into the driveway at 237. A pair of teenage girls, dressed in athletic shorts and tank tops with field hockey sticks tucked under their arms and backpacks over their shoulders, emerge from the van. Tall and lean with blonde ponytails, they look enough alike to be twins. Could these girls be her half sisters? Their mother, an older version of her daughters, is slower to get out of the car. She holds a phone to her ear and wears a scowl on her face, either angry or upset with the person on the other end.

From a distance, Presley sees no physical resemblance between the three blondes across the street and her own auburn hair and gray eyes. There's always a chance the torn envelope got stuffed in her adoption folder by accident. But not likely, since her mother's other files were in meticulous order. According to Zillow, number 237 was last sold seventy years ago. Presley assumes to this woman's parents. The official website for the town of Hope Springs identifies the owners of said property as Samuel M. and Carolyn H. Townsend. For what it's worth, the free online background check Presley conducted lists additional occupants of the home as Anna and Rita Townsend, presumably Sam and Carolyn's daughters. But this woman must be Rita because, according to Facebook, Anna Townsend—originally from Hope Springs and a graduate of Hope Springs High School—currently lives in Washington state.

This woman appears in her upper forties. No older than fifty. Presley is thirty years old. Which makes the timing right for that woman to have had an unwanted pregnancy in her late teens or early twenties.

Where are Sam and Carolyn? Do they still reside in the house? And what about this woman's husband? Is he late coming home from work? Or is she divorced?

The woman ends her call and drops her phone into her purse. Removing the mail from the black box to the right of the blue door, she sits down on the front steps and sorts through a stack of envelopes. She's smiling now, her phone conversation apparently forgotten. Presley is tempted to introduce herself. But what would she say? "Hey. You don't know me, but I think I may be your daughter."

The woman looks up from the mail and across the street at Presley. They lock eyes for a fraction of a second. A shiver runs down Presley's spine, and she averts her eyes. Did the woman see her? Is she making note of the license plate number and make and model of the rental car? Presley's not ready for this. Breathing deeply so as not to hyperventilate, she starts the engine and drives off.

ALSO BY ASHLEY FARLEY

Hope Springs Series

Dream Big, Stella!

Show Me the Way

Mistletoe and Wedding Bells

Stand Alone

Tangled in Ivy

Lies that Bind

Life on Loan

Only One Life

Home for Wounded Hearts

Nell and Lady

Sweet Tea Tuesdays

Saving Ben

Sweeney Sisters Series

Saturdays at Sweeney's

Tangle of Strings

Boots and Bedlam

Lowcountry Stranger

Her Sister's Shoes

Magnolia Series

Beyond the Garden

Magnolia Nights

Scottie's Adventures

Breaking the Story

Merry Mary

ACKNOWLEDGMENTS

I'm grateful to many people for helping make this novel possible. Foremost, to my editor, Patricia Peters, for her patience and advice and for making my work stronger without changing my voice. A great big heartfelt thank-you to my trusted beta readers —Alison Fauls, Kathy Sinclair, Anne Wolters, Laura Glenn, and Jan Klein. And to my behind-the-scenes team, Kate Rock and Geneva Agnos, for all the many things you do to manage my social media so effectively.

I am blessed to have many supportive people in my life who offer the encouragement I need to continue the pursuit of my writing career. I owe an enormous debt of gratitude to my advanced review team, the lovely ladies of Georgia's Porch, for their enthusiasm for and commitment to my work. To Leslie Rising at Levy's for being my local bookshop. Love and thanks to my family—my mother, Joanne; my husband, Ted; and the best children in the world, Cameron and Ned.

Most of all, I'm grateful to my wonderful readers for their love of women's fiction. I love hearing from you. Feel free to shoot me an email at ashleyhfarley@gmail.com or stop by my website at ashleyfarley.com for more information about my characters and upcoming releases. Don't forget to sign up for my newsletter. Your subscription will grant you exclusive content, sneak previews, and special giveaways.

ABOUT THE AUTHOR

Ashley Farley writes books about women for women. Her characters are mothers, daughters, sisters, and wives facing real-life issues. Her bestselling Sweeney Sisters series has touched the lives of many.

Ashley is a wife and mother of two young adult children. While she's lived in Richmond, Virginia for the past 21 years, a piece of her heart remains in the salty marshes of the South Carolina Lowcountry, where she still calls home. Through the eyes of her characters, she captures the moss-draped trees, delectable cuisine, and kindhearted folk with lazy drawls that make the area so unique.

Ashley loves to hear from her readers. Visit Ashley's Website @ashleyfarley.com

Get free exclusive content by signing up for her newsletter @ ashleyfarley.com/newsletter-signup/

facebook.com/ashleywfarley

twitter.com/AshleyWFarley

instagram.com/ashleyfarleyauthor

Made in United States
Orlando, FL
21 May 2022

18057838R00162